The Lost Relics:
Rise of a Guardian

By: LJ Andrews

Table of Contents

For Derek, who has my whole heart

Linnea, the reason behind every exciting creature

Andrew, for believing that architecture can have no limits

And Jarom, who helps me trust that we all have a superhero within.

Chapter 1
Destiny in Dreams

Fire burned his chest as he fled along the damp, musty corridor. Shrieks of frustration from his enemies echoed behind him, deafening the blood pounding in his ears as he ran for his life. A small halo of light glimmered ahead, signaling his freedom from the deadly pursuit. A confident smile spread across his young face; he was going to make it. They wouldn't get it and he would live.

His heavy footsteps seemed to leap across the ancient stone pathway shrouded from the warmth of sunlight. Taking one final bounding step a pain swallowed up his shoulders and neck as the eerie purple and blue mist encompassed his body, then everything went black.

****

Cheerful light seeped into the small room. A single mattress was pushed against the side wall covered in mismatched sheets and a cheap plastic box of drawers held a few simple clothes. Killian Thomas breathed deeply trying to slow his heart as the sunrise shook him from his fitful sleep. The dark, lurking figures from his nightmare had hissed and argued angrily in the moss ridden hallway. Their conversation was wicked to the core, but the deadly pursuit twisted his insides. The dream had never ended with him making it to the small lighted opening at the end of the cold tunnel. Each time he was always swallowed in the painful mist.

Rolling from the old mattress he wiped the sweat off his face and pushed back his thick mud-colored hair. The nightmares were getting worse, and the two mysterious villains seemed to be creeping into his mind more often, as if it were something Killian needed to know. Why he kept dreaming about others trying to kill him didn't make sense, he was no threat to anyone. In fact he felt quite the opposite. There was nothing extraordinary about him, just a young man with no family, a few friends—mediocre in every sense.

The thoughts toppled through his mind as he rubbed his sky-blue eyes trying to wipe out the memories of the recurring nightmare.

"Killian come eat, you're going to be late."

The wooden steps echoed as he bounded down the narrow stairway. Stepping into the bright blue and white kitchen, he brushed his wavy hair out of his eyes before Laura, his foster mother, could do it for him.

"Sorry, I overslept," Killian breathed as he plopped down in front of his cereal.

He glanced at the graying, blonde woman and immediately pursed his lips as the sun caught the side of her face. A hideous, purple bruise covered her high cheek bone underneath her thin wire-rimmed glasses. He could tell she had tried to hide it with make-up, but the swollen lump reared its ugly head on her thin face. Killian angrily dug his spoon into his cereal and shoveled the cardboard-like flakes into his mouth. He didn't know why he felt guilty about the bruise; he didn't give it to her. Scanning his lean, but defined muscles he vowed to protect Laura better. As if she knew what he was thinking, Laura placed a gentle hand on his arm, until he looked at her again.

"Did you have another dream? Those have been keeping you up a lot lately. If you don't get some sleep Donna is going to start thinking we're neglecting you and she'll take you outta here." She gave him a kind, motherly smile.

He smirked. As of last month Donna, his family service worker, no longer had a say where Killian ended up. He often wondered why he stayed. After aging out, legally there was no reason to stay. He cared about Laura; she had taken good care of him for ten years. Richard was the reason he would leave and never look back. Ironically, he was also the reason Killian wanted to stay. If he left no one would protect Laura from his rages.

"Now that you mention it, I did have a strange dream," he finally answered. "I was trapped in a cold stone hallway. As I tried to escape I overheard a conversation...I think it was two men, I'm not sure." Killian waved his hand in front of his face. "It's hard to remember everything now that I'm awake."

Killian omitted the dream attackers attempt at killing him. Laura would spend the afternoon pouring over *The Meaning of Dreams*, her favorite book. Since he'd come to live with the Petersons the dreams had been there every night, almost as if they were reminding him of his past, or warning him of his future. Laura had taken a keen interest in it, and often tried to uncover their hidden meanings.

She opened her mouth to inquire more on the subject, but was stopped by a knock at the door.

"That'll be Blake, I suppose," she said, an edge of disappointment in her voice at the interruption. "I'll read over some pages in my book while you're out. We'll get to the bottom of your dream. The part with you being trapped in darkness must mean something."

Killian rolled his eyes and slurped one last bite of cereal.

"What time will you be back?" Laura asked when he stood.

"We'll be gone for a while, I'd guess," he answered while shrugging his shoulders. "We're hoping to have a bonfire with some people on the beach."

Killian and Laura both turned their heads toward the front door that had opened.

"Laura, my love! You look more gorgeous than ever," the young man said overly dramatic. His collared shirt was unfolded, hitting just below his jaw line, but the strange black inked, double-moon tattoo was still visible on his neck.

"Blake, there is no need for your sappy sucking up, Killian's coming," Laura chuckled turning toward the flaxen-haired young man. Blake winced slightly when he glanced at the fading bruise. Laura hung her head as if feeling self-conscious and began gathering the dishes from the table. "Well, you kids take care, and pick up some salt water taffy for me."

Killian smiled. Laura asked for the candy each time he went to the boardwalk in Seaside. He'd determined she believed the taffy was only available at that location.

"Don't worry Laura we'll bring you a huge bag. Take care of yourself okay," Blake said sincerely. Killian waved and walked out the door.

"Man, he made a mess of her this time didn't he?" Blake huffed, as they drove toward the boardwalk.

"I don't know how much more I can stand, Blake. Why does she put up with it? Me, I can take it, but Laura? She's just too good, too forgiving," Killian said bitterly.

Richard had often roughed him up as a younger boy, though he had always been careful about pounding him in easy to conceal areas in order to keep the abuse hidden from Child Protective Services. In recent years, however, Killian had grown significantly larger than the man and the rages had subsided. The downside was now his pent up anger was doubled against Laura.

"Laura was joking this morning about my case worker taking me away cause I'm not sleeping. To be honest, some days, I want to leave and never look back," Killian finished as he looked out the window. His hand found the gold charm he had worn around his neck for as long as he could remember. Blake simply nodded.

They sat in a tense silence for a moment before Blake finally asked, "Why don't you leave?"

"What?" He was annoyed that Blake had the courage to point out the obvious— that he could leave. He had no reason to stay and endure the hidden abuse.

"I mean, why don't you leave? You're old enough to be on your own, dude. You can finish school somewhere else. How long have you been with them anyway?"

"Ten years. I was with a lot of different families for three years, and then placed with Richard and Laura."

"So why do you stay?"

Killian scoffed. Blake was trying to make him feel better about leaving, but the fact that it was true and he was out of the system made his gut twist in knots. Donna hadn't cared what he decided to do when he turned eighteen. She had seemed relieved when he said he was going to stay put. It made for less work and scholarship programs she was required to provide when kids stepped into the big world alone after growing up in the system. Laura had pleaded with him to stay. Wanting to see him graduate was her reasoning, but he figured she was afraid to be alone with Richard.

Laura had mentioned numerous times the idea of adopting Killian, but Richard never agreed. It was his subtle insult to Killian— he would never be good enough to be his son.

Richard was a respectable business owner in Seaside. He owned several sandwich franchises and often donated to non-profits. His status painted a loving image in the community. Killian thought Donna was rather naive. She had mentioned on numerous occasions he was fortunate to live in such a home, even if they *didn't* adopt him.

If only she knew, he thought bitterly.

"I still can't believe you don't remember your family, you weren't placed in the system until you were what—five or something?" Blake asked.

"I just don't remember. I've had weird dreams about a red-headed woman before—sometimes I've wondered if the dream was a memory but…" Killian trailed off for a moment before gathering his thoughts. "Why would I want to live with a family that just ditched me anyway? Obviously they kept me for five years then decided to call it quits."

"I get it I guess. They might be dead, though," Blake said. "I'm not trying to be crass. I just think if you found out they were alive, living with them would be better than Richard. Anything would."

"I guess not everyone can live the high life like you, Blake. How much did good ol' grandpa dish out today just to get you out of the house?" Killian teased, trying to change the direction of the conversation.

"You can't put a price on the love we share Kill," Blake laughed. "Besides, it's the only way you get to hang out with the pretty girls. I can only help you out so much, though. You've got to leave your pretty jewelry alone." Blake laughed nodding toward his incessant rubbing of the charm.

Killian gave Blake's shoulder a hard punch, causing their car to swerve slightly into the other lane. Even so, he obeyed and tucked the circular charm back underneath his shirt. He always wore it—in truth the idea of taking it off made him physically sick. He didn't understand where the connection came from. It was tacky and unattractive. The faded gold looked ancient and the circle had a hideous crack fissuring to the top of the charm.

"What?" Blake was laughing, his face lit up in his typical mischievous manner. "It's true dude, you've got to hide the necklace. And don't joke about my grandparents. I guess they give me stuff to keep me busy; I can't help it if my antics exhaust them." Blake paused for a moment waiting for the street light to change to green. "You know Kill, I have to admit, I'm glad you hang around. Us parentless kids gotta stick together."

"Thanks, Blake," Killian said, touched by the statement.

"Whoa, don't sound so gushy dude. I don't want to organize a club or anything," Blake's eyes widened. "Hey, wait!

Maybe we should. I know a little girl down the street who makes awesome elastic bracelets! We could have matching ones."

"Shut up!" Killian said, shoving him again. Blake started laughing so hard tears formed in the corners of his eyes. Killian just shook his head. Despite the joking, he often wished he could convey how much he envied Blake and his odd, but loving relationship with his grandparents.

"I need some gas; while I fill up will you go buy me some gum? Amanda is going to be there tonight—I better be prepared," Blake chuckled as he pulled into the gas station.

Within a half hour they sauntered along the beach where several other people were standing around a charcoal barbeque laughing and holding roasting sticks. Killian didn't recognize many of them, but knew some were from school. Blake scanned the small group apparently looking for Amanda. She hadn't arrived yet and Blake's disappointment was painted all over his face.

Blake was always the exuberant one, even though he'd only moved to Seaside a few years earlier he had more friends and acquaintances than Killian could ever dream.

The rushing tide and crashing waves along the rocky shore calmed Killian's nerves he experienced every time he was pushed into a crowd, especially when it was people he didn't know well.

"Blake!" a high voice called from up the beach. Spinning around Blake and Killian watched as Amanda and her brunette side kick marched up the beach, swinging two packs of beer in each hand. Killian groaned in his throat, Blake turned and gave his shoulder a friendly punch.

"Don't worry Kill, it won't get out of control," he whispered, trying to keep Killian's disgust for alcohol a secret from the others.

Killian rolled his eyes and walked toward the shore. He'd learned from experience with the Petersons, nothing could change a person more than those drinks Amanda swung around playfully.

Killian found himself standing behind a couple as Amanda passed around the beers. The young man next to a girl with long chestnut-colored hair took two cans and offered one to her. Killian watched as she shook her head and looked away.

"More for me," her date shrugged and laughed gulping down a large amount. The girl turned around, disappointment written in her smooth brown skin. Killian was instantly captivated. Her features were bright, yet also dark and fierce and her emerald-colored eyes glistened in the sunlight forcing him to keep staring at her.

To his embarrassment the girl met his gazing eye and scanned him up and down. Killian's palms started sweating when she stepped off the log, glancing back at the young man she was with, who was already working on his third can. She rolled her eyes and walked toward Killian.

"Hi," she said sweetly. "I don't think I've seen you at school before."

Killian shrugged stupidly. His stomach turned in knots when the girl's perfect smile spread across her face. "I'm Killian," he whispered.

"Good to meet you Killian. I'm Merc…"

"Dezzy! Dez," the slurred voice of the young man interrupted her. "Come on lets go have some fun." He pulled her closer to him and planted loud, wet kisses along her neck. Killian shuddered at the awkward display.

"Ugh, Kevin stop. You're a sloppy drunk." Her voice was angry and frustrated as she tried to push him away. The tone made Killian's heart pound in frustration. Kevin's face darkened and he gripped her upper arm hard.

"We're going. *Now*." He pulled her away back toward the boardwalk. Killian knew she didn't want to go with him. His skin burned as he yearned to keep her from drunk Kevin.

"Hey," he called after the two, but was drowned out by a loud shout of disgust.

12

"Ahhhh! Gross!" Blake was slowly picking up each foot and looking on in horror. "Kill! We have to go...NOW!" Killian watched as a swaying Amanda leaned in toward Blake's face. Disgusted Blake pushed her away gently and marched over to Killian.

The strong smell of vomit burned his nostrils when Blake stood next to him.

"We're outta here," Blake huffed. Killian looked to see if the emerald-eyed girl was still close, but she was gone. His heart sunk, but he still laughed at Blake and his vomit soaked shoes.

***

Blake pulled into Killian's driveway and let out an exaggerated sigh. "Sorry man, this was supposed to be an all-day thing," he pouted.

"Tell Mandy not to chug so many drinks next time, okay. Its nasty stuff anyway," Killian teased. He was amused by what had happened, but his thoughts often drifted to concern for the girl drug away by blubbering Kevin.

"Amanda didn't know you have a weird issue with alcohol," Blake said defensively.

"I told her at school I hate the stuff. Come on Blake you don't honestly *like* her do you?"

"Why do you say it as if it's a bad thing?" he asked, looking confused.

"Blake," Killian laughed and covered his face with his hands, "the girl thought she could chug five beers! She threw up on your shoes and *then* tried to kiss you."

Blake squirmed in his seat, but didn't say anything more about Amanda. "Well, have an awesome evening hanging out with Mama Laura! I've got to go wash this smell out of my shoes. Maybe you guys can watch a nice Cary Grant." Blake laughed at his own sarcasm. Killian scoffed, but couldn't help but smile at the reference to Laura's obsession.

13

Perhaps it was her escape from Richard, Killian wondered to himself. She loved to run back in time to the simplicity of the classics.

The house was dark inside, which was surprising since it was so early in the evening. Killian saw all the blinds were pulled shut and that made his hair stand on end. Setting the brown paper bag full of taffy on the kitchen table he knew something was wrong.

"Laura?" he called out as he traipsed the halls of the large house. He heard a thud upstairs toward her bedroom. Killian ran up the stairs two at a time, he hadn't seen Richard's car—unless...

Killian rushed down the hallway even faster to the master bedroom. Often times Richard would leave his car at the office, and lock his door so his employees would think he was in a meeting, then slip out on the bus when he felt a rage coming on. If anyone ever saw a battered Laura, he would have an alibi to clear his involvement. The eccentric strategy had worked numerous times; it made Killian hate the man even more. It revealed how premeditated and deliberate *all* his attacks had been.

The door to the master bedroom was cracked open. Killian paused, unsure if he dared enter the shadowed room until the hall was filled with a loud *SMACK* followed by a gurgled groan. Killian burst into the room—the sight before him made his stomach churn and he was afraid he would lose the contents on the soft Italian carpet.

Richard stood over his wife, holding a clump of her light hair in his hand. His athletic build heaving from the exertion of beating her down. His French cuffed, perfectly pressed, white shirt was splattered in fresh blood. Laura lay on the floor with her eyes closed; at least Killian imagined they were. Her face was plastered with thick, streams of blood and swelling had already started to set in. The room smelled metallic and it made Killian feel certain he would be sick.

Richard reeled around at the sound of the door opening and glared at Killian, his black eyes seething with anger and power. He

14

smirked at the younger man as if to prove how out of his hands the situation was.

"Looking to be a hero?" Richard hissed. "You—are—the most insig...insignificant waste of space I have 'er seen." The words slipped out of his mouth so slurred the insult was barely audible.

The ridiculous statement boiled beneath Killian's skin. A strange sensation overwhelmed him; he felt his insides being split in two. A strange rage filled him, followed by a seething hate. It was almost as if Killian was feeling emotions that were not his own—emotions that matched the expression on Richard's face. He hated the man to be sure, but not with such passion and viciousness as he was feeling. The sensation made Killian's head spin—he couldn't understand the strangeness of the feeling, but he quickly acted on the rage, even if it was causing discomfort. The anger built up inside him until his body seemed to perform on its own accord.

Killian immediately rushed between the two people, causing Richard to stumble for a moment. He stood over the battered, moaning woman in an attempt to protect her. Richard stumbled toward him, tripping on his feet, but caught himself. This attack was unlike others, Richard's eyes were pure black—there was no light. Killian had to protect Laura, or she may not live through the night. A strange sensation pooled in his chest, almost as if his desire to defend formed into physical matter. He coughed and weakened slightly as the feeling seeped through his pores and toward Laura. It was an insane thought, but he could almost see a barrier forming around Laura, leaving her protected for the time being. Shaking his head, he focused again on Richard. The man was attempting a charge again, and without thought, the fire that burned through his blood pushed his fist toward the side of Richard's taut jaw.

Richard stumbled backward from the blow and fell against the couple's dresser, slicing the side of his head. A clean trail of blood trickled down his temple from his scalp. Richard's mouth fell open dumbly, a flash of anger ripped through his vicious eyes. Killian recognized the hate. He had lived with it most of his life, but he also saw hesitation toward Killian's strength. Richard lifted his head toward his closet and Killian's heart pounded—he knew he kept his 9mm on the top shelf.

Killian rushed in front of his line of sight and pushed Richard back against the wall.

"Don't bother Richard, I'm leaving, you *won't* see me again. Just remember every time you beat her down, you are nothing—nothing but a worthless, sorry excuse for a man." Killian spat at the stunned man's feet then rushed out of the room.

His heart panged. *Perhaps I should stay and protect Laura,* he thought to himself. He quickly talked himself out of the idea, believing Richard may kill them both if he tried to take her. Something inside him urged him to leave, he knew the attack on Laura was over—though he didn't know how he knew it. Rushing down the stairs he quickly dialed 9-1-1 on the phone in the kitchen. His breath grew ragged as he heard Richard scuffling off the floor above him.

"9-1-1 what is your emergency?" the calm female voice sounded on the other end.

"He attacked her, 421 Blue Bell Street," he breathed into the phone. Before the operator could answer, Killian left the phone connected to the operator, but dropped it on the counter. He heard Laura's sobs, but Richard's sloshing feet on the stairs urged him to move. He had to leave now, or he wouldn't leave at all. Killian rushed out the front door and ran—he knew there was only one place he would be safe.

A half hour later, Blake shoved Killian down the stairs to his grandparents' basement.

"You really hit him Kill? Are you crazy?" Blake breathed quietly.

"You should've seen her, Blake. He was going to kill her, I know he would've." Killian was still reeling from the adrenaline rush of the entire ordeal.

"You should've called the cops man, Richard will never let you live now."

"I tried, but…" Killian didn't finish and swallowed a lump built up in his throat. Blake didn't know how true he believed that statement was. Richard was violent, and had no love in his heart for Killian. His life as he had known it was over.

The two boys rested on the soft leather couch. They sat in silence, neither knowing what to say.

A knock came to the front door and Blake shuffled upstairs to answer it. Killian recognized that Blake did a lot of work for his grandparents around the house. In truth, Killian had never met the two elderly people. Blake said they spent the majority of their days at the country club spending their vast retirement fund. He knew at this time of night they were most likely in bed, although it was still early for their grandson.

"Kill, uh—you gotta come here dude," he heard Blake's nervous voice call from the top of the stairs. He swallowed hard, readying himself to face Richard, who he was certain had sniffed him out to Blake's house.

To his surprise, he was met at the front door by a hefty dark man in a police uniform. His lanky partner leaned against the side of the house, putting on a stern, serious face that meant he was in no mood for delinquent behavior.

"Killian Thomas?" the officer asked.

"Yes."

"Killian Thomas you are under arrest for the assault on a Mrs. Laura Peterson, you have the right to remain silent…"

The man's voice blurred as he continued to read him his rights. This was not happening. He hadn't touched Laura. The police officer reached for his wrist to place the cold handcuffs around it, but Killian yanked it away.

"No, this isn't right! I stopped it! It was Richard, I called you," Killian was shouting and desperately fighting against the officer.

Blake had a hand on his forehead and just stared, not knowing what to do. The hefty officer gripped his wrist so hard Killian shouted out in pain. The second, lanky officer had joined his partner and was helping detain him.

"It's okay, Kill. It will work out," Blake shouted, trying to reassure him. "Laura will tell them what really happened! I'll talk to my Grandpa, we'll straighten this out for you! I promise." Blake's voice faded as the police officers walked Killian to their patrol car. They pushed his head briskly so he didn't hit the side and shut the door on his face.

Killian was sure he was going to be sick. His shoulders heaved up and down. "I didn't do it," he whispered obsessively under his breath. "How is this happening?"

Killian glared out the patrol car window as he held firm to a single moment of clarity. "Richard," he hissed. Inside he knew it was over— no one would ever believe him over Richard.

***

Killian looked over his shoulder. Blake and several other kids from his school sat behind him, certainly recruited by his friend. Blake gave him a thumbs up as Laura made her way to the witness box. Killian was dressed in a bright, pumpkin colored jumpsuit—his hands were still cuffed in his lap.

This was his moment. Laura was going to tell the judge what happened and it *would* match with the statement he had given the police. Blake had testified of his character, and he was certain the 9-1-1 call would help his case. He would finally be able to walk free of the prison and Richard would be trading places with him.

"Mrs. Peterson, what happened on the seventh of July, the night of the assault?" a neatly pressed lawyer asked a nervous Laura.

Laura glanced quickly at a Killian, making brief eye contact. Her eyes were glazed with pain and fear. Killian's heart sunk and he shook his head. He felt a wave of emotion overcome him. The sensation was thick and encompassing. It was guilt as he had never felt before. He believed he was going mad, but he knew the feeling was not his own. He had felt guilty for leaving Laura that night, but not in such a deep, agonizing way. He knew what was going to happen even before Laura opened her mouth.

"I was alone in my room, cleaning up before my husband came home from work. My foster son came in—he was angry I hadn't let him stay out with his friends longer," Laura began quietly, she hiccupped with emotion before continuing. "Killian, began to hit me. I don't know what would've happened if Richard hadn't come home. Killian pushed Richard against the dresser when he tried to stop him. Then he ran." She sniffled into the microphone.

Killian believed his heart would rip in two. He knew Laura wasn't his mother, but she had told him many times she wanted to be. How could she slander him in such a way? His pain and disbelief were broken by a loud shout coming from several rows behind.

"THAT'S A LIE! Richard did this and you know it, Laura!" Blake shouted, coming to his feet. The judge pounded the gavel at the commotion that had rippled through the courtroom until the bailiff forcibly led a ranting Blake from the room.

Laura had stepped down and returned to her seat next to Richard, who looked directly at Killian. His face was smug as he smiled in victory. The blackness in his eyes was pure hatred.

Killian stared at the man's face and physically felt the stone wall build itself around his heart. These people had, in technicality, raised him. Yet, there they were—one controlled by fear, the other by power, sentencing him to a life of banishment. He knew he would never forget this moment—Killian Thomas knew his faith in love and trust would be forever tainted and damaged.

Chapter 2
The Attack

One Year Later

Killian sat upright on his hard, rickety cot gasping for breath. Instinctively, he reached for the comfort of his gold charm, but his hands came up empty. He cursed remembering the small trinket had been missing for the last two days.

Laura, after his sentencing, had made a special deal with the judge, explaining his troubled childhood. She expressed the charm was a keepsake from his biological family. Eventually, he was allowed to keep the charm with him. He scowled as the memories from the trial cursed his mind. Brushing his hand through his hair he shook Laura's painful ghost from his mind.

His hands brushed against his sweat drenched T-shirt, as he rehashed images from his dream.

The little boy needed help! Killian had experienced the cold breeze and the smell of ash in the cramped, dark room where the child held his small knees against his chest. It had been so real. The red-headed woman had tried to keep him, to protect him; but the haunting, dark figures had taken the small boy from her. His brain wildly recounted the dream that had been recurring for the last month. He remembered the dream, like a ghost from his past. The same dream had come to him many times when he'd lived with Richard and Laura, but since coming to the prison, most of his dreams were replays of the horrible night that had landed him in jail.

Killian flipped his legs over the side of his makeshift bed and slowly took several deep breaths. His feet crushed the shoebox that had once been filled with smutty pictures and cookies Blake had sent. He smiled remembering what Blake had told him at his sentencing hearing.

"As long as you're locked up, just think of me as your mistress, waiting to greet you on the outside! You'll get so many care packages you won't even know you're in a cage—it'll be a vacation!"

The latest package had been intercepted by Killian's rough cellmate, Nicco. He staked his claim on the pictures and passed the cookies to Alex in the cell over. Alex had, in turn, given them to Brooks, the vicious work release guard. Killian scoffed. Alex was the biggest brown nose in the prison but it often paid off. He received less degrading comments from the cantankerous guard and lighter workloads.

"If I have to listen to your insane ramblings one more night, I promise you, *sin valor,* you will regret it!" Nicco said after several moments glaring at Killian as he stared absently at the package. His face was coated with numerous tattoos and scars. The appearance was used as a scare tactic for other inmates, although Nicco had never acted upon his threats. Killian had long ago outgrown his strategy and simply blocked him out.

"GET UP MORONS!" a voice shouted down the long corridor. Killian's skin crawled hearing Brooks' voice. "I don't have time to waste getting you trash to the worksite!"

For the last month, Killian had been involved in the work release program and was able to leave the prison three days out of the week to work his way into society before his upcoming release.

Seven inmates were selected to go to Central Oregon Community College for landscaping duty. They filed out of their cells and lined up against the bars. Nicco stood next to Killian smirking at Alex who stood straight and tall, intently listening to what Brooks had to say. Brooks paced back and forth looking each of the seven men up and down with contempt.

"You are all a waste of my time; I'm amazed the prison board believes you will make useful members of society. If I had my way, none of you would ever get out there on *my* streets. Unfortunately, until then I have to babysit you losers," Brooks spat out each word, until a string of saliva dangled from his chin. Alex was nodding, vigilant in his attention of the guard's tirade. "I want all of you to get out to the van in a single file line. Do *not* raise a hand or say a word. If you do, you'll wish you never were assigned to my crew! MOVE OUT!"

Killian couldn't help but laugh inwardly at the ridiculous speeches the guard shouted as often as possible.

The ride to the campus was uneventful; none of the men spoke to one another. The few guards assigned to their small crew sat at the front of the van at strong attention, awaiting Brooks' orders. As Killian waited for the other crew members and group of guards to pile out the door, he looked out the window at the bright campus across the street. The college was clean and busy, surrounded by beautiful wooded areas full of trails and picnic spots. Students and staff shuffled by the neatly hedged bushes next to the college marquee.

He observed how the bowed heads of the students pouring over their books, mimicked the bowed heads of the inmates. The blaring difference was the students didn't wear metal cuffs around their wrists. Killian rubbed the red grooves on his skin as he bitterly turned his attention away from the free students.

Before he left his seat in the van, Killian's hair on the back of his neck stood on end as the eerie sense of someone watching him prickled over him. The vehicle was empty, but turning his head toward the campus once again, his blood drained from his face as he locked eyes with the red-haired woman from his dream only hours earlier. Her face was outlined with worry and anxiety as her sad eyes bore into his.

"THOMAS! Don't make me drag you off this van," Brooks' voice sounded in Killian's ears, making him break eye contact from the mystery woman. When he looked back through the window again, she was gone.

Killian anxiously joined the crew outside the van. His head reeled with curiosity—he wondered if he might be losing his mind. The anxiety he felt about spotting the woman was soon buried under a slew of harsh words from Brooks.

"Alright, we are starting here by the athletic field. We will also cover the campus center and fitness building. There will be no interacting with students or staff. Fall semester is about to begin and I will not have us falling behind the *schedule I* set for the college, is that understood? I don't expect any of you nobodies to get it, but if any of the rules are broken, you'll be back in front of the judge with another year on your sentence."

Most of the young men gave a mumbled acknowledgment that they understood; Nicco had already turned his attention to a group of girls lying on the grass by the field, laughing over open text books and Diet Cokes.

"Well, *el idiotas* have a great day, I'm heading to the field," he said licking his lips and lopping toward the girls after they'd had their cuffs removed and guard assigned. Killian thought he was disgusting, but reluctantly followed him to begin work as quickly as he could.

"Thomas! Where do you think you're going?"

Killian turned around slowly to face the cantankerous man."Sir, I thought we were just told to begin at the athletic field."

"Thomas I don't know how you are going to make it without this place. You have as much brains as the roach I stepped on this morning," Brooks said, pleased at his own beastliness. Killian did not have the patience for this today.

"Sir, with all due respect I can go faster if you would just tell me *where* you want me to go."

Brooks grabbed Killian by the cuff of his shirt and pinned him against the van. Killian was nearly the same height as the man, and his toned biceps tensed in defense. Though it was probable he would be able to physically defend himself against Brooks, confrontation only brought trouble. He listened as the guard shouted a slew of obscenities describing how worthless Killian would be to society before finally shoving him hard toward the campus center with hedging duty.

Killian gave Brooks a menacing scowl, and bit out the words, "Yes, sir," to his back as he watched the large man stomp toward the athletic field. He never would admit it out loud, but after a year of hearing such degrading words it was hard not to believe them. He reached down, grabbed the hedge shears, a required walkie-talkie, a water bottle, and grumbled toward the campus center. He sighed in relief at the meager crowds of students. It was still summer semester and the campus was lacking its usual crowds.

On campus students and staff often provided a variety of expressions toward him. Some had looks of pity—some looks of wonder; he was sure they were trying to figure out what he had done to earn him a spot on the crew. But most looks—most were looks of disgust. Many students, who were in fact his peers, looked at him like he was a waste of time and space as he worked day after day beautifying their campus.

Scowling at the bitter thoughts he followed the cement walkway connected to a large circle in the center of the campus. Walkways extended from the circle like a star, leading students down different paths to the buildings. The center was lined with benches and picnic tables where students could enjoy the sun between classes or catch up on some studying outdoors before the weather turned them into cold-avoiding recluses.

As Killian moved off to the side he scanned the circle of hedges that decorated the area. Groaning, he estimated the amount of work the shapeless, overgrown shrubs would require. He glanced back at the single guard who'd accompanied him as he disappeared behind the hedges. Thankfully it was Warner. Killian remembered Warner as the bailiff present at the hearing. Warner had transferred to the work crew when Killian's turn was up. Only days into the work crew Warner had admitted to Killian he'd found it unfair to be given such a harsh sentence with no prior convictions. He allowed Killian to do his work peacefully and since Killian never caused any trouble he often took time to listen to his strange science-fiction books he stored on his phone.

Bending down, Killian placed the water and walkie-talkie behind the first section of hedges. As he came around to the front, his shoulder bumped up against another, causing him to stumble.

"Oh, I'm sorry," a female voice said. Killian looked up and met a pair of emerald eyes. A girl with beautiful bronze skin was bending down to pick up the notebook she had dropped in the collision. He bent down and grabbed the notebook firsthand handed it to her. Long chestnut waves from her ponytail brushed against his face. Despite being pulled up, her hair still reached to the center of her back.

"Thanks, again sorry for running into you. Hey, don't I know you?" She smiled up at him.

"Uh, no I don't think so," Killian said. Suddenly, a memory filled his mind. The bright smile and gorgeous eyes brought him back to the roaring bonfire, and the drunk boy planting sloppy kisses all over her neck. Killian met her brilliant green eyes and shook his head again. "Sorry, I really don't think we've met."

"I could've sworn we'd met before and I usually have a good memory—wait." Her eyes widened and twinkled delightfully. "Killian...from the beach." She laughed remembering their short intrigue months ago.

"Oh, right. Now I remember." He tried to turn away, but she adjusted her position to stand in front of him.

"So how have you been?" she continued. Her face fell when she finally focused on the words lettering his vest.

Killian pursed his lips and turned toward the hedge. Inside he wanted to disappear in a hole and never lay eyes on her perfect face again. "It's been an interesting year." His voice was gruff and uninviting. He didn't want to talk anymore, he didn't want her pity looks, or worse—disgust.

Killian scowled at the hedge as an image of how life might have been spanned his mind. She seemed to take notice of his cold body language and clutched her books tighter against her chest. Her voice was flat when she spoke again. "Oh. Well, I'm going to go study. It's good to see you again."

Killian gave a sad smile toward her back as she walked away. She didn't leave the circle, instead she found a place at the small picnic table, and she turned and gave him a quick glance before immersing herself in an exceptionally thick book. Killian cleared his throat, and walked back toward the hedge.

After an hour, he'd hedged the first ten feet of greenery. Stepping back, he critiqued his work making sure they were perfectly even. He bent down and grabbed a water bottle from his bag and wiped the dripping sweat from his forehead. In the heat he was grateful Brooks demanded short military haircuts on the crew. If he still sported his thick, longer style he'd had at the Petersons, it would be miserable.

Drinking half the bottle in one sitting he decided it was safe to move on to the next set of shrubs. Before moving to the plants, he peeked up at the emerald-eyed girl, who studiously remained at the table. To his surprise she glanced up from her textbook at the same moment. Killian's stomach doubled up again and he quickly turned back to the plants.

After several moments a tall, dark haired, pale man walked up to her table. Killian snorted in disgust. Kevin. The creep from the beach was still hanging around. Pretending to be focused on the hedges he found himself straining to hear the conversation between the two.

After catching bits and pieces, the dialogue made his blood rise to his head as memories flooded back from only a year earlier. Killian choked as a familiar feeling weighed down in his chest, he had the strongest desire to protect the girl. Quickly he dissolved the feeling—those types of thoughts led to trouble.

"Come on Dez don't make me force you. You'll have a blast tonight, just say yes." Kevin said as he twisted a piece of her hair around his finger..

"For the last time Kevin, we're done and *I don't want to go*!" she said firmly, looking right into his face. She began to pile her books into her bag. Kevin suddenly grabbed firm to her wrist, forcing her to stop what she was doing.

"Don't do that—let me go!" She shouted at him, trying to tug her arm away. Killian dropped his shears and had already started to make his way toward them on the opposite side of the circle.

"Listen, if I ask you to go with me to a party, I expect you to go," Kevin hissed, pulling her arm so their faces were inches apart. The girl pushed against him, trying to free herself. The struggle was useless; he was quickly overpowering her.

"You're hurting my arm," she snarled. "Let go now!"

"Not until you—"

"HEY!" Killian shouted, interrupting Kevin. He couldn't stop himself, the girl was in trouble. He inwardly vowed he wouldn't let the confrontation go as far as he had with Richard. "Let her go."

Kevin straightened up, releasing his grip on the girl. Killian noticed she moved a few feet away, but still close by. Kevin scoffed at Killian and folded his arms across his chest.

"Huh—I don't know if *you're* in a place to be talking to me," he laughed, pointing to Killian's jeans plastered in the same label as his shirt. "Why don't you just get back to your yard work, or I might have to let someone know a *criminal* is harassing this young lady."

Killian glared at him, but he had stopped a few feet away from the man. The billowing weight that frothed against his heart, had built up again; yet his own self-doubt shadowed the strength of the protective instinct. He'd learned even the innocent can be punished for good deeds. Killian felt a flicker of fear at his threat, if he was involved in any form of violence he could easily add another six months to his sentence. The image of walking out the prison doors, free, kept him still. It was so close to being his reality. Killian's muscles relaxed and his shoulders slumped in defeat.

Kevin laughed and made his way over to the girl, wrapping his hand around her arm. He gripped her tight as she struggled against him. His other tentacle-like arm wrapped around her shoulders, pressing her close into his body.

"That's right scum bag, just walk away—she'll be taken care of I promise," he said as he tilted his head giving the girl an unwelcome kiss on her brow. She swung a wild hand, but missed his face and twisted in his grip. Kevin laughed wickedly as if he enjoyed her struggle.

The anger inside Killian boiled over, passed the point of him caring about another six months. He felt a strange prickle of pain shoot up his back, all the way to his head. Slimy, sick desire filled his heart as if he could hear every shameful thought in Kevin's mind. Kevin flashed him a confused look as if he saw something unusual. Taking advantage of his brief loss of focus Killian's fist connected with his smirking jaw, causing him to release his grip on the girl. Before Kevin had time to recover, Killian dropped his shoulder, thrust it into his stomach tackling him to the ground.

A loud smack filled the circle as Kevin's head connected with the concrete. Kevin let out a loud groan and, Killian, straddled him and gave him one last solid punch in the nose before standing up.

"Be careful who you call a scum bag," he snarled. Kevin quickly scrambled to his feet holding his bleeding nose.

"What kind of freak are you?" He cried out and ran away from Killian, shooting him an angry glance before disappearing beyond the hedges. Killian rushed to the tall hedge and peered over. Breathing a sigh of relief that Warren was too lost in his latest Mars adventure series he hadn't even noticed the commotion.

His heart raced and his toned shoulders heaved from the exertion. The strange sensation he'd felt, and the look Kevin had given him unsettled him. He hadn't protected the girl, he'd only attacked Kevin because of his own swirling anger he'd allowed to overpower him. Pushing the anxiety aside he knew he went to check on the girl.

She was standing a few feet away from him with her hands over her mouth and her books scattered on the ground. Slowly, he made his way over to her. When he got closer he could see she had tears glistening in her eyes. She stiffened, but didn't back away from him when he came up to her. He bent down and picked up the same notebook he had earlier as well as a thick Biology textbook that had fallen.

"Sorry about that. It's Dez, right?" he asked holding the books out to her. She lowered her hands and accepted the books, but said nothing. Killian gave an awkward smile, his eyes glancing around as he slowly backed away from her. "Alright, well...glad you're okay. I was just trying to help."

"Wait..." He heard the girl behind him, his stomach clenched as he met her eyes, she stared at him for a few moments before continuing. "Thank you." She said quickly, dropping her eyes to the ground. He gave her a shy smile and moved closer to her.

"It's no problem," he said, teasing he continued, "but you should stay away from jerks like that."

"Tell me about it," she said, her shoulders relaxed as a smile spread across her face. "and it's Mercedes. Kevin calls me Dez and I hate it." Shifting the books to one hand, she stuck out the other toward Killian. Taking it, his stomach twisted even more.

"It's good to finally learn your name, it's been what a year now?" he tried to make light of the situation, but he kept feeling like he was going to double over from stomach pains. Mercedes smiled at him, and slowly let go of his hand.

"I really appreciate what you did," she said again. "Kevin isn't a nice guy, I'm sure you noticed. I finally had enough and decided to end it about a month ago. I guess he hasn't gotten the hint yet."

Killian knew from her description exactly what kind of man Kevin was. He just nodded his understanding. She headed back over to the table, giving him a small wave before turning her focus back down to her books. Killian smiled, picked up his shears, and began working on the rest of the hedges.

After about two hours, Warren had checked in once, but seeing Killian diligently hedging and receiving a little smile from Mercedes, he resumed reading his tablet. Killian put down the shears, satisfied with how the hedges looked. He grabbed his water bottle again and shifted his gaze to the table. Smiling he saw that Mercedes was still there. Over the course of the last couple hours, she had left the table and come back multiple times. This time munching on a bag of chips.

Killian smiled. He had never been a college student, but he was sure they didn't need to sit and study the same few pages for that long. Mercedes seemed to keep scanning and re-reading the same few paragraphs. She met his gaze and returned the smile.

Finally she closed her book and placed it in her shoulder bag. Killian felt like his stomach was doing summersaults when he realized Mercedes was making her way toward him. He could have sworn he saw her cheeks flush as her focus drifted to the ground then back to his ocean blue eyes. His palms were sweaty as he watched her.

Killian broke eye contact from her emerald eyes. A strange rustling was coming from the neatly trimmed hedges. The hair on his arms stood up.

"Do you hear that?" he whispered. Her brow furrowed as she searched for what he'd been hearing. "Maybe it's Kevin, he's going to get me locked up longer." His neck was tight with stress as he cracked the joints wondering how he could get out of another court hearing.

Suddenly his heart beat even faster when he heard a low rumbling growl somewhere in the plants; all around the campus the bustle from students making their way to classes appeared in one moment to come to a deadly silence.

Mercedes stopped where she was. Turning her head, she glanced at the bushes behind her. Goosebumps prickled her skin, and she quickly rushed to his side.

"What was that?" she whispered, whisking her head to both sides, listening to the deep growl.

"I don't know," he responded, instinctively placing himself in front of her. Something was behind those hedges, something that was now encircling them. The growls rippled behind the circular hedge, coming from every direction.

Killian slowly inched with Mercedes over to his water bottle where the walkie-talkie rested. He bent down grappling for his shears, and reached for the walkie-talkie. Nervously flipping the switch on, he quickly whispered into the device.

"This is Killian, something is happening over by the campus center—someone get over here quick, it sounds like...like an animal or something." He released the button and listened to the static waiting for a response, mentally cursing Warren's earplugs and novels.

Suddenly the hedges snapped apart, drowning out Brooks' sudden slew of expletives on the walkie-talkie. An enormous, hideous beast entered the campus center, displaying wicked, jagged claws. A huge wolf-like animal stood before them, with yellow mucous filled saliva dripping from its black lips and its blood-red eyes focused on nothing else, but them.

The animal had a bald scalp that was covered in deep scabbed gashes, one of the bloodied slits had a broken piece of metal protruding from the gaping wound. Its face was bald with tufts of hair trying to grow around its salivating lips. The rest of its enormous body was covered in brown, matted fur.

Two bottom fangs curled over the top lip—those were not what worried Killian, it was the two upper fangs that hung well below the animal's square chin! The creature growled, hunching its shoulders and advancing. On the sides of the circle four more of the same frightening creatures with similar scabbed heads made their way toward them.

Killian's heart beat faster as he clenched tight to his shears and watched the unearthly wolves while desperately searching for an escape route. Mercedes' breathing grew rapid next to him as she gripped onto his arm instinctively. His heart skipped a beat when his eyes picked out a small gap between the pack. It was their only chance —even if it was small.

"Mercedes," Killian whispered, eyeing the small opening, "Mercedes, run...RUN!" He finally shouted pushing her ahead of him as fast as he could through the one opening in the monstrous pack.

Chaos erupted to the side of them as the pack immediately sprang into action at their movement. Both of them darted quickly toward the unguarded hole; Killian shoved Mercedes through the hedge then quickly jumped over the bush. His left leg seared in pain as he fell to the ground; his bottom teeth cut through his lip as his face slammed into the cement walkway. Looking back all he saw was a scabbed, bald head of one of the beasts. It had dug its bottom two fangs deep into his muscle.

Killian rolled over onto his back, feeling his skin and muscle tear against the vicious teeth. He frantically reached for the shears that had landed several feet from him. Blood pounded in his head, as he desperately tried to block out the pain from the vicious gnawing on his skin. In a desperate attempt, Killian kicked his free foot at the beast's nose. He felt the sick feeling of the bones crushing in its monstrous snout. The wolf growled viciously, and dug its fangs deeper into his muscles. The kick only infuriated the beast.

Suddenly, shuffling feet flew past his head and lifted the shears from the ground. He watched in disbelief as Mercedes gouged the thick shears deep into the back of the freakish animal's neck. The creature released his leg, whining like a small dog and abandoned its prey. Behind him, Killian saw the four other beasts attack the animal that had just released him—he watched them tear long gashes into its already scabbed head as if it was some twisted punishment for failing to capture the prey. Mercedes bent down to Killian's side and wrapped his arm around her own shoulders helping him up off the ground. The two once again began their desperate escape.

"You should just leave me and get out of here," he gasped. Mercedes ignored him and slowly dragged him along.

Despite the circumstances, he couldn't help the annoying stomach twinge that filled his abdomen. He returned his focus to the distant sound of pounding feet on the ground and snapping fangs behind him.

Stumbling into a tangle of trees they stumbled desperately through the woods nearby the college, Killian's injured leg dragging useless to his side. Killian looked behind him and saw the two creatures were closing the gap between him and Mercedes with every bounding stride. He heard a loud shriek come from Mercedes and soon felt himself falling. They slid down the hard ground, twigs scratching their skin, and rocks bruised their bodies until they landed with a loud *crunch* against the ravine floor.

Gathering his wits, Killian quickly lifted his battered body, scanning his eyes up the hill to find the animals. His injured leg was throbbing after it had taken another beating falling down the ravine. He spotted the wretched pack off to his side, circling the drop off, trying to find a way down. While two of the disgusting beasts pawed the ground above them, finding their sure footing, he looked down and saw Mercedes on the ground. She had landed farther in front of him and was now crying out in pain. He saw her bare arm twisted and mangled in the sharp spikes of a barbed-wire fence that blocked off the edge of another steep drop.

Immediately Killian scooted his body toward her and gently, but hastily tried to help pry her torn skin from the fence. She sucked in a breath as he untangled the wire from around her bare skin, some of the barbs pulled and tugged as they fought against her tissues. Finally, Killian removed the final rusted, barb. The two struggled, and grappled trying to help one another stand straight again. Killian leaned against Mercedes' good arm for support. He tore off the awful jacket he wore, and crudely wrapped it around her bleeding arm. She looked into his eyes and placed her uninjured hand gratefully on his arm. He covered her hand with his and followed her eyes to the top of the ravine landing on the hideous creatures. Mercedes' breathing grew more rapid as shock overwhelmed her.

"What...what...are those...things," she gasped. "What are...we going to...to...do? We're trap...trapped down here!" Tears fell from her eyes, exaggerating their stunning color, as she clutched her injured arm close to her body. Above them, the more daring of the two pacing creatures slowly moved itself off the ledge, digging its enormous claws into the side of hill. Its fangs dripped with saliva as it anticipated its kill. Killian took a deep breath, then wrapped Mercedes in his arms.

"Hey, it's okay. We're going to be okay," he lied. Mercedes sobbed against his chest. His mind was muddled and focused on the strange beasts coming over the ledge. "Just think of the one place you would go if you could, picture yourself there."

His voice cracked, as he heard the heavy breathing of the animal getting closer. Mercedes' breath trembled against him, but she was no longer crying. She tensed her body and pulled him closer against her.

"Mercedes just close your eyes and picture that for me okay. It's going to be okay." Emotion took over, he closed his eyes bracing himself for the pain of the massive paw making contact with his head, or maybe the creature would just use its awful fangs and tear right into him. He bent his head against Mercedes and squeezed her tighter.

The low growl of the animal came close to his neck, the foul breath hit his skin. Killian tensed his body as he prepared for the fatal attack. His eyes burst open when he heard the loud howling of an injured animal followed by a sick thud next to him.

A small silver arrow was lodged inside the ear of the animal; it thrashed and howled in pain before heaving a final breath. The lifeless creature lay bleeding at his feet. The cry came again, Killian raised his head and watched the second animal that had stayed on the ledge of the ditch roll down the hill—a similar arrow jutting out from the top of its hairless scabbed skull. Mercedes lifted her head, her eyes falling on the beast at their feet, then creeping their way over to the one that had fallen to its death a moment ago.

"KILLIAN!" A familiar voice shouted above them. Killian looked up the ravine, he saw a man dressed in gray pants with a black shirt covered by a thin gray jacket. Killian could make out a thick leather strap crossing over his body holding what looked like a variety of weapons. The man quickly returned the small crossbow to the empty place on a strap behind his neck. Killian squinted, not believing what he was seeing he sputtered the name out in a shocked whisper.

"Blake?" he gasped.

Chapter 3
The Ponderi

Blake stood at the top of the hill, unraveling a spool of thin wire. Thrusting a three pronged hook deep into the ground, he heaved the wire over the side of the hill, making sure it landed just above Killian's head. Killian eyed the thin piece of metal that was connected to the wire, it formed a makeshift seat that he wagered he would be asked to sit on

Killian turned around his body trembling. "That's Blake," he said more to himself than Mercedes. "He has a crossbow. Why does he have a cross bow?" Shaking the questions from his mind he acted. Killian urged Mercedes to position herself on the metal seat through panicked protests.

"No, no you have to stay with me, I can't go up that hill— what if they are up there?" Mercedes ranted hysterically, grappling for Killian's hand. He sensed her body was going into a state of shock.

"Mercedes, I'm going to be right behind you okay. I promise. You have to hang on tight with your good arm, I know that guy up there, trust him," he tried to softly reassure her. Her emerald eyes glistened with tears, but she nodded her head. She clambered onto the thin metal rod attached to the wire, never breaking eye contact with him. The rope ascended slow and, oddly smooth up the ravine, carrying Mercedes to the top where Killian saw Blake help her over the ledge.

"Blake! There's no way you can lift me out. My leg is torn up, I can't use it to help climb up. You have to go and get help!" Killian shouted up the side of the ravine as the wire rope came back down. Blake was not a large guy, and Killian knew there was no way he could get him to the top alone.

"Don't worry about it Killian! Now get on as best you can and hang on tight!" Blake shouted back to him. Hesitating for a moment, Killian finally maneuvered himself onto the uncomfortable rod. He clutched the wire rope with all his strength, while his leg throbbed as it hung lifeless beneath him. He clenched his eyes shut anticipating the moment when Blake could no longer hold onto him and he plummeted back down the ravine.

Killian was surprised at how quickly he found himself at the top of the ravine after a jerky ride from the wire rope. Blake was bending over the edge of the ravine holding his hand out. Grasping it tight, he pulled Killian safely onto the forest floor. The remaining creatures that had pursued them lay bleeding from their bald heads, dead.

Killian's mouth hung open in disbelief as he glanced down at the wire rope. Blake had not pulled it at all, a soft motor hummed as it reeled in the remaining wire. The motor was so small, buried within the three-pronged hook, Killian would hardly know it was there had it not been for the noise. Killian turned to look at Blake, opening his mouth to inquire about the situation, but Blake put a hand up to silence him.

"There isn't any time to explain," he said. "I need you to trust me Killian. You need to come with me now. These animals attacked for a reason and there could be more coming." Glancing over at Mercedes, Blake went on, "she needs to come too—the shock of the attack will be too much for her. We can get her into the clinic to help her process all this."

"Clinic? What is happening..." His voice drifted away. Blake had already moved toward a large tree growing near the steep cliff. Opening a small device, he pressed a button; the device emitted small barbs similar to the fence that had maimed Mercedes. Amazingly the device unfolded into a small square with a translucent screen. As Blake secured the barbs into the trunk of the tree, a number pad powered up on the screen—almost as if the tree was its energy source.

As Blake typed in a numerical code, Killian made his way over to Mercedes, who was sitting on a jagged rock holding her arm. He wrapped an arm around her and she instantly hid her face against his chest and let out the emotion she'd kept bottled inside.

"It's okay...hey look—" Killian started, but was interrupted by Blake calling to them.

"Get ready Killian, get the girl...tell her to get it together... this will only stay open for ten seconds!" As he finished shouting at them the core of the tree turned brilliantly red, a slight windy force emanated from the ruby-colored trunk. The color slowly changed to a fiery orange, with an ever increasing force pulling them toward the tree as the power magnified. Suddenly the trunk of the tree burst open in furious power, knocking Killian and Mercedes from the jagged boulder. Killian felt the pull of the powerful force tugging him toward the trunk of the tree.

The tree pulsed in an electrifying white color. They both looked up from the ground, dumbfounded, at the gaping opening in the center of the tree. The tree itself seemed untouched. It didn't sway, the leaves didn't even rustle from the powerful wind that came from its core. It seemed as if only the three of them were in on the secret of the unknown portal that lit up their small area of the forest.

"COME ON! WE HAVE ONE SHOT! WE HAVE TO GO NOW!" Blake shouted back to them against the noise of the windy portal. Killian reacted, wrapping his arm around Mercedes' shoulder once again. The two of them limped and staggered as quickly as they could, taking the leap of faith into the mysterious hole that challenged any law of physics he had ever understood.

Instantly, as they passed through the opening, the air around them felt thick and humid. Killian could feel Mercedes' body move closer into his as the matter around them seemed to threaten their air supply. The unpleasant feeling was coming to a point that was hard to bear. Coming from behind them they heard the powerful force of the portal suctioning them back toward the opening.

Suddenly the world around them fell silent. The powerful suction ceased and calm surrounded them. Killian and Mercedes seemed to stay airborne for a small moment before falling; their feet crunching onto a steel walkway. Killian groaned as his leg seared in pain. Mercedes cried out when the shining steel splattered with her blood from landing on her injured arm. The fall was only two feet at most, but Killian had been sure he was plummeting to his death. Releasing the breath he had held in the entire time through the portal, he looked around, trying to take in their surroundings.

The sky was different. It was full of brilliant blues, dazzling reds, and radiant greens. All the colors swirled together against a back drop of an ebony universe littered with stars. In the center of the magnificent sky was a glowing orb. It shone brightly and warmed their faces. The same hues of the sky swirled in beautiful patterns in the large, gaseous sun emitting a soft lavender hue. All around them were plants and bright foliage. The flowers that stood out amongst the green plants were tall and brilliant with rainbow patterns along their petals. The plants didn't seem to fit any botanical design he had ever imagined; they seemed to be a cross between tropical and woodland shrubs.

The colorful sky reflected off an enormous building directly in front of them. Killian marveled at the unbelievable structure towering in the center of the magnificent garden. It was one of the strangest buildings he'd ever seen, made of glass and beautiful smooth steel. Huge beams jutted out at unique angles with enormous glass windows randomly scattered between the steel. The building reminded Killian of a block game he had played as a child with the objective to leave the tower standing as long as possible while removing blocks and re-stacking them on top. The large windows created translucent openings between the steel beams causing some concern inside whether the building would topple as the blocks had.

Blake had landed softly behind them, a content smile painted on his face. "You guys okay? It's pretty intense the first time through." Blake smiled, ignoring the contemptuous glares from the other two. "Come on inside. You both should get to the clinic. I'll make sure you get there. We can take care of those nasty cuts for you." He stated the words simply.

"We...who is we, Blake?" asked Killian fiercely, as he pushed himself off the ground with difficulty.

Stopping, Blake slowly turned and looked Killian in the eye. "Killian, I know you have no idea what is happening right now, but I really need you to trust me. Everything is going to be explained to you." He smiled and punched his arm like he used to. "Have I ever given you cause to mistrust me?"

Killian just stared back at him. "What about your grandparents, do they know about any of this?"

Blake gave him a sympathetic look. "Kill, I'll tell you about them later, I promise." He then turned around and opened a numbered key pad that was next to a set of giant wooden doors with steel bars covering them. After the code had been entered the huge steel hinges groaned as the doors swung open letting them enter.

"There better be some explaining," Mercedes' shaky voice broke with frustrated emotion. "You expect us just to follow you when we...we just...jumped through a tree!" Killian glanced over at her, the pitch of her voice increased as well as the color of her cheeks.

Blake turned around again, a flash of annoyance was present in his eyes. "I promise, before you know it you'll be home and comfortable; this will all be a bad memory." He turned briskly, leading them into the odd building, silencing further protests.

The room inside the door resembled a typical office entryway, with potted plants and a desk in the center of the room. A woman sat behind the desk. Killian stared at her; she was not the typical secretary he was used to seeing. Her hair was fire red, with the tips burning in bright orange. Her hair hung over her shoulders, blending in with the brilliant orange and fitted blue dress that revealed much of her legs. Her tan skin was covered in intricate, orange tattoos of fire. Both eyebrows had piercings that were connected by a gold chain, the glass charm from the chain dangled so it set in the center of her forehead. Her red lips curled into a big smile when she saw Blake.

"Blake! Oh my, I wondered when I would *ever* see you again," She said in an airy voice and a slight hint of an accent Killian couldn't place. The woman gave a gentle kiss on Blake's sweat covered forehead. The sweet sign of affection was strange to see between Blake, who typically viewed women as a prize.

"Fia my love! It has been so long since I've seen your beautiful face," Blake teased, stroking a strand of her bright hair. Killian almost smiled, that was the Blake he knew. Even in this strange place Blake still was a relentless flirt. The woman slapped him playfully, releasing all the sweet, soft affection she'd given earlier. "Fia, these friends of mine need to be taken to the clinic, would you mind calling Connor or Shannon to come and get them?" He pointed at Killian and Mercedes before bending in and nibbling her ear.

Giving a squeal of delight, Fia pushed Blake away from her. Turning her attention to Killian, her eyes widened. Killian couldn't help but stare into them. Her brown eyes were beautiful yes, but he could have sworn there was a faint flicker of flames moving behind her pupils.

"Blake...oh my I can't believe *he's* here." Her eyes looked worried as she kept staring at Killian, speaking as if he wasn't there. "Times can't be good if he has come home."

Blake shook his head when her gaze shifted back to him. She picked up a phone on the desk, typing in an extension, she asked for someone named Shannon. Killian raised his eyebrows. Home? What was this woman talking about?

"Shannon—file two, eight, zero, eight. Yes...*yes* Shannon he's here. He was brought in with a young woman. They will both need some medical attention." That was all she said before she hung up the phone. Killian felt overwhelmed, this strange, eccentric woman seemed to know him. He was unnerved that she implied she knew something dangerous was happening that involved him, something he didn't know.

Fia walked toward Killian, staring at him with her glowing fire eyes; the flames grew brighter as she stared deep into his blue eyes. Biting her lip, she took his free hand that wasn't around Mercedes' shoulders, and clasped it in her ring covered fingers, holding it close against her chest. Killian could hear Mercedes clear her throat loudly from the side of him. Fia ignored her, squeezing his hand tighter against her tan skin.

"You are what we have been waiting for. We're so thankful you've come to help us with the search." She leaned in and kissed his cheek with the same softness she'd bestowed to Blake. Holding his face between her hands, she looked like she was about to kiss his lips when Blake interrupted.

"Okay Fia, take it easy. Killian's been through a rough day. Why don't we let him unwind a bit?" Blake winked at Killian, as he grabbed Fia's hand and played with her hair again. Losing the intensity she'd had moments before, she began teasing and flirting with Blake.

Taking a deep breath, Killian glanced at Mercedes, whose eyes looked directly into his. She was looking at him with suspicious eyes.

"What is this?" she whispered sounding flustered.

"Mercedes, I have no idea. I promise." He shrugged and whispered back, exasperated. He wasn't sure if she was upset for being drug into a new world, or that Fia had kissed him.

"Well, they seem to know *you* pretty well." She nodded toward Fia.

"Mercedes, I promise I don't know what's going on. You act like I've been here before—I haven't," he stated firmly. The hurt from Laura crept into his heart. How long would the pain and anger at her betrayal stay? How often would it rear its ugly head whenever he opened his heart up to someone else?

Mercedes bit her bottom lip as her face softened. Her eyes scanned the blood stained shirt wrapped around her injured arm; she seemed to accept the answer and actually believe him. Silently she moved closer to his body, squeezing his hand that she held around her shoulders. The familiar twist in his stomach came as he squeezed her fingers tight and gave her a small smile.

A woman with strawberry blonde hair arrived shortly after, wearing large outdated glasses. She stepped out of an elevator they hadn't noticed had been there. The doors closed and the wall looked the same as it had before. The woman's hair bobbed up and down as she walked briskly toward them pushing a sleek silver wheelchair. The lab coat she wore was billowing behind her; it was much too big for her small frame.

"Hello, I'm Shannon. I'm going to take you to the clinic downstairs and make sure you both are cleared medically," she said, shaking both of their hands. "Please, Killian you really shouldn't be walking on that leg." She gestured to the chair. Killian glanced back and forth between Mercedes and Shannon, his leg was throbbing with each breath now that adrenaline was fleeing his body. Reluctantly he listened to her and plopped down into the surprisingly comfortable chair. "Now young lady if you would follow me." Shannon wheeled Killian toward the empty wall.

"Wait," Mercedes' voice trembled. "I…I don't feel good going…anywhere away… from him." She pointed at Blake, who couldn't help but smile boldly. Mercedes' anxiety fed into Killian, like everything she felt he experienced in sync with her.

Blake stepped toward her and placed his hand on the small of her back, gently urging her forward. "Shannon is going to help you. You can trust her, but you need her to check you out okay."

Mercedes' emerald eyes glazed with fresh tears but she nodded feebly before joining Shannon and Killian by the wall. Killian didn't want to admit it, but he needed Mercedes to stay by him. She was helping calm his nerves, and feeling much like an invalid he needed her to help him just as much as she needed support.

Fia ran ahead of them and stepped between them and the steel wall. He couldn't see what she did, but moments later the elevator doors dinged open once again.

They witnessed the entry of the building fade as the doors closed on them. Shannon typed a six-digit number onto a translucent numbered touch screen. The interior of the elevator was not like typical elevators, the list of floor numbers was absent on the wall and the walls and floor were completely made of glass. After she had typed in the number the elevator lurched and sped downward, much faster than a normal elevator. Killian's stomach rose into his throat as the car plummeted downward. Shannon stood still, obviously she had made the trip several times before and was quite accustomed to the sensation.

"Just for your information so you can move freely around, since we have no staircases, to summon the elevator you simply put your hand on the wall. The elevators run on a neuro-sensor system. A keypad should open up shortly after your touch. Each area has its own six digit number; we will provide a list for you soon so you can use the elevator at will, but even if you forget the floor number the car usually understands where you want to go." The woman said without a hint of jest in her tone. Killian stared at her incredulously. She spoke about the elevator car like it was a living thing.

"What is this place?" Mercedes asked quietly.

"This is the Praetorium." Shannon said, assuming they should just know what that meant. Mercedes looked at Killian, her face scrunched in confusion. Catching the exchange out of the corner of her eye, Shannon turned her face toward them.

"This is our headquarters," she said.

"Whose headquarters? Who are you people?" Mercedes asked louder than before. The pitch in her voice gave way to the anxiety she was feeling. Killian felt his pulse pound in his neck as his pressure rose as the small car plummeted downward, seeming to increase speed each moment they were trapped inside.

45

"We are all members of the Ponderi." Seeing this cleared nothing up for the two younger people, Shannon sighed and continued, "Look, I'm not the one who should or can explain it all to you. I'm in charge of making sure you are fine physically and mentally. Someone will answer your questions after we're done, I promise." She said facing the doors again as the elevator dinged to a stop.

Killian and Mercedes both seemed to accept this vague, partial answer. Killian calmed his breathing from the impending panic attack and reached out to give Mercedes' hand a reassuring squeeze.

Shannon wheeled Killian out of the elevator when the car suddenly stopped. Mercedes hobbled behind them as they found themselves in a room with glass walls and steel floors. There were hospital beds that lined three separate treatment rooms. It was a typical clinic. In the corner, typing on a computer, a man with thinning brown hair stood up. He wore similar glasses like Shannon, although his were significantly thicker.

"This is Connor, my colleague," Shannon said.

"Colleague? Pfft...try *amazing, attractive* husband!" Connor teased, giving Shannon a friendly swat on her behind. She glared at him, but the sparkle in her eye gave her true feelings away.

"Excuse me, meet Connor, my husband and very *unprofessional* colleague." He nodded toward her, accepting her new introduction of him. "Killian, Connor will be checking you, we need to do a full physical so I assumed this young lady might feel more comfortable with a woman." Mercedes' eyes opened wide as Shannon wheeled Killian toward Connor, then led her to a separate room and pulled the curtain over the glass wall.

"Wait can't I stay with him?" he heard Mercedes frantically ask. Shannon closed the glass door to their room before he could make out her mumbled assurances.

Connor turned toward Killian. Smiling he slapped some rubber exam gloves on his hand.

"Well... let's begin." Connor helped Killian up to a paper lined exam table and proceeded to poke and prod his body. He checked joints and bones, looking for possible fractures from the fall. Connor cleaned and disinfected the gashes in Killian's leg and stuffed a small piece of gauze inside his bottom lip. The gashes on his leg were enormous gaping wounds that made Killian's stomach queasy, the smell of necrotic tissue didn't help. Connor opened up an aluminum tube and applied a white sticky salve across his entire lower leg. The salve soothed the aching and throbbing he had felt earlier.

After a moment his skin was numb where the white paste was, then Connor laid across each open wound a thin strip of bristled, scratchy material. He held a long fluorescent bulb. Grabbing onto a metal end of the bulb, Connor brought the light toward Killian's leg. The bulb radiated uncomfortable heat, almost steaming as it inched closer to his skin. Killian quickly jerked it away.

"What are you doing?" he shouted.

"Hold still, trust me it doesn't hurt. It looks strange, but I promise these will be the quickest set of sutures you've ever gotten." Connor smiled and pulled Killian's leg toward him again.

Sweeping the hot light just above the ugly material, the uncomfortable heat ceased and a warm sensation flowed up and down his leg. He watched as Connor moved the light back and forth along the material until it shriveled and sputtered against the heat. As the material crackled, Killian could feel his skin tugging and pulling together. Connor lifted the light away from his leg after a moment or two; tiny charred pieces of material were left that quickly fell to the ground. The long, ugly gashes were now long thin lines of shiny skin; they were the only indication there had even been a gaping, bleeding cut.

Once he had impressively closed the gashes in his leg, Connor proceeded to apply a small piece of the scratchy, burlap type material to his lower lip. Connor's face looked disgusted as he inspected the gash his teeth had cut. Within a minute, the heated light had sutured the cut in his lip. He then checked Killian's blood pressure explaining that the type of stress he had just been under could cause his body to go into a period of shock.

Killian scoffed. "I think I'm coming out of the shock period, my mind is clearing up a bit." Connor took his glasses off and rubbed his nose where they had rested.

"Well, now I just want to ask you a few questions, then I'll send you up to Miller and Nathaniel."

"I'm not answering any questions until I get some answers first!" Killian blurted out. "I'm not going to be sent to two different people after we're done, have them examine me in some way, avoid all my questions, and send me to someone else promising I'll get answers very soon." He finished sarcastically. Connor curled his lip up into a half smile while he grabbed a thin, translucent tablet and laid it on his lap.

"Those two will be the ones to answer your questions." Killian closed his mouth, feeling a little sheepish for getting so short with Connor. "But I would be happy to try and answer any questions you have first."

Killian pondered for a moment. His mind was swimming with questions, but he blurted out the first thing that came to the forefront, "What kind of doctor are you exactly? Medical or a mental kind of doctor? How is it that I've never seen any of this equipment before? "

Connor chuckled. "Okay, I'll answer more than one. The answer to your first question, I am neither actually. I'm a Bioengineer to be exact, but Shannon is an M.D. with a secondary degree in Psychology. She taught me a thing or two," Connor answered simply. Killian was sure he was joking, but he didn't smile. "And the reason you haven't seen these things in other doctor's offices is because I invented them. Anything I have invented I have given to the Ponderi for the use of helping its members. So do you have any other questions?"

"Yes. I have tons of questions, but I'm pretty sure you're not the guy who's going to answer them right?" Connor nodded his head, giving Killian a sympathetic smile that he was getting quite tired of.

"Okay, are you ready to get started?" Killian just shrugged. Connor opened a screen on his device and quickly scanned through an open file.

"So, Killian Thomas, Blake has entered his report from earlier today. I'm aware you don't understand what has happened to you or your young lady friend," Connor smiled kindly. "I want to explain what the creatures are that you, unfortunately, met this afternoon."

Killian leaned forward in his chair anxious to hear what Connor had to say. He knew the creatures were not of his world.

"They are called Malumian Wolves. They roam independently throughout the four realms. They are very vicious and attack in an almost obsessive manner until they get their assigned prey." Connor's eyebrows furrowed. "The strange thing about your attack though is...well Malumian Wolves don't just attack by themselves. It's almost like they are animal versions of assassins. Do you know what I mean?" Killian stared back at him with his mouth slightly open. How could he possibly know what he had meant? His blood pressure pulsed again. He fought against the frustration that came so easily since he'd been sent to prison.

Connor seemed to grasp the ridiculousness of his question and waving his hand to erase his last statement he continued. "No, of course you wouldn't. The wolves...they have to be *sent by someone*. Someone programs the creatures to kill another and they do it with no reward it's just their nature. The wolves are placed onto another's scent and they won't stop until they are found, almost robotic. That's the problem we have, you see. We have no idea who would have sought out the wolves and sent them after you. You haven't been in the Praetorium since you were five-years-old." Connor sat back in his chair, tapping a pencil against his knee.

"What? I have never been here before. I was in the foster system since I was five. You are wrong. I have no idea where I am." He shifted nervously in the chair. "The only people I know are Blake, the work crew, and some CPS workers. Not counting my foster families."

"Killian, what do you remember about your life as a young child? Where were you before you went to your first family, before the Petersons, it was the Tubbs' right?" Killian nodded, confused how Connor would know that, and quickly answered.

"Well..." He began, trying to think back before the plump Tubbs family, "I guess I was with another family, or a home, or something. I was so little it's hard to remember. Why? What does that have to do with anything?"

"I think you'd be interested to know that there is more to your very young years than you may have thought." Connor glanced back down to his glowing screen and scanned the document in front of him again. "You have a greater connection to the Praetorium than you know. In fact, you were born here."

"What? How…how do you know that?"

"Killian Thomas…the Thomas family is the founder of the Ponderi, but as I said you will hear more—"

"Upstairs," Killian interrupted, "I know, that's what everyone keeps telling me."

"I know it's frustrating for you, but it's true." Connor smiled sympathetically. "I will tell you this attack from the wolves has me worried Killian. We have to get to the bottom of it, and we must assume you were attacked because of your connection to the Ponderi. Can you think of anyone that may wish you dead, or has connections to this place?"

His blue eyes widened as he looked back at Connor, registering what he'd suggested. "You think someone really wants me dead?" Connor shrugged. "I never knew this place existed so how would I know if anyone had a connection here?"

"It's worth asking," Connor said, a hint of frustration in his voice.

Killian thought for a moment. "The only person I know who hates me that much is Richard...and Laura it would seem," he said bitterly, "but the person who has any connection to this place is Blake. You aren't suggesting Blake could be a part of this are you? Because he saved us."

"No Blake was assigned to you by Nathaniel and Miller. He has been checked and rechecked for his loyalty and commitment to the Ponderi. Richard and Laura are out of the picture, they have no connection to anything. We checked." He eyed Killian warily, deciphering how he would handle the information. "We'll have to check on others throughout your history," Connor said quickly. Killian nodded.

"You said something about the wolves roaming the realms. What do you mean, like outer space or something?"

"No. There are three main realms in our Celestial Hemisphere. I'm sure Nathaniel and Miller will explain it more. Ignisia, you met Fia, that's where she is from, Glaciem and Cimmerian. Earth is a half realm, we call it Terrene. It's a half realm since it never fully joined into our Hemisphere. Each realm has a specific atmosphere and climate and each has their own specific duties to help keep our Hemisphere in balance."

Killian couldn't wrap his head around what was happening. His jaw clenched. He rubbed a hand over his face, scraping along prickly whiskers of his unshaved chin. He glanced down at the shiny, thin scars on his leg, the only evidence that disgusting creatures *had* attacked him. Standing up from the chair he was sitting on, and surprised by the lack of pain in his leg, he paced back and forth.

"Killian, I know this is so much to process, but I really need to ask you a few more questions, okay."

"How do I know that I can trust you?" Killian shouted. "What does *any* of this have to *DO WITH ME*?"

Connor stood up next to a pacing Killian. He put both hands on his arms, trying to stop him from moving.

"Killian, please sit down," he said softly. "I am going to try and help you understand. I promise after I get some answers I will take you to Nathaniel and Miller myself, where you can ask all the questions you want. I know since...your incident—"

"You mean since the only mother I knew sent me to prison...you can say it," he retorted.

Connor nodded nervously. "I comprehend it must be difficult to trust people. I can't imagine how unbelievable this is to you, but may we continue?"

Reluctantly Killian obliged and plopped down into the steel chair. His heart was pounding. He believed there was more that Connor knew, and he wanted to see the report Blake had written. His patience was wearing thin with the secrecy and lack of explanation he had received since arriving at this strange place.

"Whew...okay, that got a little intense didn't it?" Connor smiled trying to lighten the mood. Killian gave him a quick smirk as he sat again in his chair. "Killian, I think you are medically fine. How are you feeling otherwise, I mean emotionally?"

"I don't know how to answer that. How would you feel if you had all this thrown on you?" Killian bit; he took a deep breath trying to bury the frustration inside.

Connor's smile faded. He nodded, then stood and placed his tablet on the desk next to his chair.

"Well, I think considering the circumstances, I can say you're ready to move on. I'll take you up and I promise I won't pester you with silly questions." Killian stood as Connor pushed his chair back under his desk. They headed out into the cold hallway outside the clinic doors.

"I think maybe I should wait for Mercedes," he told Connor looking back into the clinic hoping to catch a glimpse of her.

"She's going to be just fine. It's not just my bias because Shannon is my wife; she really is the most brilliant physician I've ever seen. Please, Miller and Nathaniel are very anxious to meet you."

52

Killian had a weight in the pit of his stomach, but he couldn't muster the energy to argue though he wanted to. Connor placed a hand quickly on the wall, then just stood, staring at the empty steel. Suddenly Killian saw a small screen appear on the wall. The screen showed a series of numbers which Connor quickly typed in the six-digit number to open the doors.

Inside the glass box, Connor typed in the tenth floor code and the doors closed. They rode the fast moving elevator in silence.

The elevator accelerated upward and before a minute had passed the doors dinged open. Connor stepped out of the elevator with him. The hallway they entered was exquisite, with marble floors and pillars lining the hall. Killian saw flecks of gold leaf shimmering in the marble. It was so masterfully polished that he could see his reflection almost perfectly in the shining floor. Hanging on the walls there were huge portraits that had different landscapes framed in what appeared to be solid gold.

"The office is down the hall, second door on your left. They'll be waiting for you." Connor gave Killian a big smile and held out his hand. "I hope you get the answers you're searching for." He stepped back into the open elevator after a brief handshake and typed in his floor number. Killian nodded, then suddenly turned around back toward Connor.

"Wait! Where is Mercedes going to be?"

"Don't worry, Shannon will take good care of her. She'll make sure she gets home safely," was all Connor had time to say before the elevator closed, completely disappearing behind the wall. The only hint that it was even behind the wall was the whoosh behind the painting that had split in half when the doors opened.

Alone, Killian made his way down the majestic hallway, feeling a little unnerved by the silence. He found it strange that the enormous building was filled with the constant eerie quiet. For a building so large, there certainly weren't a lot of people in the hallways.

He examined the paintings as he walked. One painting showed a beautiful land full of snow covered mountains that lined a great green sea. Another looked like a desert, a very lovely desert. It had large flowering cacti, and beautiful red-rock mountains, with rolling sand hills along the base of the rocks. The last painting that rested next to the second door on the left was a painting of a scene at night. Killian could see shadows of a forest and rolling hills. It could have been a painting of anywhere had it not been for the two moons in the sky.

Turning away from the impressive paintings he knocked rapidly on the door, wringing his hands as he nervously waited to meet the mysterious men. After several moments, the brilliant gold knob creaked as someone turned it from the inside. As the door swung open, Killian was met by a man with a thick ashen mustache and twinkling gray eyes.

Chapter 4
The Two Master's Tale

"Killian Thomas! I cannot express how *thrilled,* just *thrilled* we are to see you here...and safely I might add." The man chuckled cheerfully. "We've been looking forward to speaking with you for so long. My how you have grown." The man seemed so excited he could scarcely contain himself as he fussed over Killian.

He helped Killian sit in a small wooden chair and swiftly clamored to an enormous wooden desk, the top of which was covered in the same beautiful marble as the hallway. He propped one thin knobby hip onto the corner of the remarkable desk, then simply beamed across the room from atop the perch.

Killian met his gaze for a moment. The man was incredibly dressed in an expensive looking burgundy vest, perfectly tailored for his shape. He wore a crisp white button down shirt that boasted a pair of cufflinks neatly shaped in the form of two stars. His black shoes were polished and reflected the bright sunlight that had filled the magnificent room as it lowered into the greenish-purple sky.

Behind the desk and the enthusiastic man, an enormous glass window allowed the incredible sunset to pour in across the carpeted floor. As Killian marveled at the room, a large red office

55

chair that was placed behind the desk, swiveled around toward him. A man with a short, perfectly trimmed black beard smiled. He looked familiar to Killian, but he knew he had never met someone before who dressed so fine. He had dressed in a similar style to his counterpart, albeit his vest and shirt were a smooth black, matching his beard. The few streaks of gray in his short, dark hair stood out against the darkness of his attire and added to his sophistication. He looked younger than the first man, but his face showed signs of age and stress.

"Killian, welcome. We are sure you have many questions for us," the man said in a formal tone. Killian slowly nodded, glancing back and forth between the two men. "Perhaps we should begin by telling you who we are, and I think you will be most interested in learning how important *you* are to...well all of us."

"Killian, you don't recognize us, but *we* have known you since your infancy. We have kept you under watchful eye. I am Miller and this is Nathaniel." The man with the mustache pointed, first to himself than to the second dark-haired man. "Nathaniel is the Director, I am the Regent, or second in command here. We knew we would see you once again, but we had no idea when. We're sorry for the unfortunate circumstances that brought you here." Miller finished, rubbing his fingers over his mustache.

Killian shifted his eyes between the two men. He was unnerved that people had been somehow watching him his entire life. Shifting his thoughts, he had many questions for these strange men. Nothing made any sense to him.

"First, we'd like to let you know your prison sentence has been eradicated," Miller said.

"What?" Killian choked out. "What do you mean eradicated?"

"It's done. You're not a fugitive. In fact, the prisons have no record of you ever being there. Weren't you concerned there may be a warrant from your abrupt escape from your work crew?" Miller raised his eyebrows. Killian's face blushed. So much had happened and Brooks' work crew was the furthest thing from his mind.

"Honestly, I hadn't even thought about it. I'm not sure how you could dissolve my charges and sentence, though."

"Ah, well perhaps over time we may show you many unique aspects we house here in the Praetorium," dark-haired Nathaniel said. "Now, do you have any pressing questions you need answered?" He smiled kindly at Killian from his handsome chair.

"Where are we?" he asked with a sigh. Exhaustion from the stressful experience was beginning to seep through his body. All he wanted was truthful, straight answers and a place to sleep.

Nathaniel stood and held a small silver rod toward the grand window. Immediately the brilliant glass dimmed to a tinted black. "Killian, your earth, or Terrene as we call it is not alone in the universe." Nathaniel began tracing the rod in the air. As he moved his hand shapes and symbols formed on the tinted window. He pointed to one large circle in the center. "The Praetorium is nestled directly in the center of all realms. It's not part of any realm, but forms the balance between them. It is a neutral ground, so basically we are in a limbo," he explained. "In fact you can liken it to the Sun you see on Terrene, just like your planets, the four realms orbit around the Praetorium." Nathaniel drew four lines from the Praetorium circle to four smaller circles. He labeled them strange names before pocketing the small rod and turning toward Killian.

"Who are you?" he finally asked.

"The Ponderi is an organization that maintains order, upholds the laws of Cimmerian, Glaciem, Ignisia and Terrene. The realms. We defend the safety, cultures and freedoms of all the races. There are millions of people throughout the Hemisphere you don't know about."

"You keep saying Hemisphere? I thought this was called the Praetorium."

"The Hemisphere is the grand universe each realm, including the Praetorium limbo, is in. Each realm has their own small solar system, but the Hemisphere encompasses everything."

57

Killian didn't respond. His head was spinning.

"Our society is very similar to what you were raised in. People who live in the Praetorium with us have employment according to their different skills. Our children attend school much like the ones you attended until they are eight, from then on they become Potentials in departments throughout the Praetorium. Potentials will be trained and taught in various skills." Nathaniel smiled kindly at him, bringing Killian to the realization he was subconsciously shaking his head in disbelief. "Killian, you will find that things you once thought fantasy are in fact real." Nathaniel looked at him, his eyes blazing with truth.

Killian stared at the greenish orb through the magnificent window that had lost the tinted color. He wondered to himself why the sun was so strange, if it even was a sun. After several silent moments he pushed the irrelevant thought aside and mustered up the nerve to ask the question plaguing his mind.

"You said you've known me since I was young, so you must know my family. Who are they...*where* are they?" Killian asked, looking away from Miller and back to Nathaniel. Nathaniel leaned back into the padded red chair and crossed his leg over his knee.

"Killian, I wonder if our tale may be better received if you could *see* what we are about to tell you," He said. Nathaniel promptly stood from the chair and made three long strides to a small end table placed cozily next to an overstuffed sofa. From the drawer, Nathaniel retrieved a small, brown vial with a thick, clear liquid swirling inside.

"What do you mean see?" Killian questioned as Nathaniel brought the small vial toward him.

"Killian, the Ponderi have always been masters of design," Nathaniel said proudly. "We have many amazing, and useful tools available to us. This is one of them." Holding the vial out for Killian to see, he sat on a small stool Miller had pulled next to Killian's chair. "This particular tool is called Supraserum. It is a serum designed to share information across realms and councils. You can imagine that passing information across such distances can, at times, blur the message. This beautiful serum allows the message receiver to see the tale that is being recited to them. This way nothing is left out."

"This will allow you to see the events that we have seen, people we have encountered, and tales we have been told. It's lovely and so advanced in its technology. With the serum you may look upon events that you may not have been able to remember otherwise." Miller chimed in, giving Killian a melancholy glance.

"I don't understand how that's possible. I can see things from the past?" Killian asked.

"Yes. The serum connects with the neurotransmitters of the story teller," Nathaniel said pointing to himself, "then it connects to the one listening. The information will play out right before your eyes like a video. There is a great history before our time that is valuable to helping you understand our world."

"Would you like to give it a go?" Miller asked, excitedly. Killian shrugged, then giving a nod of consent, he turned to speak to Nathaniel.

"Is this like time travel?"

"Oh my dear boy, not at all," Nathaniel chuckled, a light European accent coming through his voice. "You will not leave this room. Perhaps you will understand as we begin." Nathaniel silenced any further questions from Killian.

He watched as Nathaniel unscrewed the top of the vial. The lid revealed a dropper that was coated in the liquid. First, Nathaniel tilted his own head back, holding the dropper over his eye. He gave it a slight shake causing several drops of the serum to fall. He blinked several times while the thick serum spread over the surface of his eye. Satisfied the serum was adequately coated, he turned toward Killian.

Nathaniel tilted Killian's forehead back and held the sticky tube over his eye. He shook the small dropper causing a cascade of falling drops to gush in. He repeated the same steps in the other eye before twisting the top back onto the vial.

The serum was not a pleasant feeling. It crept from uncomfortable warmth to a frigid frost coating his eyes. His brain hurt from the chilly temperature and it seemed to be seeping into the crevices of his mind. After several moments, the thick potion absorbed into his eyes and the discomfort subsided.

"You will know that what we say is true," Nathaniel stated. "This serum was designed with a defense mechanism to distinguish liars and traitors among us. If the images dim and fade, you can be certain the tale being told is untrue. Are you ready?" Killian nodded, looking at the faces of the two men.

"First I would like to tell you of the four realms and the beginning days of the Ponderi." Killian saw Nathaniel in front of him, but was astonished to see in the corner of the room other images coming into focus. Before him he saw a group of men, dressed in old fashioned clothing—some in very strange clothing—standing in line in front of a pale man. The man had long black hair, with shimmering silver streaks throughout. His hair was pulled back tightly in a low ponytail. His eyes were like nothing Killian had ever seen. They gleamed in a shocking silver color, almost glowing in their paleness.

The walls of the office seemed to fade into the background, and Killian found himself completely immersed in the scene where the mysterious people were. The group of men stood on bright green grass, fresh after a rainstorm. The atmosphere was cloudy and damp and Killian could feel the chill in the air as if he were with the men. The circle of huddled men was surrounded with large structural stones placed strategically in a circle. The stones were thick and rectangular; some were bridged together by other large stones. Sitting on a pile of throne-like boulders, the silver-eyed man glared out among the crowd.

"Wait...isn't that...what is it called...in England?"

Nathaniel nodded. "You'll learn the Stonehenge structure served a great purpose for the realms— watch." He directed Killian's attention back to the ghostly images in the room. The unique silver eyes glared at the men in front of him menacingly as one man stepped forward to address him.

"Terrene is the youngest realm. This story takes place when the other three realms were under the rule of a Grand Master named Claec. He was from Cimmerian, a mystical land full of magic. They live in shadows and darkness, but it is a land of beauty and is very valuable to the balance of our world. You'll learn the specifics of each realm at a later date. The man with silver eyes is Claec." Nathaniel explained obviously connecting to Killian's visual experience. "Thousands of years ago, the realm people desired to create one realm where they could live in a united group. Ancient leaders in Cimmerian developed the idea of a realm with all different climates for each unique person to live."

The people called it the Terrene Venture. They wanted a unified community where resources were available to all, without traveling through three different solar systems to address problems. Cimmerian was placed at the helm of the project. It was their leader's suggestion, but also they were the only ones with the magical abilities to begin the world formation."

"Magic, different realms? Seriously, it sounds like I've stepped into the Twilight Zone," Killian said.

Nathaniel chuckled. "In a way you have, my boy. At this moment you are seeing, the Terrene Venture was almost complete, the only step that remained was to merge Terrene into the Hemisphere. For several years prior to this setting, however, there had been corruption."

As we've explained, Cimmerians are magical. They are strong in their spells so naturally they were the leaders. But it went to the extreme. Claec had placed Cimmerians above everyone and kept valuable resources from the other people. Other races besides Cimmerians lived in squalor during the final years of the venture."

The people were afraid to question Cimmerian authority, though there had been challengers. A rumor had formed—a man from the realm of Glaciem had developed a formula to create a power that could rival the magic of Cimmerians. He used science to battle magic."

"Well, what happened?" Killian asked after Nathaniel paused.

61

"From what we know, the formula was successful...for a while. The man disappeared, but the damage was done. His successful formula convinced people from other realms that magic had become a means to enslave the people to the will of the Cimmerians. They also had been given a way to combat the rule of Cimmerian magic—by using science and their own designs. So of course, there were contentions that were quickly becoming violent."

Killian watched as the projected images ignited into vicious altercations, each unique race against another. The smell of the room had a dingy metallic smell of fresh blood. "James Thomas, founder of the Ponderi, introduced the idea that the realms were designed to govern themselves and their own people, and together the realms would work to bring balance to the Hemisphere. They would each add value through their own governments," Miller said smiling at Killian's furrowed brow. "Due to the uprisings, Thomas was suggesting returning the realms to their original systems, but also to create a society to be the mediator between the realms. He hoped the mediating society would extinguish previous problems with distribution and help meet the needs of all the people."

"Wait, James *Thomas*?" Killian asked. Miller smiled and nodded confirming the relation of their last names. "Connor mentioned the Thomas family founded the Ponderi."

"It's true. Now, at this great council meeting with the people on the Terrene Venture, James Thomas provided testimony from realm leaders from Ignisia, Glaciem, even Cimmerian." Killian observed as the three projections floated mysteriously in front of him. One was a burly, tanned man with vibrant orange hair and a matching beard. He was bare chested and looked angry. A peaceful looking man stood next to him with billowing white hair, but a young face. His long white robes looked angelic with a brilliant blue and gold sash fastening them around his body. The third man had long black hair and fascinating silver eyes, just like the leader, Claec.

"Killian the man you see with the orange hair was chief of Ignisia. The man in the white robe is Emperor of Glaciem. Both testified of Claec's greed. They explained no resources were being sent to the people remaining on Glaciem and Ignisia preparing to move to Terrene. Their people were dying because Claec was sending all resources to Cimmerian. Claec was turning into a dictator; he was going against everything the Terrene Venture stood for, unity and peace."

"What about the silver-eyed man, he looks like Claec."

"Ah, yes. He is most important to our story. You may recognize his name, Merlin of Cimmerian.

"Merlin? You don't expect me to believe he's the wizard from the King Arthur legends do you?" he asked.

"The one and the same! After this council meeting, he fled the Venture for his life for betraying Claec." Nathaniel smiled. "The legends of Merlin come from reports of his oddities during the venture. He was a powerful Cimmerian. He performed works people on Terrene had never witnessed before. He is the foundation for all Terrene's ideas and legends of magic."

Killian rolled his eyes. This was beginning to drift between absurd and delusional. He watched Merlin square his shoulders and face Claec. Behind the image of Claec, a dark man seethed.

"You see Claec's brother now, Rowan. He is the one behind him," Nathaniel continued. "Merlin was the master of distributions on the venture. He was in charge of seeing that all the resources were distributed to the distant realms for all the people." The image of Merlin bowed low to the two Cimmerian leaders. Killian could see his pleading eyes as he silently spoke to the men. He wished the Serum allowed him to actually hear what was said. "His testimony sealed the destruction of the venture. He told the people how Rowan and Claec had altered the amount of resources, especially materials to build weapons and food, to the different realms, and how everything was sent to Cimmerian."

Around him, Killian saw the images of the crowd huddled in the boulders of Stonehenge rise into an uproar. It seemed to be an impressive conflict, with no one knowing what to do.

"The testimony of Merlin was a great betrayal to Rowan and Claec. He was threatened and had to go into hiding from the

63

brothers," Nathaniel said. "The Terrene Venture was abolished after this council; Claec was overthrown." As he finished the tale, the projected images disappeared as well as the film over his eyes from the serum.

"What happened then? How do people still live on Earth...or Terrene...or whatever?"

"Stonehenge was the gateway. As I said, the landmark is more than meets the eye. The gateway was where people from the distant realms traveled to help build the new realm, as well as passing resources back to the other three main realms. When the Venture was abandoned, the gateway sealed itself, trapping the remaining people on unfinished Terrene. These people lived and populated the realm, forming their own histories to the formation of their world. As time passed the truth blurred, since Terrene is not fully joined into the Hemisphere, knowledge of other realms faded from their memories. Limited amounts of people on Terrene truly know of the other realms existence. Earth is diverse because of the different races mixing together."

"Killian," Miller chimed in, "three groups evolved from the end of the venture, the Ponderi, the Deshuits, and the Trinity. You know *we* are the Ponderi, the creation of your ancestor. Deshuits are rebels, people who run wild throughout the Hemisphere believing no one should belong to any realm. They fight against us with extreme violence."

"Why do they fight you?"

"They believe we rule the realms and force the different races to never be truly free, when in reality we are simply a mediation group. We help realms work through issues as well as provide the track system for resources to pass fairly to the realms. We also protect people from threats. I suppose you could name us the guardians of the realms." Miller smiled.

"Well, if that is true, why haven't you tried to form a truce with them and explain your reasons?" Killian asked skeptically. He didn't know these two men. For all he knew the Deshuit group could be right, maybe the Ponderi did try to rule the realms.

"We have tried for centuries. The Deshuits aren't easy to speak with. Many Ponderi recruits have been lost to their violence. For the sake of our members now, we try to avoid them," Nathaniel answered.

"Okay, well what about the third group?"

"Yes, the Trinity. This is why *you are* of great importance my boy," Nathaniel said. "The Trinity is a brotherhood that despises what the venture did to the realms. They feel the venture divided a people that wished to be unified, and they hate Terrene still. They are hunters of certain artifacts that will be able to once and for all destroy Terrene. Killian, they want to obliterate the entire realm. Billions of people will fall from existence if they have their way."

"How could they even have the power to do this and what does it have to do with me?"

"Merlin has much to do with this. The Venture created unbalanced power. People had learned it was possible to create abnormal abilities like the rogue Glacien man. This created awful conflicts and power struggles. Merlin, being highly skilled in his magic, created a relic individual to each realm so the races would each be able to have a weapon with equal power. They were to be used as defense against those seeking to dominate the Hemisphere. Each relic is infused with unique, strong forces specialized to every realm. But the downside to having such powerful relics is if they are ever joined together, they could obliterate worlds, races...anything! The owner of all four relics would be unstoppable."

"So I'm assuming this Trinity society is after these relics then they will used them against Ear...I mean Terrene, right?" Nathaniel nodded.

"Which is why we brought you here...your family was tasked with guarding the Cimmerian relic."

Killian's eyes widened. "What? I don't know what that means?"

"Your parents, Killian, were appointed relic guardians." Nathaniel bit his lip as he paused and Miller looked at the ground. Killian's heart beat in his chest. He wasn't sure he was ready to hear what Nathaniel was going to tell him.

"You parents surprised us by asking for permission to bequeath the relic to you temporarily. They assured us it was temporary. The relic could only have been passed to you from your father. The relics can only be passed down a line, never up or to a different family. Even for temporary guardianship. You were the only choice. Temporary guardianship can be awarded and returned back to the original guardian if there is an emergency."

We felt assured your parents had good reason or they wouldn't have asked, so we authorized the temporary guardianship—you were only two-years-old." Nathaniel paused allowing Killian time to absorb the information. "Killian, a week later...your...parents were killed. It appeared to be an accident, but we aren't sure since they had passed on the guardianship. It seemed strange after the guardianship transfer, they were killed so quickly. Your mother was a brilliant analyst and scientist, and one of the electrical lines in her lab caught fire and both your parents..." He looked away from Killian's disappointed eyes. "Anyway, I'm sorry to tell you this story, but you have to know about the relic. It was stolen from you recently."

Killian gasped and instinctively grabbed his neck. "My necklace...with...with the gold charm on it?"

Miller nodded and picked up where Nathaniel left off. "Yes, that charm was the Cimmerian relic. It was bonded to you, which is why you never wanted to part with it...am I right?" Killian gave a quick nod. "When it was stolen, it gave us reason to believe the Trinity had found you and taken the relic. The attack from the wolves sealed this in our minds. They want you out of the picture, most likely to destroy the Thomas bloodline."

"You say I have grandparents, then where are they. And if the relic was so important, why did you send me away? Wouldn't I have been safer here?" Killian frantically replied.

Miller and Nathaniel glanced carefully at one another. "Killian, several weeks after your parents died, your grandfather passed as well," Miller explained in a somber whisper. "You have a grandmother, your father's mother, named Rhetta. Rhetta panicked and fled with you. She believed it would keep you safer. It took us nearly three years to find you both, but with such a valuable relic, we couldn't let you be lost to us in the Hemisphere. Rhetta spoke with us. She believed her identity had been compromised. She also made valid points about not knowing who to trust at the Praetorium, so we all decided you would be safer on Terrene without her, under watchful eyes. When we learned from Blake the relic was stolen, we were preparing to extract you anyway. Then you were attacked; you were no longer safe there either."

Killian closed his eyes and dropped his head in his hands. "So you sent me away as a little boy from the only family I had left." Slowly he lifted his head and glared at the two men.

"Killian, please. The Trinity is a *secret society*. It was difficult to determine who to trust at the time. We promised Rhetta we would never lose sight of you—"

"You watched how I grew up then," he interrupted, his voice dripping with bitterness. "You saw how miserable I was, but when it benefits *you*, that is when you bring me here." Killian felt the same pin-pricks along the back of his neck and scalp. "Everyone here seems to have an ulterior motive. That's why you brought me here isn't it? You need help finding the charm?"

"Yes, my boy," Nathaniel answered in a firm, truthful declaration. "We hated learning you were mistreated, and perhaps we should have handled things differently looking back, but we can't go back. And now there is a greater cause. We must find the relic—Terrene depends on it."

"Killian, try to understand. We thought you would be safer on Terrene, but we were wrong," Miller said with emotion. "Now, you may be the most qualified to help us retrieve the relic since, as its guardian, *it is* bonded with you. You may be able to sense it along the way."

A long silence ensued—Killian felt awkward as Nathaniel and Miller gazed at him, waiting for his answer. Finally after several minutes he spoke.

"I will have to think about it. Everything I know is back home. I have to be honest, I don't know if I care to involve myself in this fight. I don't mean to add to your guilt, but if I'd been aware of the significance of the charm, maybe I would have cared for it more. I was the one who was in the dark, it's not on my shoulders."

The two men both dropped their heads. Nathaniel nodded slightly.

"We understand my boy. Take the night and think it over. You can come to us tomorrow with your decision." He turned to his desk and pressed a small white button. "Connor will take you to the room we've arranged for you." He sat down and pulled out a small blue tablet and began working on it. Killian gave a curt nod and turned toward the door. He could see the severe disappointment in the men's countenances, but he didn't believe he could help them find these relics. Killian opened the grand door and made his way to the hall. Instantly, the elevator doors slid open with Connor smiling at him.

"Ready to head to your room?" he asked cheerily.

"Sure."

The ride down was silent for only a moment before Connor began jabbering to Killian. "You are really going to fit in great here, Killian, I have a feeling. The food is to die for and there are so many things to learn and do...trust me it isn't all work, work, work. We have an entire outer arena dedicated to amusement—"

"I don't think I'm staying," Killian said abruptly. Connor stopped mid breath and scrunched his eyebrows.

"What do you mean? Did they explain to you the significance of your charm?" Connor stepped out into a magnificent carpeted hallway, keeping his bewildered expression on his face. Killian followed and stayed shoulder to shoulder with Connor.

"They explained everything — how my parents were the guardians, how they died, how I was thrown into a world with no family! I know you think I can help, but I can't. There isn't really enough reason to stay. You guys have dealt with the realms for a long time now. I'm sure you'll manage just fine without me." They both stopped at a fine, ornately carved door.

"Killian, would you mind placing your hand on the door? Please hold it for about ten seconds or so." Connor directed in a flat voice, ignoring his excuse. As Killian held his hand against the wood, Connor typed something into a small tablet he carried in his pocket. The screen was a deep blue translucent color that flashed red fingerprint shapes every few seconds. Finally, the device beeped. "Thank you. That should do it," Connor said as Killian lowered his hand. "No one will have access to your room but you. Just make sure you place your hand against the door and it will open. Well, I hope you will enjoy your room. We pride ourselves in making sure all members are provided the highest quality comforts."

Killian nodded his understanding. He felt at ease with Connor, though he knew by his expression he was disappointed. Connor stepped back as Killian opened his door. He didn't turn to leave, he just stood looking thoughtful.

"Well thanks, Connor, for everything," he said, slowly closing the door.

"Wait Killian." Connor shuffled his feet a bit before stepping to the doorway. "You have to stay. There are a few things I think you should know...you can't tell anyone I told you though, understand?" Killian was taken aback by the sharp tone in his voice.

"I understand."

"Your parents...I was a certified Potential, or an intern as you would say on Terrene, in the labs when they were here...I remember them, especially your mother. I...well, I don't think a fire would have taken them out. They were special recruits. They went on the most dangerous missions you can imagine trying to bring down the Trinity."

69

"What are you saying?" Killian asked, feeling his blood pressure rise.

"I don't want to give you false hope. They may be gone, but we never saw their bodies. I just find it odd they passed ownership to you right before they died, almost as if they knew they were going to leave." Killian held his breath remembering Nathaniel's insinuation the timing of their death seemed strange too.

"Killian," Connor continued, "if you help us find Merlin's relic, your relic, we might be able to find out what happened to your parents. I have a feeling the people who stole the relic are involved in the disappearance of your mom and dad."

"Why do you think that? They died here, right? The accident was here. So how could the Trinity be involved."

Connor continued to gnaw on his lip. "That's why we need your help. No one, I mean no one except some Ponderi members and your grandmother knew where you were on Terrene, *no one* but the Ponderi knew about your relic before it was stolen and you were almost killed." Connor hesitated and shifted his eyes up and down the empty hall.

"Connor," Killian whispered, "are you thinking there is a member of the Trinity in the Ponderi?"

Connor shrugged. "How else would they know where to send the wolves and what the relic looked like? I think since your parent's accident was here, if there is still a spy; if you help us find the relic, you'll get answers to what happened to your family. There's more Killian. Your mother was working on something...something big. When you were given the relic, my instructor had the opportunity to assist in the transfer of guardianship. He said there was something different about the charm, something more powerful. He even brought in a second opinion from Cimmerian. The woman was a supposed expert on the relics and she agreed with my instructor." Connor paused, pushing his glasses up the bridge of his nose.

"You've had strange dreams and have experienced anomalies in your emotions, true?" Killian was breathless but

70

nodded. "Well, if something was odd about the charm and it affected you, I'd say there is another mystery that needs to be solved too." Killian leaned against the wall, his mind was whirling.

"Can I still take tonight and process this?"

"Of course, just think hard Killian. If you go back to Terrene without Ponderi protection, how long do you think it'll be before the Trinity finds you? The way they go about stealing relics is destroying the bloodline of every guardian family. You're the last Thomas, so even if there is a spy, you are probably safer here where you can learn to defend yourself." Connor turned and began walking away. "Oh, I should tell you, the young lady you arrived with is back home and safe. Sleep well Killian, I promise you'll be safe in the room." He smiled and headed for the wall, leaving Killian alone to his thoughts.

After a long while, Killian turned into the grand room he'd been assigned. It was immaculate, with a towering cherry-wood dresser with at least a dozen empty drawers. The closet next to the bed was as big as his dingey cell had been. It had more space to hang clothing than a department store. Killian didn't know what they expected. He had about two shirts and two pairs of pants to his name and they weren't even with him.

He saw a bathroom next to the massive closet. Inside was a beautiful old-fashioned tub that looked like a small swimming pool to him. The shower was magnificent with glamorous hand cut tile mosaics covering the floor and walls. Killian turned the bronze handle and watched as sprays of warm water flowed from every direction as well as waterfall spouts pouring in along the bottom, making sure his feet would constantly be covered in water.

Killian smiled thinking he could definitely get used to this way of living. Before leaving the bathroom, he glanced at his reflection in a gilded mirror. His tanned skin was scratched and torn from his fall down the ravine. The reddish-brown whiskers looked thick on his chin, and irritated his face. The brown color in his short, military style haircut looked darker from the dirt and debris coating his scalp.

After self-criticizing his gaunt face for several moments, the mirror fogged from the steamy shower. Turning off the water, he left the bathroom and sat down on the cloud-like bed. He rested on the mattress planning to just relax for a moment before getting ready for bed. His thoughts drifted to Mercedes, he hoped she was alright. Part of him wished she could've stayed, he would have liked to get to know her more. But he knew her place was at home. He assumed she had a loving family waiting for her. He wanted to go home and find her again, but Connor's theory was haunting him. He knew if he left he would wonder for the rest of his life what had truly happened to his family. If he wanted answers, this was the place he would find them.

Chapter 5
Realm School

Lavender sunlight filtered through the thin cream colored shades and warmed Killian's face. Stretching, he couldn't remember the last time he had slept so sound. He sauntered into the bathroom and soaked for much too long in the multi faucet shower. He peered at his tattered clothing from the day before. There were still deep, burgundy stains from where the wolves mauled him and the smell was rank. Sighing, although he knew the drawers were empty, he pulled one open.

To his surprise, there were several fresh gray T-shirts, with matching gray sweat pants. Opening the enormous closet door, he found an array of tan, gray and white shirts in various lengths with similar pants. There were even three different pairs of shoes: tall, thin black boots that reminded him of riding boots, thin black sneaker looking shoes that looked so light he wondered how they would protect his feet, and a pair of comfortable looking black sandals. Jumping into the slip-on sandals, he dressed, inspecting his faded scars from the day before. He was amazed; it was almost as if mucous coated fangs had never torn his skin.

Killian looked at the large stone clock on his wall. It was late morning and he needed to speak with Nathaniel and Miller about his decision. Just as he was about to step out his door, a pounding knock caused him to jump back.

Timidly, Killian opened the door. A large young man, about his age, stood in front of him. He was dressed in similar gray clothing, but everything else on him was eccentric and colorful, just like Fia had dressed. He had bright red hair with blue tips, gold earrings in both ears, and a blue jeweled ring in his brow. But his eyes were what stopped Killian, for just as Fia, he had deep brown eyes with bright, jubilant orange flames behind the color.

"Killian Thomas?" he asked in a deep voice, hinted with a strange accent. The burly young man crossed his fist along his chest. It appeared to be a greeting. Killian would rather have the odd salute compared to the soft kisses Fia gave.

"Uh...yes."

"Please come with me." The young visitor turned on his heel and began to walk away.

"Where? I'm not sure I should go with someone apart from Connor or the Director. Who are you and then maybe I'll come with you."

"My name is Dax. And I don't appreciate your tone, Thomas. Ponderi recruits show respect, and you seem to have little of that." The man's tan face literally appeared to let off steam.

"Excuse me? I don't know who you are and why you want me to follow you. Maybe it's just me being new here, but most people give others a little more information to go on."

The tan young man huffed and tensed his shoulders, causing the muscles in his neck to bulge. "That's what I'm here to do; I was given orders to escort you to the upper floor. I follow my orders and I expect you to follow yours."

Killian felt angry. He could feel his face scrunching up in annoyance. "What orders? I just woke up buddy, so don't come here all soldier-like telling me what to do." Dax's expression changed slightly, he seemed to believe Killian truly didn't know who he was. After a small awkward pause, a cheery *ding* sounded from Killian's room. Dax darted into the room with Killian shuffling behind. On the bedside table, the wooden top had lit up into a blue screen. Dax gulped and tapped the screen revealing a message. Stepping back sheepishly, Dax nodded for Killian to read the odd tabletop message.

Killian,

One of our head recruits, Dax, will be coming to escort you to my office so you can inform us of your decision. Please follow him to the upper floors. Hope you slept well.

Nathaniel

Killian turned around smugly. "So, want to try asking me to come with you again...Dax was it?"

Dax pursed his lips before turning on his heel and marching out of the room. Killian chuckled, pleased he'd brought the haughty recruit down a little bit.

The ride to the upper floor with Dax was awkward, they didn't speak. The only words Dax said to him was a reminder of which door was the office before he whizzed away in the hidden elevator.

Killian knocked hard on the thick door and was quickly met by Miller, who ushered him into the room.

"Good morning, my boy," Nathaniel bellowed in a cheerful voice. "Would you care for a hot drink? There is tea, coffee, even hot cocoa over near the window there," he said pointing to a small coffee cart. It was covered in small baskets that held various assortments of garnishes for the drinks. Killian waved a hand in refusal and sat in the same chair he had used the night before.

He shifted nervously in his seat as Nathaniel peered at him over his drink.

"I trust you slept well?" Killian nodded as the two older men sipped from their mugs.

"Are there any questions you have for us after our conversation last night?" Miller asked with a kind smile.

He wanted to ask him about the possibility of his parents being alive, but he didn't want to let on Connor had told him. Suddenly he remembered another person. "Mercedes...have you heard anything else about her. I...just want to make sure she's okay."

"Mercedes Forino is safe at home and one of our scientists has seen to it that she believes the events of yesterday were all a dream."

"What? She won't remember it was real? How?"

"Another serum. It was given to her as she left yesterday. It's better this way. Imagine how Miss Forino would live her life, knowing there are horrific creatures roaming the Hemisphere. She will go to her summer classes on Terrene this morning, thinking she had a horrible nightmare. Of course, as a precaution, we have two recruits keeping watch over her at a distance. It's standard precaution since the Malumians picked up her scent as well during the attack. We are certain they won't bother her again, however, since it seemed they were programmed to attack you."

Killian nodded, but still felt a twinge of sadness in his heart. He was grateful she was being protected, but Mercedes had touched him somehow. She had saved him from the wolf and was the first person in a long while he felt could be trusted. Now he would simply be a memory from a nightmare to her.

Killian breathed out loudly, allowing his body to relax into the metal chair.

"Well, I suppose we should cut to the chase. Are you going to stay with us in the Praetorium?" Nathaniel gazed over his silver mug at him.

Killian processed Connor's advice once more; he wouldn't be safe at home, there is a small chance his parents were alive, and he had to learn if Merlin's relic had affected him in some way by the odd power Connor's instructor had mentioned.

"I have decided to stay."

Nathaniel clapped his hands together and Miller beamed. He couldn't tell who was more pleased with his decision. "Marvelous, I cannot begin to tell you what a relief this is. You will be most valuable in the search for the relic, and possibly other relics," Nathaniel exclaimed.

"I don't know about that, but I'll try."

"No you don't understand Killian, you are connected to your relic. It will be far easier for you to find it than one of us."

"Okay, I'll go with that for now. What do I need to do?"

"I want to enroll you in Recruit training."

"What does that mean?"

"Oh, my, you will be trained on everything. You'll learn weaponry, hand to hand combat, proper realm etiquette, oh, and of course survival skills. The different realms each house their own dangers. You need to go through realm school first, though."

"What's realm school?"

"It's just a small class covering each realm. It will explain what makes individual realms special—it's only a few days, but beneficial. Remember how we mentioned our young members become Potentials?" Killian nodded. "You are going straight to realm school and skipping the Potential period altogether. In order to find your relic you *will need* to be trained as a recruit."

Nathaniel sat back in his chair, noticeably tired. He held a small roll of papers in his hand that he'd pulled from his drawer. "I wish I could give you the opportunity to visit all the different departments, but you will need skills as a recruit to find your relic. So, my boy, take these orders down to the fifth floor. Forgive the paper, some things I still like to do 'old-school'. A least that's what the young people say." Nathaniel chuckled. "I will send them your file; the information of your background. When you arrive, don't head into the recruit training door, go to the classroom next to it. Your instructors will meet you there. They will direct you on what to do after you complete the class." Nathaniel powered up his computer built into the fine marble top of his desk. The older man moved in such haste Killian knew the conversation was over, but he wanted to make them aware of one thing more.

"Sir?" Nathaniel looked up from his desk. "I...uh...well sometimes odd things happen with me. I'm wondering if it could be affects from wearing such a powerful relic for so long?" As he spoke, he had also caught Miller's undivided attention.

"What kinds of things Killian?" Miller asked.

He shifted his eyes between the two older men. "Well, sometimes I *feel* too much. I know it sounds strange, but it's like at times I can feel what everyone else around me is feeling...it can be overwhelming and make me feel physically sick." The two men stole a quick glance to one another. Nathaniel appeared calm, but Miller looked worried. "And...and I also have had a lot of strange dreams before. Maybe I'm over-thinking it, but it's been almost like I physically go somewhere, like it's not just a dream. From what you've described of me being separated from my grandmother as a kid, I'm pretty sure I've dreamed of her and witnessed the moment I was taken." He didn't expound that he believed he had also seen her the day he was attacked. "Does she have red hair?"

Miller's eyes widened and nodded slowly. "It's been years, but yes Rhetta had cinnamon colored hair."

Nathaniel cleared his throat, almost appearing reluctant to speak further about a strange ability. "Killian, I'd like you to monitor and inform me if you experience anything strange from here on out, but don't think too much on it. These things are most likely coincidences and effects from emotional stress in your life. But I assure you if anything continues, we will follow through with neurological testing and mental simulations. Now don't worry, and please enjoy your time today with the instructors. We are so glad to have you with us, my boy."

He bristled at the rushed conversation, but nodded and stood, making his way out the brilliant doors to catch the elevator to the fifth floor.

The training floor was much colder, with none of the charm from the upper floors. The walls and walkway were made of shining steel similar to the exterior of the building. Small, square windows high on the walls were the only source of light along the cool hallway. Walking on the smooth steel, Killian saw an unmanned desk nestled against the back wall in front of a large double door. Approaching the two doors, Killian could make out the black, bold lettering "Recruit Training" directly over the doorframe. Off to the side he noted the classroom. Inside, he saw three people huddled in a circle speaking to one another. When the door creaked open, they all turned to face him.

One woman had long black hair and glowing silver eyes. She smiled at Killian revealing faint lines in the corners of her lips. Another woman with bluish-purple hair tipped red gazed at him. Her eyebrows were completely made up of gold piercings, along with both nostrils. All the eccentric piercings were shadowed by her flame-red lipstick that accentuated her lips. The third was a pink-cheeked man. He wore a blue bandana on his head that held his long white hair out of his face. It was easy to figure he had one instructor from each of the main realms. Although each instructor was dressed in bland, gray or brown uniforms, each one had added something to differentiate themselves from the others. The Cimmerian woman had a dark ebony necklace filled with sparkling stones around her neck. The Ignisian woman had a colorful, yet attractive, scarf tied fashionably around her throat, and, of course, the Glacien had a similar sash around his waist just as the emperor from the Supraserum vision.

"Hello, Killian. Nathaniel said you would be attending realm school this afternoon. We're so pleased to have you join us," the Cimmerian said. Her voice was whimsical and enchanting, like a whispered song.

"You guys get messages quick here," Killian chuckled, handing her the rolled papers.

The woman nodded. "My name is Sasha, as you can see, I am from Cimmerian. This is Serefina, she is from Ignisia." The bright haired woman smiled excitedly at him and waved as she took a few short steps toward him, planting a soft kiss on his cheek. "And finally, this gentleman is Janus. He comes to us from Glaciem." The kind faced man smiled at Killian and bent low at the waist. The customs of the Ponderi were strange, but he enjoyed the obvious cultural greetings from each race.

"Please have a seat," Sasha said, ushering him with her hand. Killian followed her direction and found a soft chair in the center of the room.

"I suppose I will begin the lesson. This class is to simply give you an idea of each distinguishing factor in the three main realms. It will help you if you are a Custodis to understand what is important and special about each culture, does that make sense?"

Killian shook his head. "What's a Custodis?"

The teachers glanced at one another before Sasha spoke. "Nathaniel didn't tell you what a Custodis was?" Killian shook his head. "Strange. Your father was a Custodis. Killian we assume you were told our society is full of different talents and jobs right?"

"Yes, Nathaniel briefly mentioned something about young kids being Potentials in different departments."

"True," Janus said taking over dialogue. His voice was soft and calm, yet carried a brash Scandinavian accent. "Ve have many areas of employment. To name a few ve have engineers, medical staff, chefs, analysts and scientists, Beastians, recruits and finally Custodis recruits. I'm sure you can figure out vat most of zose departments control, but since you'll be joining za recruits ve'll discuss zat department."

"The recruits are in charge of realm defense, and defense of the Praetorium. If there were ever an unlikely combat situation our recruits would lead us. They are skilled in many different areas," Serefina explained.

"Nathaniel told me about weapons and combat training. It seems like a soldier."

"In a way they are. But Custodis recruits, those are the realm jumpers."

Killian scrunched his face and got lost in Serefina's gold facial jewelry.

Sasha cleared her throat. "Custodis are the only recruits that travel through the track systems to other realms. In your forms here," she said looking at the rolled paper, "it seems Nathaniel suspects you may be a Custodis too."

"They want me to travel to the other realms?" Killian was flabbergasted.

"If you are able, not everyone can be a Custodis. Only certain blood types can link with the track system. If everyone could jump, the tracks would eventually use too much energy and collapse," Janus said simply. "Does our explanation answer your question?"

Killian nodded slowly, unsure if he understood anything that had happened in the last twenty-four hours.

"Alright, let's begin." Sasha opened a case and pulled out what looked like a fluorescent light tube. She pressed a small silver button and immediately the walls in the room burst into enormous holographic screens. It was as if the room had formed a bubble around him and every direction was allowing him to experience a new realm. Killian gawked in awe as he saw two magnificent moons above him as the ceiling transformed into a brilliant night sky. One burst in ghostly pink light, while the second, smaller moon was a peaceful blue. An earthy smell filled his nose, the smell of twilight mixed with a fresh breeze.

"Cimmerian—or the magic realm—is the last Monarchy," Sasha began, waving her arms around the impressive screens. "The Queen's name is Maurelle, and she leads the Cimmerian people today. She comes from a grand line of wonderful leaders."

Killian saw a stunning woman walk the surrounding black stone streets. He could hear the bustle of the busy shops and the Queen's steps. She had flowing ebony hair and floated amongst her people with a regal grace. Every sparkling diamond sewn into her impressive purple gown glimmered in the moonlight and reflecting off her pale, flawless skin. She seemed so real, as if she were in the room with him. Killian locked onto her silver eyes that swirled like brilliant stars. She was truly one of the most beautiful women he had ever seen.

"Of course it's not necessary for you to know her lineage, only that her father was Claec."

Killian tore his gaze away from the beautiful queen. "Wait, Claec? The ancient ruler...he lived like hundreds of years ago, how can his daughter still be alive?"

Sasha smiled. "Killian not every realm ages the same. Cimmerian's have the longest lifespan, and we count our years in seasons, three seasons make up one of your years. We can live for thousands of seasons. Queen Maurelle has been alive for nearly seven centuries according to Terrenian time." Killian didn't know how to react; he didn't know if this was even possible. The Queen looked close to his age, but she was seven hundred- years-old! Sasha didn't wait for him to process the astronomical age difference, she continued with her lesson. "Each realm has their own language, but since the Ponderi's birth most have learned James Thomas's common language."

"English?" Killian verified, understanding why everyone had unique accents. Sasha nodded and smiled.

"You were told Claec lost his position as Grand Master and the Ponderi was formed under his rule, correct?" Killian nodded. "Cimmerian's are a proud people and treasure their magic. I admit personally it's been hard for me not to summon my abilities. It is ingrained within us, but it's for the better good we don't. There *is* danger with magic. Remember these terms—Summoning, Binding, Extracting."

The images surrounding him altered to nothing more than the beautiful Cimmerian sky, glittered with pink, purple, blue, and white stars.

"These are the three spells Cimmerian's are experts at. Let me first explain summoning. A Cimmerian has the ability to summon unprotected artifacts or objects. It is very helpful if you need to find something and of course, it can make a person rather lazy." Sasha chuckled as if she were referring to herself. Killian smiled along with the other instructors.

"What do you mean unprotected?" He asked.

"Well, if something is hidden by a spell or highly guarded in multiple ways, summoning would not be able to access the object," Sasha explained. Killian thought of the relics. It would make it much easier if a Cimmerian could simply summon one of the artifacts, but he was certain they all were heavily guarded. "Now for this class I've been given permission to provide an example. I may be a little rusty, so bear with me."

Sasha focused hard at one of the desks in the back of the room, with a loud crack the desk evaporated and reappeared in front of the room on its side. Sasha's lips turned down into a frown.

"Wow!" Killian was astounded. "That was amazing. Miller and Nathaniel said there was magic, but I...I never could imagine something like that." Sasha waved a hand in front of her, blushing at his praise.

"If I was practicing regularly, the spell would be silent, I could summon from a different room, *and* it wouldn't land in an atrocious way—you get the idea, though." She quickly corrected the desk and continued her lesson. "Do you have any questions so far about Cimmerian?" Killian shook his head. "Right. The other two charms are more dangerous and can unintentionally cause harm, so I won't be demonstrating. Binding" −an image of a Cimmerian appeared in front of him. The person crouched over another resting on a black tabletop− "is connecting another ability with your own. This is often used to keep unique traits within families. For example, as a family member begins to pass away, the living relative may bind the dying's power with their own. It adds upon one another. The Royal family is one of the longest in our history, so Maurelle, in theory, would be the most powerful person in the Hemisphere if she had bound powers to herself from her family. Binding is not public knowledge, we can only speculate whether she has bound her loved one's powers to her or not. A person may also bind their energy and power to someone who is ill, or requires healing. It can greatly help someone in a dire state

83

of health. This form of binding takes great skill, and I would wager Maurelle may be one of the few skilled enough to successfully do it. Our queen *is* powerful. We are blessed to have her—she generously uses her abilities to better Cimmerian and other realms." The other two instructors nodded their agreement.

"She is generous," Janus said quietly.

"The last spell is Extracting," Sasha said as two more holographic Cimmerians seemed to appear in the room. "This is tricky and caused a lot of problems during the Terrene Venture. The basic principle is: a Cimmerian may forcibly extract another's powers, memories, illnesses, or even their life. It can be performed on any race. During the Terrene Venture this power is what others experimented with creating harmful, fatal mutations."

Killian saw one of the projected Cimmerians place their hand upon the chest of the other. A brilliant, white light pierced the screen until the second collapsed at the feet of the extractor. As the images faded, he imagined the silver-eyed warriors stepping onto the battlefield. While the opponent raised their sword, the Cimmerian simply sucked their life away.

"But of course," Sasha continued, interrupting his thoughts, "many of these spells were corrupted during the venture. They are rarely used now." Sasha seemed sad her beloved abilities had to be so closely guarded and Killian felt sad for her. She seemed like she would be someone who would use them for the benefit of others.

"A few last Cimmerian points I'll explain. To most, Cimmerian is also named the dark realm. You see my gorgeous eyes," she teased, "they are accustomed to see in dim lighting. Anything brighter than this room I would have to wear protective glasses. It would feel as if my eyes were being burned."

"Why is it so dark?" Killian asked.

"Cimmerian doesn't have a sun. We have two moons instead, as you see above you." Sasha pointed to the ceiling as the unique moons appeared again on the invisible screen. "We grow many plants that would shrivel under sunlight. Emerald Fruit is our most valued crop. It has healing properties. In fact, Connor's salve he put on your cuts when you arrived has Emerald Fruit extract," she said proudly. "Our largest moon is nicknamed the Pink Giant, or as Cimmerian's call it, the sharing moon. As I said, Cimmerian is divided into three seasons: light season, harvest, and the dark season. In Terrene measurements, I've been told you would say each season was four moths."

"Do you mean months?" Killian chuckled.

"Oh, I always miss that word." Sasha grimaced. "Anyway, during the dark season the Pink Giant disappears from the Cimmerian sky and naturally offers more light to the other two main realms. This happens to fall during *their growing seasons*. The extra light from our moon creates healthy crops for Glaciem and Ignisia. Everything is balanced." She finished.

"If it's so balanced why did the ancient leaders want to create the Earth...I mean Terrene?" The three instructors shifted slightly, thinking of how to answer. Janus spoke, his voice barely above a whisper.

"There *is an* ancient balance of za realms. However, there were many difficulties negotiating vith za realm people. Many needs vere left unaddressed simply because of za distance of za realms. So za idea vas to create a place where everyone could live. Zat is why za Ponderi, in today's world, have provided an added balance. Zay have provided za solution to ancient problems without joining Terrene. It is almost like a train system you vould have on Terrene. Za Praetorium is za station. Anything that needs addressing is brought to za Praetorium, and sent to za needy realm by way of za 'track', or portals Custodis pass through." He said making quotations with his fingers.

"I guess that makes sense," Killian concluded.

"Well, I suppose I may begin za Glaciem lesson, of course unless you have further questions for Sasha?" Janus said motioning to the Cimmerian. Killian shook his head. "Perfect. Killian, you may liken Glaciem's environment to your territory of Alaska, I'm told it is called, but in some parts it may feel like za territory of your arctic circle." The holographic room shifted in a cold blast of air. The earthy smell was replaced with the fresh, salty smell of an ocean. Killian's skin prickled against the breeze and he noticed how Serefina closed her eyes, obviously uncomfortable in the cold.

"Za glaciers," Janus continued, "bring forth fierce winds zat are violent and vell below freezing temperatures. If a Terrenian were to step into our coldest canyons wearing zere thickest protective gear, zay would freeze to death in moments."

"How could anyone survive living there if it gets so cold?" Killian asked staring at Janus's wind burned cheeks.

"Our bodies have adapted over time. Our greatest evolutionary aspect is our hot blood."

"You mean warm blood?"

Janus shook his head slowly. "No, Glaciens are hot-blooded. It helps us maintain regular body temperatures zat other races cannot tolerate." Killian's eyebrows scrunched together in disbelief. Janus gave a soft laugh at his expression. "I understand it is strange to you, but it's true. Even Terrenians have some remnant of hot blood. Zat is why some people on Terrene prefer za colder climates."

Now, Glaciens can adapt to any other realm too, except Ignisia," he said giving Serefina a quick nod. "Ignisia's sun is too much for us. Ve could survive in Cimmerian though ve vould be blind as bats in their dark areas, and Terrene, ve vould find comfortable."

Janus pressed the button on the tube changing the holograph to an image of a beautiful glacier dotted forest; Killian could feel the drip of freezing water rolling from the trees. It was amazing, and so real—but so impossible all at once. There were bright icy mountains, but they were littered with tall pines. Below Killian recognized the green sea he'd seen in the painting in the upper hallway.

"I vill describe two points about Glacien culture. Ve have certain abilities that make us beneficial during unrest." As he spoke, Killian felt himself slouching in his chair. His muscles seemed to relax—*this chair is so comfortable*, he thought to himself.

His mind drifted away from Janus's soothing voice. Instinctively, he wanted to think about what made him happy— what brought him peace. The green Glaciem sea filled his mind. It was calm and the sound of small waves made him feel such serenity. A pair of emerald eyes were next to him—Mercedes. In his mind, she sat next to him, laughing and throwing small shells into the peaceful water.

"Killian—Mr. Thomas," Janus's voice broke through his daydream. "How do you feel at zis moment?"

Killian sat up straight, he could feel the heat rising in his cheeks. He was mortified to have dozed off, dreaming about Mercedes, whom he would most likely never see again.

"I am so sorry, sir. I don't know why I dozed so quickly, I—"

Janus interrupted Killian with a surprisingly loud laugh. The man's face was red when he finally caught his breath. "Forgive me, Mr. Thomas, I haven't put someone into such a relaxed state in such a long while. I vasn't sure if the demonstration vould vork. It appears I still have my touch."

"Demonstration? What are you talking about?" Killian asked feeling more embarrassed.

"Glaciens, Mr. Thomas, are experts in meditation, relaxation and focus. In stressful moments, ve can actually place people in a relaxed state of mind. Of course, it takes particular skills to reach zat level of mental control. Glaciens who choose zis route, choose it as a profession. They must attend rigorous training to reach their mastered calm state of mind. Not every personality is suited for it. I vent through za training as a young adult—it filled five rotations of my life. So zat is the equivalent of fifteen years on Terrene." Killian's mouth dropped at the length of study the man had accomplished.

"You're like a Zen Master," he said.

"I'm afraid I'm not familiar vith zat term, but if it means peace and focus, then Zen Master it is." Janus smiled as the room shifted to the salty waters of the green sea. Killian felt the spray of waves on his face, each restful swell added to his yearning to travel to this realm as soon as possible. Janus's voice broke through his relaxation once more.

"Now, za other point I'd like to focus on is za Glaciem contribution. Glaciem has za purest resources available in za Hemisphere. Ve provide healthy nutrition for all varieties of plants; ve vork vith all manner of animal life as vell. In simple terms, Glaciens provide za seeds for all realms. Even Emerald Fruit seedlings are vashed and tended in Glaciem before being transported to Cimmerian. Our blue pebbles are sent to each realm to place into their bodies of water. Za pebbles provide a cleansing reaction ensuring all water is fresh and pure for other races to drink." Janus scooped his hand into the green water and scooped up several holographic translucent blue stones. Though Killian knew they weren't really in his hand, they glimmered like sapphires against the water.

"But how can your realm be compatible with the other realms?" Killian asked. Janus appeared confused by the question. "I mean, wouldn't Emerald Fruit only grow in Cimmerian? Wouldn't your pebble things melt in Ignisia if it's so hot?"

"Ve don't grow za plants, ve *prepare* za seedlings. Glaciens have a way vith plants, ve focus za seedlings on their purpose so they provide suitable crops. Ve cleanse and protect za new seeds from infection or poisons in za soils. And yes, actually our blue pebbles do melt in Ignisia. But when zay dissolve zay release za minerals needed to cleanse za dust and sand from za water. It also gives Ignisia's water za most stunning blue color you've ever seen." Janus finished proudly. "Any other questions before I turn za time over to Serefina? Main take away points: Glaciem is za soul behind life in za realms, and *ve are* Zen Creatures." Killian laughed as Janus finished.

"Zen Masters."

Janus shrugged and chuckled before moving aside for Serefina to step forward.

"Killian Thomas!" she shouted excitedly, "I am thrilled to teach you about my realm!" The cold was instantly replaced by a dry, desert heat. Killian began feeling uncomfortable as each minute passed.

"I can see that," Killian said as Serefina brought her nose to almost touching his. She beamed at him.

"Ignisia is a powerful, proud realm. We have provided light and heat since the Hemisphere's beginning. Though Ignisian's can't calm or practice magic, we are skilled fighters." The walls filled with lines of eccentric, colorful people shooting metal bows, clashing swords, and throwing spears. "Our strength has made us masters of battle for millennia."

Serefina pulled out two shimmering gold daggers from a thin leather belt around her waist. Killian hadn't even noticed the weapons during the entire class. Serefina suddenly spun in a furious circle, spinning several times, before releasing the brilliant weapons with a ferocious cry. The daggers sliced through the air at an amazing speed, before slamming with such force into two leather squares tacked on the wall, Killian heard the ding of the gold hitting the steel behind the patches. He let out a long whistle at the impressive marksmanship.

"As I said, Ignisians are a proud people Killian," she continued. "We pride ourselves on our ancient tribal bonds. We have one tribal leader for the entire realm. Young Ignisians are schooled on battle strategies and fighting techniques before they utter their first word." Serefina smiled at Killian's stunned expression. "Yes, Killian it's true. We are fierce warriors. Neighboring realms avoid conflict with Ignisians *at all cost*."

"Ignisians are also very humble if you can't tell," Sasha teased.

Serefina laughed. "Ah, Sasha you only tease because I have conquered you on the training field for ninety seasons—three decades in Terrenian time Killian." Serefina smiled while Sasha scoffed in the corner.

"One main point to remember about Ignisia is: the realm becomes uncomfortably warm to most other races." The images shifted on the holographic walls to a beautiful desert dotted with brilliant blue ponds as Janus had promised. Killian could smell fabulous scents from desert flowers and watched as a small blue lizard -like creature with two heads and large black eyes, padded near his face on the wall.

"The realm is made from fine ruby sands with beautiful oasis', but it is a vast desert. Ignisian's have adapted and live quite comfortably. We are masters of heat and are responsible for the development of each realm's sun, or moons in Cimmerian's case. We've helped shape the light so their realms flourish. If there is ever a problem with their fires, suns or any light or heat source, Ignisians can tolerate the extreme temperatures to repair the issues."

Light is our life, Killian. We dress brightly to honor our source of existence— fire, light and heat are beautiful and sacred to Ignisians. Without our expertise and services the other realms would fall into cold and darkness—*the hemisphere would ultimately die.*" Serefina finished with such fervor Killian pulled back from her intense flaming eyes.

"Well, I suppose that's a good reason to have some pride," Killian teased.

"I wholeheartedly agree," Serefina said. Her exuberance caused all her piercings to glimmer in the overhead lighting—the gold jewelry cast a gilded hue over her tan skin. Killian stared at each instructor. They were all so different, yet he could see how they each made such valuable contributions. The more he observed the different races, the more he saw traces of evidence on Earth that each realm had once been a part of its creation. It felt like, for the first time, things were beginning to make sense.

"Just so I'm on the same page," he began, "Cimmerian is magic, dark, shares their moon, and grows healing plants?" Sasha smiled and nodded. "Glaciem is full of peace and Zen, and they

90

purify all the plant and water sources so things can grow and people have fresh water?"

"Correct," Janus answered.

"Ignisia is a desert, which has an awesome control over light and heat. You guys build suns and are unbeatable fighters." Serfina bobbed her head up and down, causing her jewelry to clang together.

"Killian, the purpose of this course is to teach that each realm is crucial to the balance of the Hemisphere. We contribute in our own unique ways and for centuries, with the Ponderi's help, have found peace with our roles," Sasha said, repackaging the light bar and the walls instantly faded from the beautiful desert to the boring steel.

"What about the issue with Earth…I mean Terrene? What will happen to the realms if Terrene is destroyed by the relics?" Killian asked softly.

The instructors glanced at each other for a moment before Janus spoke. "It is a real problem—zat is true. Since Terrene is still a part of za Hemisphere, if za worst should happen, we don't know how it vould affect za rest of us. You vill learn more in training, but our Custodis recruits, or realm jumpers, are valuable in assisting us to resolve zat issue. Killian, if you are anything like your relatives I believe you vill be a valuable recruit." Sasha and Serefina nodded in agreement with Janus.

"I *wish I could* learn more about my relatives," he said sarcastically.

"All in good time Killian. You will have many of your questions answered here in the Praetorium," Sasha said.

"That's what they keep telling me."

Serefina stepped to the steel door leading out of the classroom. "Killian, it's time for our midday meal," she informed him as she headed toward the door. "If you are hungry take the elevator to the third floor. The entire floor is the dining area, we're sure you'll find something you enjoy eating."

Killian nodded, suddenly focusing on his wrenching stomach. He couldn't remember the last time he'd eaten. Because of oversleeping that morning, he'd missed breakfast, and last night after he'd arrived he hadn't even thought to eat. He thanked each instructor. He was surprised to find how fascinated he was during each brief lesson. The realms were mysterious and, in his opinion, each one was magical in their own way. After the first realm school lesson he admitted traveling to the realms sounded thrilling. He mentally stored a reminder to ask the instructors how you learned if you were one of the Custodis recruits; the realm jumpers. He left the cool classroom with the strange hope that soon he'd be visiting each one of the mystic realms.

"Killian! Finally, I found you!" A familiar voice shook him from his thoughts. Blake was running toward him waving. His dirty blond hair was shorter, revealing the two-moon tattoo even more on his neck. Killian's eyes widened. Blake was wearing two gold rings in each ear. He'd never seen earrings on him before. Forgetting about the added accessories he smiled widely at his friend.

"Blake! Man, I feel like I haven't seen you in forever, where have you been? You bring me to this crazy place then disappear," Killian teased, but also had a hint of seriousness.

"Sorry. I was told to leave you to Miller and Nathaniel for a few days. I wanted to be there the whole time, thinking that seeing a familiar face would help, but they said they needed to help orient you."

"Well you were right, it would've been nice."

"I know, I'm sorry. I've been dying to see how you've been adjusting, but your here now. I'm starving and I'm ready to hear everything you've been told. So, I'm heading up for the midday meal, let's go. You're going to freak when you see the dining hall. No more prison food for you my friend."

Blake pressed his hand against the steel wall to signal the elevator. He was obviously brimming with excitement at what Killian was going to experience.

Chapter 6
Unexpected Arrival

Killian and Blake arrived at the third floor in a matter of seconds. Before the doors opened from the elevator, Killian was overwhelmed with the delicious, distinct aromas from a variety of foods.

The doors disappeared into the walls, allowing them entry to the dining area. Killian let out an audible gasp as he took in the extravagance. Hanging from the vaulted ceilings were glorious gold chandeliers that cast an ethereal glow among the thick cherry wood tables. Upon each table rested a satin cloth in different shades of blue. There had to be every type of ethnic cuisine he could imagine. Each food cart sat behind quaint brick alcoves, shaped to look like a corner cafe. He recognized most foods, but some, he'd never seen.

"Look, Kill," Blake said pointing to a gray bricked alcove. "That's Cimmerian food, looks like he's whipping up some silver eel scampi." Blake laughed at Killian's disgusted face. "Hey you have to try it before you write it off. Cimmerian's make some of the best seafood I've ever had."

"Uh, I think I'll stick to some things I know first," Killian answered eying a spicy smelling Italian Bistro. "Maybe later I'll brave some of that...stuff." He gulped again as a silver-eyed chef butchered a thin, worm-like creature covered in silver barbs. Blake laughed and shoved his shoulder before turning to order his choice of the odd Cimmerian food.

Killian made it to the Bistro after dodging herds of other Ponderi members. Staring at the food on the pewter trays made his mouth water and his stomach wrench with longing. Stuffed crust pizza covered in every delectable topping he could imagine— creamy, cheesy Italian crusted chicken, ten layered lasagna—he didn't know how he could choose. His last meal had been a stale protein bar with watered down orange juice. Killian felt he would die happy after eating even a small bit of the food on the trays.

"*Buon pomeriggio* what would you-a-like?" A plump, gray-haired, beady-eyed woman asked him. Her accent was a thick Italian and she smiled pleasantly waiting for his selection.

"Oh, I don't even know how I could choose," Killian responded, never taking his eyes off the trays.

The woman beamed in delight. "Ah, take-a it all, *si*?"

"You mean I can have some of everything...for free?" Killian's day was turning out much better.

"*Si, si*," the woman answered excitedly. She began scooping up a portion of every tray without waiting for him to make a firm decision. She topped off the large china plate with a sprig of parsley before handing it to Killian. "*Molto Bene!* Here you-a go."

"Thank you!" The kind Italian woman smiled jubilantly. Killian scanned the grand dining hall before seeing Blake sitting at a table waving toward him. Sitting next to him, he scrunched his nose as he watched Blake shovel the gray fish with strange black rice into his mouth.

"So Kill, what do you think of this place? Pretty nice huh?" Blake said through a mouthful. "I heard the girl that came in with you got home okay."

95

"Her name is Mercedes," Killian answered. Blake shrugged in response and continued eating. Killian stared at him. He was still in disbelief at the fact that he had known Blake for years and had never noticed anything out of the ordinary.

"It all makes sense now."

"What does?" Blake asked, scrunching his forehead.

"Everything. Why you became friends with me right after you moved into town. You knew who I was the whole time didn't you?" Blake awkwardly wiped his face with his napkin and looked down at his plate. "So your whole *story* about your messed up parents and staying with your grandparents wasn't true? Do you even have grandparents Blake?" Killian didn't know why he was getting so upset.

Clearing his throat Blake squared his shoulders. "No Killian. The story wasn't true. I *did* know who you were the entire time, but I wasn't pretending to be your friend, I could've protected you from a distance. Our families merged together a long time ago. My ancestor was one of the original Ponderi leaders too. He was an advisor for James Thomas. I don't know what to say to make it alright with you, or to get you to believe me Kill. I *had* to protect you, but I protected a friend, not an assignment. I'm alone here too. The Ponderi is the only family I have left." Killian looked away digesting what Blake had said.

"Just—can you explain your family and house in Oregon for me?"

"It was just a stage. I was there alone. I figured you always wondered why you had never met Grandpa, huh?" Blake smiled.

"It was a mystery," Killian laughed. "What happened to your family here, if you don't mind me asking?" Blake's lips tightened as he sliced through his fish.

"Being a member of the Ponderi requires sacrifice sometimes. My parents were brave and skilled recruits, but they were killed doing things that were honorable. It was one of the hardest moments in my life." Blake's tone was dry and empty. It was obvious he did not want to expound on the story. Killian felt

96

the sting of emotions fill his heart and mind. *Agony*. He bent over from the overwhelming sensation that had overtaken his body.

"What's the matter Kill?" Blake asked. Killian took several deep breaths trying to stifle the rampage of emotions.

"I...sometimes...get strange feelings. That's all. It overwhelms me without warning," he answered, being as vague as he could without lying. As the waves pulsed over him, he remembered Connor insinuating these odd occurrences could be effects from the relic. Nathaniel had said to monitor any strange moments, and this moment seemed strange to him. He was sure most people didn't react in such a way. After another moment, he recovered. Killian empathized with Blake; he only had the Ponderi to live for too.

"Okay. That's a good enough answer about your life story, thanks Blake," he finally said, giving Blake a nudge on the shoulder with his elbow as he dug into his pasta.

Soon they were joined by a beautiful raven-haired girl; her stunning silver eyes protected under the shaded lenses of her glasses gave away her origins immediately. Killian frowned. The arrogant Ignisian, Dax, sat down next to her as she began reprimanding him from training earlier.

"Dax, stop! I hit the target closer to the center, and my speed was faster," the girl argued in a poetic voice, just like Sasha.

"Soph, get real. It's charted that I was faster *and* closer, check with Aidan," Dax taunted the dark haired girl. Her silver eyes grew brighter in her annoyance; she quickly dropped her head and stuffed a forkful of a spinach-looking leaf coated in thick silver dressing into her mouth.

"Kill, meet the two most competitive people in the Ponderi. Sophia has made it her personal mission to represent all female Ponderi and prove they are the more superior sex in the Praetorium. Much stronger than the weak male recruits," Blake teased. Sophia gulped down her spinach and glared at Blake.

"For your information, I am not competing...I just want it to be acknowledged who the *actual winner* was," she answered more to Dax than to Blake. Killian smiled. Although they were arguing, he could tell they seemed like good friends who had a healthy competition against each other. He enjoyed seeing this version of Dax. He appeared to let go of the haughty accusatory tone he'd thrown at Killian before.

As if he'd read his mind Dax glanced at Killian. His red hair was almost as distracting as the bright flames spurting behind the deep brown of his eyes. "I wanted to apologize to you Thomas...for my behavior this morning. I shouldn't have been so quick to judge you. Lucan had told us you were...well to be blunt, he said you were a disrespectful, lazy guy who is trying to rise to the top because of your name. I hope you'll accept my apology," Dax said reaching his hand across the table. Killian took it, but could feel his mouth gaping open.

"Lucan? I haven't met anyone with that name. Why would someone who doesn't know me say that?"

"Ah, don't worry about it. Lucan is the first Custodis recruit in his family and a good one. He sometimes has the attitude that people will beat him and rise above him and he'll be kicked out or something. He's probably just threatened by you," Dax reassured him and patted him on the shoulder.

"Oh Dax, how sweet," Sophia began. "You're so sensitive and considerate when you help others feel good about themselves." Her sarcasm was thick, and immediately caused Dax's flaming eyes to burst in bright, frothing bolts of fire.

"Sensitive? You didn't call me sensitive when I was beating you on the practice field today!" Sophia hit his shoulder and the two instantly immersed themselves in their previous argument.

Blake laughed and stuffed some black rice in his mouth. Looking up from his plate his eye caught the strawberry blonde running frantically around the tables.

"Hey, look...what's up with her?" Blake nudged Killian and pointed to the front of the dining hall.

Shannon ran down the line of tables, dodging Ponderi members returning their china plates to the large dispensing system and dishwasher. Her shoulders heaved with deep breaths as she frantically searched for something, or someone.

Killian slowly made his way toward Shannon. He bumped a few recruits shuffling through the crammed tables. He hoped he could help her, she seemed distraught.

"Shannon!" He shouted over the last three tables, getting frustrated with the overcrowded conditions of the dining area. She hadn't heard him; her hair was flipping from side to side as she desperately scanned the tables.

"SHANNON!" He shouted louder, and this time she'd heard him. Meeting his eyes, he saw her soft expression show relief, but was also disconcerted at the sight of him. She immediately took a more aggressive stance and pushed herself through the swarms of recruits, most looking back at her in annoyance.

"Killian," she breathed heavy when she finally reached him. "Killian, I'm so glad I found you. I...I've been looking for you everywhere. You have to come with me...now! Something has happened." Shannon grabbed Killian's arm and began shoving her way through the crowd again.

"Shannon, what is it? Is it Connor?" Killian's stomach sunk. Could something have happened to Connor for telling him his theory about his family and the relic? Shannon didn't turn to answer him. Dropping her grip on his arm, she kept her pace and ran ahead, expecting him to follow. She pushed through the dining hall doors and out into the cold hallway beyond the training facility. Killian looked back at the trio still sitting at the table. They all looked concerned. Sophia held a forkful of lunch midway to her mouth as her silver eyes widened in anxiety. Killian shrugged and smirked back at them. He didn't want them to worry just yet, so giving a quick wave, he quickly followed Shannon.

Several feet in front of him, once he made his way outside, he saw Shannon place a hand on the cold, steel wall wringing her fingers as she waited for the elevator. Before he could catch up to her, the elevator appeared and she took a quick step inside.

Holding her hand over the door she anxiously motioned for him to hurry up.

Within seconds they shot down toward the lower levels. The doors dinged before Killian had a chance to even ask Shannon again what was happening. Although he hadn't known Shannon long, she did not seem the type to lose control. He knew they were on the first floor which was the clinic floor. This reinforced his belief that something had happened to someone that was close to both him and Shannon. The only person in his mind was Connor.

"Shannon, wait!" he called after her as she snapped open the clinic doors and ran inside. Killian ran through the door that had stayed open behind her and looking side to side he saw the tails of her white lab coat jutting out from behind one of the ivory curtains. Two other white coat medical workers were bustling checking wires and monitors and fetching supplies for Shannon.

Killian heard gasps and tears and mumbled words between Shannon and her patient. Pulling back the curtain his stomach dropped like a lead weight inside.

It was not Connor lying on the padded steel. Killian's mouth gaped open in disbelief. Mercedes lay sobbing on her side clutching her stomach, trying to fight the pain. Tear streaks flowed down her bloodied cheeks, landing on the steel floor of the clinic in large, wet, red drops.

Killian rushed to the side of the steel gurney. Bile burned his throat as he scanned his eyes over Mercedes' slashed cheeks and scalp. The deep gashes were gushing blood into her beautiful chestnut hair. Chunks of mangled skin revealed three, long bald areas where her hair had been torn out. She was sobbing hysterically and fighting against the patches monitoring her blood pressure, heart rate, and oxygen. She raised her brilliant eyes to Killian's face. She looked frightened, which reminded him that, to her, he was an image from a nightmare. He fell to his knees and softly placed a hand in her hair, stroking it on instinct.

"Shannon…Shannon. Get that healing light…get it she needs help," Killian's voice raised into hysterics.

100

"Connor is on his way, Killian, he will be here any moment," Shannon said softly, applying the thick white salve on to Mercedes' open wounds. "Here now. This will help with the pain, sweetie. Try not to move."

"What happened Shannon? You said you were going to get her home safely!" Killian shouted, obsessively stroking Mercedes' long hair. He wasn't sure how to act or feel—he was useless. This girl meant something to him although they knew nothing about each other. They had been forced together by the vicious attack from the wolves. Killian felt responsible for her and believed this somehow was his fault and he alone had brought this pain into her life.

"Killian, my boy, Miss Forino *was* returned safely," Miller's soft voice came from behind them as both he and Nathaniel entered the clinic. "We could never have predicted this."

Mercedes let out a ragged breath. Killian watched as her eyes rolled back into her skull. In horror, he watched as her body went limp on the steel gurney.

"Mercedes, MERCEDES!" Killian shouted.

"Killian, she's okay. I gave her a sedative to help her sleep and help with the pain," Shannon said as Connor arrived and applied the ugly material over Mercedes' wounds.

With tears on his cheeks, Killian turned to face Miller and Nathaniel. "What happened? Why is she back...and like this?"

"Killian, we sent protection for Miss Forino and her aunt and uncle, whom she lived with just as a precaution. We believe the fact our recruits were there saved her life." Nathaniel nodded toward a young, chiseled faced Glacien man standing in the corner. His face was bruised and scratched, but calm. "Speron, was one of the guards of Miss Forino, he brought her back to us, nearly killing himself in the process. If they hadn't been there...well I believe we would be reporting a different situation."

"You're stalling, just tell me what happened!" Killian's anger boiled beneath the surface of his skin.

101

Miller sighed. Speron looked at the ground, shaken as well. "A hole in the barriers opened again. Someone is actively sending dangers to you through hidden track systems *and now* we also believe to those connected to you. It wasn't Malumian wolves that attacked her, or she would most certainly not be here on this table. There are many creatures that travel the realms and wreak havoc and pain. Our recruit noted that the attack was from a troop of Shadow Imps. They are disgusting, half-living creatures that are very difficult to kill. They are vicious alone, but deadly together. The imps are nearly impossible to detect when they're hunting. It is almost always too late to stop a group attack once it's begun."

The worst thing about these demons is they attack for a reward, unlike the Malumians who simply follow their instinct to serve. But the imps don't just destroy their target, they enjoy leaving as much collateral damage as possible. The imps are sadistic creatures that cause pain for the pleasure of it." Miller's face looked angry as he spoke of the beasts. "Killian, Miss Forino's aunt and uncle did not survive."

Killian felt like someone had just punched him in his stomach. He braced himself against the steel wall, barely breathing.

"We are incredibly sorry my boy, for you and Miss Forino—"

"Mercedes. Her name is Mercedes," Killian said through gritted teeth.

"Of course. She will be staying here for now. We…we know the deceased were her only living family on Terrene," Nathaniel said quietly. Killian turned away not wanting the present company to see him wipe tears. Being alone was a familiar curse for him, and now she would be forced to walk the same path as he had for so many years.

"Why…why is someone trying to hurt people around me?" Killian's voice cracked as he asked. Nathaniel slowly shook his head. Shannon and Connor had stopped attending to sleeping Mercedes and watched the dialogue.

"My boy…I don't know. *Blast*, Miller and I have been searching for anything so we may answer that question," Nathaniel said in frustration. His European accent came out thicker when his emotions were heightened. "Other than her being brought here with you, who is a direct descendant of James Thomas and relic guardians, we can't find anything that would instigate an attack on this innocent young woman."

"Unless there really is something the relic did to me and someone wants me and everyone I've associated with dead."

"As I said, we will watch for anything out of the ordinary and if needs be we can run some neurological testing," said Nathaniel.

"Killian, please…let's let Miss…I mean Mercedes rest," Miller said, reaching for Killian's elbow.

"No! I'm not leaving her alone again," he huffed backing toward the gurney.

"Killian, please…" Miller continued.

"No!"

"Miller," Nathaniel said quietly to his Regent. "We can permit him to stay for the evening. Come." Killian smiled gratefully at Nathaniel then turned his back to the others and resumed stroking Mercedes' hair.

"Killian," Shannon whispered to his back, "I'll be in my office down the hall if she wakes up tonight. Please come get me, she'll need to have an evaluation. I'll be honest Killian, her injuries were extensive. Even if she wakes, I don't know if she'll pull through."

Killian's eyes burned with hot moisture, but he nodded his understanding. His eyes were glued to Mercedes' bloodied face. As soon as he heard the swoosh of the automatic door closing behind the others he released a painful sob from his chest.

"I'm sorry Mercedes. All you've ever been was kind to me and look at what I've done to you." Killian leaned forward and gave her forehead a small kiss. In the corner, there was a steel bin full of fluffy gray towels. He rushed over and took several out; their fresh scent was intoxicating. Ignoring the urge to hug them to his face, he rinsed them in the large steel sink with warm water.

Slowly and gently he washed Mercedes' face with the towels. The gray color turned a sick muddy orange from all the blood he washed off her soft, brown skin. Her cheeks were pink and looked fresh, although severely beaten when he'd finished her face. Rinsing another batch of towels, Killian gently wiped her hair that was caked with dried blood. He was careful to avoid the ugly suture material, but wiped the excess scabs around the healing salve. By tomorrow he hoped her deep gashes along her scalp would be nothing but shiny, taut lines.

Satisfied with her cleansing, he returned to the silver bins and removed a lilac scented tan blanket to cover her while she slept. Killian sat next to her and held her warm hand for several hours, he was content and relieved to just watch her chest fall and rise with each peaceful breath.

Before long his head bobbed to his chest, although he fought exhaustion, sleep eventually took over.

Killian's mind drifted to a dim empty space. Taking in the cold surroundings his heart pounded against his chest as he locked eyes with a white-haired stranger in a billowing white robe. The man's eyes were a deep blue, with a terrifying madness tainting the vibrant color.

He was frozen under the man's gaze as the air around them swirled in: electric blues and oranges, pastel pinks and purples, and deep browns and grays.

"Killian." His name echoed around him though he couldn't pin point who had said it. The strange man's cheeks were flushed with windburn pegging him as a Glacien, and Killian saw strange red marks coming from the back of his neck. They looked like scars, but he couldn't be sure. The usual peaceful demeanor of Glaciens was not present in his countenance. Suddenly the man lifted his hands out from his chest, and the dirt below their feet swirled furiously. The earth blinded Killian, and blocked his view of the curious stranger. All at once the earth stopped. The billowing dirt fell down, back to the silent ground. The wild man stood, untouched by the furious torrent of sand and dirt. In his hands were crude, jagged blades the color of rusted metal.

Killian's breath caught in his throat as the crazed man lifted the daggers above his head and threw them into the brilliant surrounding sky, straight at Killian's heart. He watched in fear as the weapons, forged from the dirt, sliced toward him, bringing death on their point.

As soon as the rusted tip hit his chest, he jerked up in the hard chair, finding he was safely back in the clinic. He wiped the perspiration from his forehead and tried to catch his breath from the upsetting dream.

"Killian," the hoarse voice shook him upright. He looked at the gurney, Mercedes' bright emerald eyes were gazing up at him.

"Mercedes! You're awake…how are you feeling? Are you hurting?" Killian rambled rushing next to her again.

She squinted her eyes, and slowly brought a hand to her head. "My head is throbbing, I don't know if I'm dreaming again, or if you're real. I want to wake up!" She sobbed to herself.

Killian noted he was again stroking her hair. He pulled his hand back, unsure if she would appreciate his touch once she found out what had happened.

"Mercedes, I'm sorry. This isn't a dream, and neither was the last time we were together, you only thought that." Her piercing eyes cut through him, but she said nothing. Wiping a stray tear on her gashed cheek he continued. "What do you remember from this attack Mercedes?"

She grimaced as she struggled to recall how she'd again come to the Praetorium. "I remember laughing…awful, horrible laughing. My uncle locked me in my room then," she paused as her eyes widened. "Scratching…at my door. I heard screams! Killian where are my aunt and uncle?" Her breathing was frantic. The ball of painful emotion lodged itself in his chest again. He hadn't wanted to be the one to tell her. Perhaps it was justice. Perhaps he

105

deserved to be the one to feel the guilt for his role in her pain. He knew she would hate him. If they had never met she wouldn't have lost her only family.

"Mercedes…the scratching…" his voice caught in his throat. How could he tell her they were dead?

"Killian what?" her voice cracked as if she already knew.

"Creatures called Shadow Imps…attacked you and your family. Mercedes your aunt and uncle…"

"No." She turned her face away and slowly sat on the edge of the table. "No, they can't be gone." She whispered under her breath more to herself than to Killian.

"Mercedes," he said while hesitantly placing his hand on her shoulder. "I am so sorry. I wish—"

Before he could answer Mercedes wrapped her arms around his neck, despite the wires still monitoring her vitals, and sobbed. She cried for her aunt and uncle, she cried in pain, she cried in anger. Killian held her against his chest and let her cry. He clamped his eyes tight, trying to hold back the emotion as he thought of Shannon's warning of her condition. He pushed the thoughts away, grateful she was conscious and near him. He prayed inwardly that she would be fine and healthy, but he dreaded what the next few days could bring.

Chapter 7
The New Recruits

Mercedes went into cardiac arrest soon after she woke for the first time. Killian seemed to literally feel her pain, and it nearly destroyed him. Shannon was one of the swiftest physician's he'd ever seen. Immediately she was at her side with two nurses and had stabilized Mercedes in minutes.

To Killian's relief from that moment Mercedes seemed to be on the mend. When she regained consciousness again, Killian had made sure he was the first one by her side. It had been a week since her attack and she'd remained carefully monitored in the clinic. Finally, Shannon had cleared her earlier to be released. Killian had selfishly stolen quiet hours with Mercedes in her recovery room each night after he had attended lessons from realm school.

For the last few days, he'd studied the relics, learning how they worked and the power one would have if all four were ever joined. Each relic was seemingly ordinary in appearance, the relic from Glaciem was a simple green pearl, yet it could control minerals, water, and creatures. The Ignisian relic appeared to be a black stone with burning scars throughout the surface like a dying ember. It had the ability to create fire, remove heat or bring heat. It even had the power to extinguish suns. He knew about the Cimmerian relic, it was his after all. The Cimmerian relic provided protections. It allowed the user to create barriers around the object they wished to protect, but it also could affect the mind, creating hallucinations, or bending someone to the owner's will. Killian imagined it would be frightening if the wrong person obtained the relic. His throat was dry imagining the Trinity holding such a powerful weapon. The instructors had run out of time before explaining about the Terrenian relic, but promised to explain it later on through his training.

Killian hadn't noticed anything out of the ordinary with his emotions since Mercedes had flat lined, but every now and again Connor would covertly ask him questions about his dreams, feelings and any other odd occurrences, then wall himself up in his lab for several days. Killian tried not to worry over the possibility something else had been embedded in Merlin's relic, but deep inside he knew there was more to the mystery then he'd yet uncovered.

His relationship with Mercedes developed into an easy friendship, once she was oriented with the fact the Praetorium was not a place from a nightmare. Mercedes was calm and caring and was the easiest person Killian had met and felt he could trust. She originally had great goals to be a Marine Biologist but of course, those dreams had changed. To Killian's relief, she had never asked about his prison sentence. Most of the time he listened and steered the conversations back to her before they dug into the raw wounds of his past.

Mercedes had confided in Killian she never wanted to return to Terrene. How could she? It would be too painful. At times, their conversations were difficult for Killian. They would be laughing and joking until something reminded Mercedes her family was dead. For a portion of their visits, it would be spent with Mercedes crying on his shoulder. It had not been so many days since Killian was alone, angry, imprisoned and cut off from society. During these emotional moments, he gulped down his apprehensions and hoped he was comforting her in an appropriate way. A year in prison often made close contact uncomfortable.

Wringing his hands together, he waited in the hallway for Mercedes to come back. She'd been in a meeting with Nathaniel for over an hour. During that time, Miller and a woman with rosy cheeks and an exceptionally intricate white braid in her hair had entered the room, smiling swiftly at Killian. He stared at the glamorous carpet which was twisted with shimmering gold leaf thread—the upper hall of the Praetorium certainly had a regal atmosphere. Killian was growing anxious just as the solid gold knob twisted and the four people emerged. Nathaniel patted Mercedes' hand.

"Ah, Killian," Nathaniel said, "have you been waiting this whole time?"

"Yes, I…just wanted to make sure everything was okay."

"It's better than okay!" Mercedes shrieked. For the first time since she'd been attacked her face actually showed pure happiness. The shadow of grief was not written anywhere at the moment. "Forget marine biologist I'm going to be a…a… Beastian!" She said finally remembering the odd term.

Killian chuckled at her excitement. "A what?"

"Cora," Nathaniel began, "is taking charge of our dear Mercedes. She is the director of the Beastian department in the Praetorium. Our Beasties, as we call them, are the absolute experts on all creatures in the Hemisphere. When the Malumians attacked you, Beasties went out to survey the scene. They help train our Custodis before jumps on how to handle creatures and defend themselves. There are incredible creatures in each realm, not just Grizzlies and mountain lions. Miss Forino has agreed to the charge, and I feel she'll be a delightful addition."

"I agree," Cora whispered.

"Wow, that sounds cool. You get to work with animals after all," Killian said.

"Not just animals—*monsters*! Cora showed me some images on this awesome light bulb screen…thing…anyway there are some incredible, unbelievable creatures out there," said Mercedes with excitement.

109

"Mercedes has promised she will follow Cora's orders and not seek out certain creatures. Miss Forino assured us she is not on a revenge mission," Miller chimed in soberly.

Mercedes nodded slowly, a bit of the grief apparent in her countenance again. Killian felt agitated with Miller. He wasn't the one in charge of whether she stayed, but it almost seemed as if he'd rather she return back home.

"Yes, of course, she will listen to Cora," Nathaniel said, briefly rolling his eyes away from his Regent. Killian chuckled at the difference in their personalities. "Killian I'm actually glad you're here. Since you passed through realm school, it's time for you to begin your recruit training and hopefully Custodis training. Cora will be taking Miss Forino's time this afternoon and you will be heading down to the training center. Aidan will be waiting for you." The older man smiled at him, obviously excited for him to begin.

Killian's stomach knotted. He knew he would be trained in weapons and fighting, but now that it was here he was suddenly nervous. Mercedes stepped next to him and gave his hand an excited squeeze before walking toward the elevator car Cora had opened.

"Am I supposed to leave now?" Killian asked once Mercedes had disappeared behind the wall.

"Yes. The sooner the better. Aidan will observe you today and let us know if you are a Custodis. You'll also receive your recruit clothing."

Killian looked down at his baggy gray pants. The material was light and airy. The tan shirts were not exceptional looking, but just like the blankets in the clinic, they always smelled of fresh forest flowers. He had never seen anyone pick up his laundry, but each day the bin was emptied with fresh, folded clothes returned to the drawers. He mentally noted to ask where the dirty clothes went.

A few minutes later he wandered on the cool fifth floor again. This time passing the classroom, he nervously pushed against the double doors of the recruit training center. The doors

110

easily gave against his weight, brushing along the steel floor. The training center was astronomical in size, with incredible training materials that would amaze even the greatest athletes. Killian looked from the floor to the ceiling in awe. The room was bustling and busy, full of different races of Ponderi recruits. Seeing so many people from the different races in one setting was quite a sight. The calm, white-haired Glaciens were quite the contrast standing next to their tan-skinned, vibrant, eccentric Ignisian counterparts. He watched as the dark Cimmerians raced gracefully around in the different sections of the unbelievable room. Each Cimmerian wore a pair of glasses on their eyes. The lenses were dimmed, but not completely black and the rims were thin, looking like the glasses would break if they were hit too hard.

Each section was divided by large glass walls. Walking by the first glass room, he saw clouds of breath coming from what he assumed were recruits. The glass walls were dusted top to bottom with a thin layer of frost. In the center of the pool, a long line of anchored white cylinders bobbed along in the freezing water. Killian watched as a small group of recruits began inching their way across a large pool. Small chunks of ice floated throughout the water. A black rope was suspended above the cylinders and recruits were making their way slow and careful from platform to platform.

Killian watched as one small, auburn-haired recruit stumbled and nearly fell from the cylindrical platform; quickly reacting she grasped the rope overhead to save her the pain of falling into the freezing water. Killian jumped when a loud siren sounded. A large man with tan arms, bright blue hair, dressed in a black wetsuit came over to the recruits from the far corner. Killian listened to him shout something at the dangling girl—the glass muffled the voices so he couldn't make out what was said.

He grimaced as the young girl reluctantly let go and landed into the painful, cold water with a splash. The girl surfaced, her face contorted in agony. She treaded the water for several moments as the other recruits passed her by on the safety of their floating platforms. Killian watched anxiously until the final recruit passed the freezing girl and she was finally allowed to climb back onto her cylinder.

111

The girl's long ponytail already looked like it had a layer of frost encasing it. Watching the young recruit, he stood feeling melancholy as his thoughts drifted to Mercedes. The recruit had an uncanny resemblance to her. Killian silently reprimanded himself for spending so much time wondering if Mercedes thought of him as well. Shaking his head, he brought his thoughts back to the training facility and continued walking. The Ponderi seemed vicious and painful in their training methods.

The next glass room was full of multiple rock walls with gray suited recruits decorating the many sides. The walls seemed less intense than the ice pool, until Killian saw the solid wall full of black lava rock shift, without warning, into cold chunks of rock and ice. The recruit who had been climbing stumbled for only a moment before grasping tightly to the new set of rocks and continuing his climb.

The neighboring wall was undergoing similar surprising shifts. A rocky glacier suddenly fell into complete darkness, the only light came from small bulbs attached to the recruit's belt. The small beams indicated the man was continuing his climb slowly and carefully in the darkness. Other walls were ruby red sandstone—another, full of pines and boulders. It was easy to gather the ever-changing climbing walls represented different terrain on each realm.

Across the large hallway between the glass boxes, Killian saw a field dotted in gray uniforms. Recruits were dueling with one another with long, double bladed spears. Others had long daggers and knives. Killian watched two young women join in intimate combat with the sharp weapons. The girls crouched and lunged aiming at their opponent in fury.

Further back on the field, Ponderi recruits were throwing all manner of dangerous weapons at odd shaped targets; he was amazed at the distance these people could accurately throw such weapons. If Nathaniel thought he was going to be able to roll along with the skill these recruits had, he'd be sorely disappointed.

Across the field in a distant corner, recruits were aiming sleek crossbows; the same he had seen Blake use to kill the

Malumian wolves. Killian recognized the current shooter as Dax. He shot a series of arrows with perfect grouping on the target—all fatal shots if the cloth target had been a live victim.

"HEY!" a gruff, angry voice yelled from behind. "Only recruits down here, what are you doing?" Turning Killian saw a short stalky man dressed in tight fitting gray pants coming toward him. His bare chest was tan with a long chain around his neck. Killian was mesmerized by the charm on the end. It had flames sputtering and flickering, trapped in a crystal prison. The man had bright flames glowing behind his brown eyes and his bright orange hair was impossible not to stare at.

"Can you hear? Only recruits down here!" he shouted again as he came nose to nose with Killian.

"I...I was sent by Nathaniel. My name is Killian Thomas," he stuttered.

"Ah, so you're the new recruit," he said looking over the orders that had beeped to life on a small translucent tablet in his pocket. Squaring his shoulders he quickly crossed his fist over his taut chest, just as Dax had when they met. "I actually had been told earlier you may be coming from Blake. I am Aidan. I am the director of the recruiting office. Come and speak with me for a moment before we set you to work."

Aidan swiftly turned on his heel and began walking back the same direction Killian had come from. Killian followed him back toward the main doors. As he made his way passed the ice pool, he noticed the freezing recruit that had been forced to tread the icy water stood shuddering in a thin gray towel. The instructor stood over her pointing at the rope then the water in an apparent reprimand for her mistake.

Back at the main doors, Aidan led Killian past three oddly shaped doorways. One was an open arched doorway labeled *Changing Room* —that room was obvious. He stopped and stared at the door next to the changing room. It was a bright red, circular door and an obvious heat emanated from behind the entrance. Aidan was turning into the third, massive black door, with a charred log over the frame. It had a name plate with his credentials off to the side. He glanced behind him seeing Killian staring at the red door.

"That's the simulation room, obviously it is on Ignisian settings. Come on, I stick to a strict schedule, let's get this over with."

Inside Aidan's office, Killian felt a rush of warm air overwhelm him. Heat blew in from every vent in the small steel office. Aidan sat down on a steel office chair, and Killian nervously found a seat on an uncomfortable metal stool in front of the desk.

The desk was covered in a translucent computer monitor. Laying his large palm on the screen, Aidan woke the computer up by his touch. He pulled up a file that looked similar to the one Connor had read the day before. Briefly scanning the document, he raised his eyebrows as he read the last paragraph.

"Well, Mr. Thomas. Nathaniel is very specific on the training you should receive. I am not surprised, given your lineage that you will need to be trained as a Custodis."

"Well, Nathaniel mentioned I would need to undergo some observation to be sure...although he and Miller are pretty convinced I am," Killian said. Aidan raised one eyebrow and gave Killian a strange look.

"Are you telling me how to do my job? Are you telling me I need to *observe you*?"

Killian's face flattened almost instinctively. *Please don't be a Ponderi version of Brooks*, he thought to himself.

"No, sir, I was just passing on what I've been told. I'm pretty new and am not sure how often you meet with—"

"Ah, Thomas lighten up," Aidan chuckled slapping his muscular thigh. "I just wanted to make you a little tense. Glad you were paying attention to what Nathaniel was telling you, though." His face returned to the serious demeanor he had kept. "Right. I will get you a set of training clothes. You will be called *Recruit* and be tested to your limits in every aspect. Do *not* think for one

114

moment, Mr. Thomas the fact that you have a strong bloodline in the Ponderi that you will receive *any* special treatment from me, or your fellow recruits. Understood?" Killian nodded briskly. Aidan stood from his chair and reached in to a deep wooden cabinet behind him. Pulling out two pairs of plain gray clothes and a pair of thin black boots he handed them to Killian. "Take these. They are designed to be one size fits all so I would advise against tightening the belt. The combination for the locker is on the inside of the neck. Alright, come with me Thomas, get dressed and I will show you around. Then we'll get straight to work."

Aidan stood outside the changing rooms while Killian made his way in to put on the uniform. Inside the changing room, there were rows and rows of thin lockers. He wasn't sure how he was going to fit his clothes *and* the extra uniform in the sleek, thin space. He glanced at the number on the inside cuff of the neck of one of the uniforms. He saw each space had a vertical set of numbered buttons. Typing in the three digit number the locker released and jutted out as if it was a vertical, wheeled tray.

Killian saw small hooks he assumed were there to hang his clothing. Laying aside the black boots and a uniform he quickly undressed. Once his clothes were hanging on the hooks, he typed the same combination into the open tray. He didn't know how they would fit into the small space, yet as he observed his flailing hanging clothes an amazing suction from somewhere within the locker flattened them into paper thin sections. The tray slowly made its way back into the slot easily fitting into the thin slat in the wall. The Ponderi's gadgets and unusual technology continued to bewilder him. Killian scoffed at the idea of one size fits all. The pants Aidan had supplied him with were incredibly large. He'd never considered himself a small person but still the uniform was drowning his lower body.

As soon as he fastened the belt to the furthest notch the fabric began shrinking and suctioning to his skin. The belt dug into his sides and stomach until it was unbearable. The thin fabric fastened itself around his legs like a new layer of skin. Killian desperately tried to loosen the belt, believing his insides would be crushed. Finally finding the snap that dug into his core he pulled it apart and gratefully found relief from the pants. Pulling on the baggy long-sleeved gray shirt, the fabric mimicked the lower body until it was skin tight against his biceps.

Killian glanced at his reflection on his way out. His mud-colored hair was not as trim, but still quite short from the military-style he'd had for a year. The gaunt, sullen look he'd had when he'd first arrived was filling in with more vibrancy. His whiskered chin could use a good shave, and his blue eyes seemed to have more life. The gray uniform was tight but so comfortable. The belt was a thick slab of leather, though it felt weightless. He noted the loops for various weapons and wondered what use he would have for such things. He looked so different and almost didn't recognize himself. Perhaps being attacked by the vicious wolves was a blessing in disguise.

"Alright, Thomas, stick out your finger," Aidan instructed after he'd returned to the hallway. He held a vial filled with purple liquid in his hands. Killian hesitated but eventually held out a finger. Aidan pricked the tip with a small needle bringing a bead of blood to the surface. Flipping Killian's hand over the vial he pushed against his finger tip until several drops plopped into the vial. The dark blood swirled and frothed as the purple mixture turned to a pastel blue with small flecks of glittering gold. "Hmm, the gold is out of place. I'm not sure what that means, but it's mostly blue," Aidan murmured as he studied the vial. "So that means Thomas, you are our newest Custodis. You must have something strange in your blood to have flecks of gold in the vial." Aidan chuckled, but Killian sucked in a breath. He knew Aidan meant it in a teasing manner, but it caused his mind to speed with questions about the gold charm and the power it held.

"Now," Aidan continued, "as I said earlier, this is the simulation room." He was pointing to the formerly red circular door which now was a deep ebony color. "We use it during our annual Peridus tournament, you'll learn about that later, but it's also used if a recruit disconnects in the realms."

"Disconnect in the realms? What do you mean?"

"Some recruits have difficulties connecting with other realms. When this happens it usually means they either get seriously injured, have locals attack them, have an inability to communicate with realm leaders, or they die." Killian choked a little. Aidan ignored him and continued. "The simulation helps us discover their weakness—it shows us what that specific recruit needs during training. Some recruits exhibit unique abilities at times as well, we use the simulator to break it down mentally so we can chart and analyze any anomaly."

Aidan stopped walking and pointed to the ice pool he'd passed earlier apparently anxious to change subjects. "This is the ice pool. It resembles water on the high mountains on Glaciem." Killian scanned the pool, a new group of gray-suited recruits had lined up along the side. He watched as one by one they grabbed the rope above their heads. With white knuckles, the group of young people slowly inched their way across the freezing pool. The exercise appeared to be the opposite of the one earlier. This time, the goal was to *not* touch the floating cylinders. Killian shuddered imagining the training he would have to go through.

"So are only Custodis trained here? If other recruits never cross into a different realm, why would they need to train in the pool?"

Aidan looked a little exasperated at the question. "We train each recruit on all the facilities here. It's better to be trained to handle any situation wouldn't you agree?" Killian nodded quickly before Aidan continued. "We also have other sections, such as Beasties that learn to work with creatures in the different environments—possibly even fight creatures, so it isn't only recruits that use this facility."

Killian acknowledged he understood. He was excited to know he would hopefully see Mercedes in the training center when she trained as well.

"Realm school explained a lot about the other realms, but I admit I still find it amazing Glacien's can survive if the temperatures are so cold." Aidan shrugged then pointed at a boy with spiked white hair dangling from the rope.

"When you look at some of the Glacien recruits, notice their skin. They have a fine layer of hair; it's almost invisible to an

117

untrained eye. It protects their skin and keeps them warm. They have thick skin as well; thick and rough in order to withstand windburn."

"Impressive that a thin layer of fur could keep them warm." Janus had never mentioned this during realm school.

"Hair, Thomas—not fur. It's not *just* the hair," Aidan said. His tone was perturbed as if Killian was an imbecile for not thinking another race in the realms could have an extra layer of hair.

"So Glaciens aren't like humans then?" Killian asked, slightly confused. Janus had explained Glaciens related to creatures, perhaps they were more animal-like.

"*Gah!* Thomas, I do not have all day to assist you in your history of the realms. You should have taken greater care for these inquiries during Realm School. Glaciens are *humans*. Accept that fact. They are *another race of human*! I know most Terrenian's think they are the single greatest species in the Hemisphere, but wipe that from your mind immediately. Each realm is home to different races. Color of skin, as you classify on Terrene, is not the only factor in distinguishing race." Aidan's face had gotten red and hot in frustration. Killian nodded, not wanting to upset the volatile trainer more.

Moving on, Aidan brought him to the ever changing rock walls. "Whenever you have the opportunity to visit another realm you will notice the terrain can be treacherous. You have to be prepared for any physical exertion required. Each realm has many mountainous regions with their own dangers. It is imperative that you are an experienced climber, Thomas. You need to have the skills to maneuver in any weather *and* with all your gear, alright?" Killian nodded keeping his silence. "Good, moving on. Over here as you saw earlier is the practice field, don't worry about hurting the grass during exercises...it's manufactured right here in the Praetorium. It looks and feels much like Terrenian grass, but is one hundred percent artificial. I will begin your training here today. I need to get an idea of where you stand with a weapon—"

"Wait!" Killian interrupted. "I have never used a weapon...ever."

Aidan eyed him up and down. "Well, then all the more reason to begin on the field. If you are going to exercise your Custodis abilities you need to be able to handle yourself in a combat situation. There are ferocious creatures throughout the realms, Ignisia has many," Aidan said with a sense of pride. "Also you most certainly will come in contact with Deshuits." Aidan turned and began making his way to the field.

Ending any further explanation Aidan opened the large glass door and entered the practice field. He led Killian over to a small group of recruits holding knives and daggers. Killian's stomach dropped as he watched a fierce recruit pin down a small red-headed boy. The man had dark hair tied low in a short ponytail. His eyes were focused as he straddled his fellow recruit, holding the knife to the pale boy's throat. Instinctively, Killian wanted to help the smaller recruit; The older man looked like a vicious bully to him, but he stopped walking toward them. He doubted he could do anything to help the boy. Life had taught him when you step in where it isn't your business you pay for it in the end.

"Everyone, this is our new recruit, Killian Thomas. He is going to be a great asset for the Ponderi," Aidan said loudly to the knife fighting group. The recruit glared at Killian from under his dark, bushy eyebrows. "He is joining the Custodis to train. He has never jumped, and is fairly new to the Ponderi so I expect each one of you to give him thorough instruction."

The group of recruits stared blankly between Aidan and Killian. The dark recruit scowled and threw his knife into the soft field, showing his disdain for the idea. Aidan scanned the group, Killian's mouth went dry when he called the angry man by name.

"Lucan, you are the most seasoned recruit. I want you to take Thomas today and show him the ropes. Start off with a little knife play. Thomas, you are in for a treat, Lucan is the *best* knife fighter we have. He is a fellow Custodis as well, so he'll show you the way to fight from firsthand experience."

Killian doubted Lucan would want to help him, this was the recruit Dax had told him was spreading rumors. Killian wanted to protest, but Aidan had already turned toward the recruits using the crossbows. From across the field, Killian spotted Blake. He was watching Killian with a long spear in his hand. Blake gave him a wide smile and a small wave before thrusting his spear deep into a realistic, disgusting looking target that resembled a disfigured, winged boar.

"I think recruit Thomas is considering running away," Lucan said sarcastically. A rippled chuckle ran through the group. Turning around, Killian put up the defensive walls he had always carried in his life.

"You wish," he shot back. Lucan scowled and threw a jagged knife at Killian's feet, it landed inches from his boot, sticking into the grass.

"Here, wear this," A small, mousy haired boy said handing Killian a soft, but firm black leather wristband. When he put the band on his wrist, the knife pulled from the ground on its own and stuck to the band. Killian stared at it with awe.

"Well, Thomas if you're so special why don't you show us something. You and me right now. Let's see if your *bloodline* holds true," Lucan spat the word bloodline like it was dirty. He grabbed the steel hilt of his knife, and locked it onto his own band and began circling Killian.. Killian's palms were sweating as he danced in a wide circle, never breaking eye contact with Lucan.

Killian knew this could go on forever, it was clear Lucan was just playing with him. He felt the frustration and anger boiling beneath the surface, and the calm facade he'd kept since arriving was waning. The constant unknown, the truth of his dead parents and now this dancing bully in front of him spilled out. He stopped in his tracks and foolishly took the first move, lunging his entire body at Lucan.

As he lunged, he tried to take the knife off the band, but it wouldn't budge. Lucan easily thwarted the amateur attack, as Killian stumbled Lucan held his palm open and Killian watched as his knife flew from the band into his open palm. Quickly Lucan hit

120

the back of Killian's head with the butt of his knife. Grabbing the back notch of his skull, Killian felt a warm trickle of blood where his scalp had split from the blow. He glared at Lucan. The bystanders had circled the two recruits and a low rumble of surprised voices sounded through the small crowd.

"What was that Lucan? This is training, not combat," Killian growled wiping the streak of blood from his palm onto his new pants. He didn't know how he would beat Lucan if he couldn't figure out how to get the dagger off his wrist. It was as if an incredibly strong magnet was holding it in place and only by using a release mechanism would it be useful. He wanted his knife free to penetrate Lucan's skin. Killian surprised himself by the thought, trying to calm his emotions he took a deep breath.

"This *is* training Thomas, now learn from it!" Lucan lunged swiftly and expertly. He wrapped an arm around Killian's neck while swinging his body away from Killian's flailing arms. In one swift motion, Lucan twisted Killian so his feet came out from underneath his body and he landed with a loud *thud*. Lucan raised his knife and swiftly stabbed it into the ground next to Killian's ribs, slicing his skin on the way down.

"*Ahhh*," Killian cried out against as the sharp blade opened his skin, spilling bright red blood over the green field. Lucan brought his face directly next to Killian's, seething he whispered so only Killian would hear.

"You don't belong here, Thomas! We don't need you."

Standing, he left Killian bleeding on the ground. The other recruits were speechless; a young blonde girl had a hand over her mouth with tears glistening in her eyes. Killian knew this wasn't normal training and he didn't know what to do.

"That's all for now recruits, we'll meet up again after mid-meal. One hour! Move!" Lucan shouted to the shocked group, he spoke softer to the crying girl. "Ann, get it together, he's fine." The blonde girl turned and jogged away from Lucan trying to hide the tears on her cheeks.

Lucan walked passed Killian, bending down to grab his knife from the ground. He smirked at his wounded opponent while wiping his blade clean across his thigh leaving a red stain on his gray pants. Laying his head back down on the soft grass of the field Killian closed his eyes. For the first time he actually wished he was back on the campus hedging bushes with Brooks breathing degrading comments down his neck. The grass crunched as someone walked near him.

"Rough day," the familiar sarcastic voice came from above him. Opening his eyes, Killian saw Blake smiling down at him, an annoying laugh written on his face.

"You could say that," Killian said accepting Blake's outstretched hand. He winced as his torn skin pulled further apart upon standing. Angrily he tore off the band with his untouched dagger and threw it to the ground.

"We better patch you up, then we'll head to get something to eat…are you going to brave some Cimmerian food today?" Killian scrunched his face up bringing a laugh from Blake.

Blake and Killian sauntered out into the hall where the first aid cart waited. He moved slowly, with each step his skin felt like it split further apart. Blake ruffled through the drawers on the steel cart looking for a bandage.

"Killian, what happened?"

Killian's stomach leapt to his throat. Turning he saw Mercedes rushing toward him. She looked amazing. He'd seen her this morning, but somehow she still looked different. Her long wavy hair was pulled up high in a tight ponytail. The fading lines on her face from her attack were almost gone. She wore a similar suit as he did, though hers was a dusty sand color with a gray belt extenuating her athletic figure.

"Hi—you look great," he blurted out as she placed a hand gently on his side. She didn't acknowledge his comment, but continued to inspect the cut.

"Found one that should do the trick," Blake said proudly lifting his head from the drawer. "Oh, hello again," he smiled at Mercedes.

"Hi," she answered. "I'm glad to see you again. I never had a chance to thank you for saving us."

"Ah, it wasn't a big deal." Blake shrugged it away. Mercedes just smiled. "Alright bud, lift the shirt—I'll put this over it."

"Wait," Mercedes put out a hand. "We can't just bandage it, it should be cleaned. Blood is everywhere, the bandage won't fasten right. Killian, can you take off your shirt, please?"

Killian's face flushed and he gave Blake a nervous look. Blake shrugged and laughed quietly. He'd never felt self-conscious about his figure until now. He'd always thought he had a good form, not too bulky, but toned and in shape. Mercedes' emerald eyes were insistent so slowly he took off the tight gray top. Mercedes was right; most of the blood was wet, while some had dried, all around the wound. She dug through the drawers as Blake had until finally retrieving cleansing wipes. She slowly and gently wiped his skin, placing her hands on his abdomen. His heart pounded dulling the sting he felt from the wipe.

"There, all done. Turns out those intro to nursing classes before switching degrees paid off." She said patting his wound gently after she'd applied a clean white bandage. She slowly lifted her eyes to his face and he wondered what she was thinking. Was her stomach in knots like his was?

"Thanks," he whispered. She beamed at him and looked at the steel floor shyly.

"So…can we go eat now?" Blake asked

"Would you mind if I joined?" Mercedes piped. "I actually was coming to see if Killian wanted to go eat with me, I admit I'm still a little nervous so I wanted to be with a familiar face."

"Sure, you can meet Dax and Sophia too," Blake answered. Killian just nodded in agreement. His heart was still returning to its regular speed.

"Okay then, let's go. I can't wait to try all this amazing Cimmerian food people keep telling me about," she said excitedly.

Blake laughed until he cried, Killian just rolled his eyes. He wasn't interested in eating. He couldn't shake the unnerving feeling that Lucan wanted to harm him. The thought of the violent recruit roaming the Praetorium sent chills down his spine. Someone wanted him dead, and Lucan seemed to have the same goal in mind.

Chapter 8
Training

  Killian wasn't surprised Mercedes had gotten along well with Dax and Sophia. Ever since she'd arrived, people were drawn to her. Killian had noticed most sections in the Ponderi stuck with their own associates. Beastians stayed near Beastians, Recruits with Recruits, analysts with analysts—but not Mercedes. She spoke to everyone; she showed an interest in everything. In turn, others wanted to be around her. Killian found it difficult at times to ever be one on one with her, it often bothered him.

  Aidan had thrown Killian straight back into training, despite his disastrous conflict with Lucan. He avoided knife fighting, more to avoid Lucan, and typically stuck with spears and bows. Blake, Dax, and Sophia were all experts with the weapons. On the field, Dax tossed him a small metal rod. Knowing the truth of the rod, Killian pressed a small flat button on the side and two dangerous points ejected creating a long, sleek spear.

  The spear felt like air in his hands, practically weighing nothing. Killian was paired up with a rather fierce looking red-headed girl. She was small and didn't look intimidating in the least, but she was amazingly swift. Seconds after Aidan blew his whistle to begin, he landed flat on his back after the red head swiped her spear across his ankles knocking his feet from underneath him. A small group of her friends, raven-haired Sophia included, chuckled and gave her multiple high fives. Killian let out a breath in frustration as he stood from the ground. His pride was wounded and it showed as his skin turned a deep red.

"Come on Thomas, you can do better than that!" Aidan shouted, embarrassed for Killian. "Blake! Get in there and show this recruit how to fight!" Blake gave Killian a mischievous smile as he came forward to go against his friend.

"Yes, sir." Blake was laughing as he jogged over to Killian. "Will you close up half the spear Kill?"

"How do I close half of it?"

"Just hit the lower half of the button, you don't know all the tricks this baby can do?" Killian shook his head and pressed lightly on the lower part of the button. The bottom half of the spear disappeared into the shaft with a rush of air.

"The spear is ultra-strong Kill. If you need to you can eject that lower half and push yourself into the air. Look at Jean over there." He pointed to a tall, pale woman with ebony hair streaked in the radiant Cimmerian silver. She was on her back and as the attacking recruit approached her Killian watched as the lower half of her spear jutted into the soft field propelling the woman up and away from the second recruit. Jean landed softly behind her attacker, released both points and held one end of the sharp steel against the opposing recruit's neck signaling she had won. It was impressive that the spear had such power to launch a person into the air. He gripped the metal tightly against him feeling safer with it near him. "I wanted you to understand the button so you can use it if you're ever in a jam. Okay, Kill, hold the spear tight in both hands like this." Blake demonstrated the grip after he had released both ends. "Keep your hands a little more than shoulder width apart. Stay on the balls of your feet, not back on your heels. You have to be constantly on the defensive! Don't let anyone hit the sides of your spear like…this!" Blake lunged at Killian, hitting the center of his spear on the wing of Killian's. The force of it broke

Killian's grip from the opposite hand and his control over his spear was lost.

"Could you feel how weak the spear gets when the flanks are hit? You need to will the spear to hit where you want."

"What do you mean *will the spear*?"

"I mean, these aren't normal spears Kill. They run off your nervous system. You learn your strategy and basically think the spear where you want it to go. It'll listen to you. When you form a connection with a weapon, you will *always* use that weapon. Some people get so close to their weapons they actually name them."

"Yes, my bow is named Medusa," Dax chimed in, quite serious about the name. He and Sophia had jogged over when Blake had begun his instruction curious to how Killian would do. "Because if you really think about it," Dax continued, "Medusa is terrifying." He smiled and raced Sophia and the red-haired girl to the targets with their arrows, causing yet another argument between them. Killian laughed. Dax had been more accepting of him since their awkward introduction and he had learned he was a loyal friend. Not the arrogant, pompous Ignisian he'd originally thought.

Blake laughed. "You might think he's kidding...he isn't. Before we move on, do you feel confident the spear is your weapon?" Killian passed the sleek steel rod in his hands inspecting the smooth metal. Something warmed his palm, almost as if the spear was committing to his protection as he gently stroked the weapon like it was a living being. Glancing at Blake he nodded softly. "Okay, then with the spear, if you are the better man at strategy, the moves will just happen and your opponent doesn't stand a chance. Here I'll show you, let's try the target."

Blake signaled to a small Glacien Potential with snow white hair to bring the target in front of them. When the young boy arrived with the target, he bowed low on one knee in front of them and Blake quickly returned the gesture.

"Okay, now just urge the spear to hit where you want it to hit," Blake said pushing himself back up from the ground. "It takes some practice to develop the connection, but just try."

Killian looked at the steel spear in his hand. He felt foolish trying to talk to the weapon in his mind. Looking at the dot in the center of the Malumian wolf shaped target, he thought how desperate he was to hit the target and not make of fool out of himself again. Imagining the spear hitting the center, he raised his throwing arm up above his head. Reeling back, he carried his arm passed the side of his head releasing the spear toward the target. It stuck deep into the material, two circles out from the center, directly into the stomach of the Malumian wolf. Blake clapped from behind him.

"Not bad, not bad. I think with practice you are going to have no problem with spear fighting."

"Are all the weapons like this? Do they all need a connection with you?"

"Pretty much. You can't just depend on the connection though. All of them require skill. You can better your chances with a few of the weapons with some extra tips. Knife fighting depends on how well you take care of them, they are picky about their blades. The more you clean and sharpen them the easier it is to aim and attack."

"I don't get the wrist bands, though."

"Oh, it just attracts them back to you. So if you throw your knife, the bands will bring them back when you signal it instead of you having to go find it. If you want to release the knife you just command them. The deeper the connection you have with the knife the swifter the reaction time. Most knife fighters can command them mentally which is dangerous since the target won't know when an attack is coming."

"Makes sense why I couldn't get the knife to respond to me the other day."

Blake nodded. "Sword fighting all depends on your confidence. The swords like to feel heroic. They are pretty arrogant and don't work as well when they sense nervous, or unconfident feelings. Take a look over there," Blake said pointing to a young recruit holding a magnificent gilded sword. "That's Nelson, he's a squirrely little guy, and is petrified of fighting, but he comes from a long line of recruits and his dear old dad won't stand for him to be in any other department. Watch the sword in his hand."

Killian obeyed and observed the blond boy. He watched as he lifted the large blade and charged a holographic target projected on the field. Any onlooker could see the uncertainty written on the boy's face. Before the sword stuck into the heel of a strange, winged-horse target, the young boy swerved—or more like the sword swerved—away from the target. Trying once more the young recruit held the sword straight out from his chest, closing his eyes he charged again. The sword flew up over his head, avoiding the target again, and landing poor Nelson on his back.

Blake chuckled. "See. The sword can sense Nelson isn't dedicated to attacking even the hologram. It will not perform if the attack won't end in some type of glory. Even if a recruit were to die in battle against an enemy, the sword would be satisfied if they gave it their all. It would be a hero's death."

They are tricky too, swords would not be my first pick because in the event you do use it against an enemy the swords eject smaller, barbed blades from the side of the main blade into a victim and...when they are removed...well it's pretty messy." Killian shuddered at the thought.

"You need to have good footwork with all of them too, though. You can't just tell the weapons what to do and stand back to watch. You will have to learn how to stay light on your feet like Sheena over there...she's the one who took you out."

"Funny," Killian smirked. "Why use such, I don't know, low tech weapons?" Blake scrunched his face confused at the question. "I mean, you don't have guns or anything like that."

Blake smiled. "I'm surprised that question came from you, I thought you didn't like guns?"

"No, I didn't like *Richard* with a gun."

129

"Ah, I see. The Ponderi have no reason for Terrenian weapons, as we call them. The main realms believe in honorable face to face combat that comes from fighting with swords and spears, it's tradition. So the Ponderi follow suit, it wouldn't be fair in the Ponderi's eyes if we held a weapon greater than others in the Hemisphere. It would create us as the superpower over them, and we have fought hard to create a feeling of equality throughout the realms. Besides, there are powers in the Hemisphere that Terrenian weapons would be useless against anyway, so there is simply no use for such things."

Killian raised an eyebrow. The Ponderi had the technology, he was sure, to make a super-weapon that could frighten anyone into submission. The fact that they hadn't created such a thing offered a little more trust toward the people in the Praetorium.

"So what is *your* most useful weapon?" he asked Blake.

"Oh, that would be the cross bow. They are forged in the black caves on Cimmerian. When I first worked with my bow, it just felt…perfect. All bows have the ability to have perfect aim if the user is skilled enough. The arrows are designed to hit the target even if something is standing in the way." Blake gave Killian a longing smile as he drifted to another place.

"Like the arrow can go around something and still hit a target?"

"Exactly. Some recruits are given a special bow called an Infinite arrow. They have little cartridges like these," he said pulling out a small, smooth rectangular piece of steel. "You notch the cartridge into the bow like this and pull back." Killian watched as Blake pulled the string back. Amazingly, the steel cartridge molded into a small, perfectly sized arrow. Blake released the string and the arrow pierced the target in the center. The rectangular steel was left in the catch of the crossbow.

"How did it do that?" Killian asked whisking his head from the arrow to the remaining piece of steel.

"It's all a sensor system. It molds according to which bow you use and will fit an arrow perfectly, then you just keep

130

shooting. As long as you keep a good eye on this little piece of metal you'll always have arrows."

"How did you get one?"

"It's kind of a long story…" Blake paused for a moment gathering his thoughts.

"Recruits!" Aidan's voice echoed through a small microphone device he had clipped to his shirt. The noise broke Blake's daze. "Custodis groups need to come with me. The rest of you rotate stations. Field recruits head to the pool with Ivy, pool and rock wall recruits head to the field with J.J.!"

"Sweet! Ivy is the best pool trainer," Blake said, placing his spear back on the rack.

"Why is that?"

"She is soft. Glaciens, you will find, are soft-spoken, love everyone kind of people. She can't stand it when a recruit fails. Her reprimands are firm, but never above a whisper." Blake winked back at Killian, loving the good luck he was given. Glancing up he saw Aidan waving his thick arm for Killian to follow his group. His face was shadowed with annoyance, so Killian quickly followed.

"Recruits, you will be working on the climbing walls this afternoon and we're going to have a little fun with it too," Aidan smirked, obviously excited. "You will race one another and whoever wins will earn the code to the training center for a week!"

The other recruits gasped excitedly and murmured amongst themselves, but Killian couldn't see why this was such a great prize. Aidan noted his lack of reaction and frowned.

"For those of *you unaware* at what a *rare opportunity* this is, this will give you an opportunity to train harder for the Peridus." Apparently Killian still lacked the reaction he desired so he growled again. "And again, for those who still don't know *what Peridus* is, who would like to explain?" Lucan's hand shot up from the group.

"Peridus is a tournament where each department competes for leadership positions and unlimited access in the Praetorium. It is the only way to advance in the Ponderi. It brings a sense of honor and prestige as well as financial compensation."

"Correct." Killian saw Lucan cast an angry sneer toward him. "The Peridus is a chance for recruits, beasties, analysts, even engineers to compete. Winning the codes to the training center will give you the upper hand in preparing for the games. I *expect all of you* to participate in the Peridus," he finished with his flaming eyes resting on Killian. Killian gulped. He was horrible at weapons, and from the healing wound on his side from the knives, hand to hand combat was not his forte either. Aidan's gaze pierced him. Killian liked Aidan, he was stern but just as passionate. Deep inside he didn't want to participate in Peridus because he didn't want to disappoint his trainer.

"Alright let's begin—Sam, Ansel you first."

Two recruits stepped forward. One was husky and muscular with short spiky brown hair, the other was long and lanky. His white hair was brushed neatly across his head, and he emitted a peace that calmed Killian's nerves instantly as he walked by.

"Remember recruits, a full week of codes to the training center." Killian watched as brown-haired Sam sneered at Ansel, although his face was tough and competitive he got the sense that the recruits were enjoying the friendly competition. Aidan blew his high pitched silver whistle and in moments the two recruits were moving up the walls.

Sam was quick and strong, but Ansel had the length. Ansel was nearly halfway up his rocky cliff when suddenly the wall shifted textures. Ansel was hanging onto clear, ruby red rocks, littered with small grains of red sand. He cried out in pain as Sam closed the gap between them. His side of the wall had shifted to a frozen glacier. Gritting his teeth, Ansel continued upward. Killian thought perhaps the Ignisian rock was too hot for his skin. He had been told Glacien's struggled the most in Ignisia.

The surrounding recruits gasped as Sam slipped almost falling to the padded floor but quickly grabbed hold of a jagged stone jutting from the side of his glacier. As soon as he latched onto the stone, the rock wall fell into darkness. Both recruits made their way slowly up the dark wall, the small bulbs of light the only indication of their progress. Both recruits were neck and neck and almost to the top when the shift happened again. Ansel's rock wall shifted to pine covered, rocky terrain while Sam's shifted to the ruby red Ignisian sand stone.

As Sam reached his hand onto the final ledge several feet ahead of Ansel, his hand slipped on the fine red sand blanketing the already slick stone. Sam fell, free falling a three story distance toward the padded floor. Killian held his breath as he watched him helplessly. Sam would not be leaving today without a few broken bones. As Sam fell, Killian noted he was slowing down little by little. Before he reached the padded floor, he was practically floating before landing softly on the ground. Sam slammed his fists in frustration at his defeat, then stood back to observe Ansel's descent down the Terrenian landscape.

Killian's mouth gaped. "How did he fall so slow?" He whispered to a bubbly girl next to him. She flipped her auburn hair, whipping him in the face.

"The floor is connected to sensor's in our belts, silly," she chirped. "If we fall the sensors measure our velocity and decelerate our fall by pressurizing the air around us. The faster we fall the more pressure builds up. I'm sure Sam's fall was rather uncomfortable, it probably felt like he was being squeezed in a tube."

"Wow, that's genius," Killian said in awe.

"I know right!" She gasped. "Sometimes I would love to just go spend a week with all the brilliant engineers here! Fascinating! I mean who would think—*hey let's not have any more broken recruits from the rock walls. Let's break their falls with a super awesome sensor*!"

Killian smiled at the girl's enthusiasm until Aidan blew his whistle silencing the group. Two more recruits went up the wall, each one faring well. Killian was nervous, Lucan hadn't climbed yet and neither had he. His stomach dropped with only four recruits left. Two were called leaving Lucan to be his climbing competitor. Killian rolled his eyes. Aidan knew what had happened during training the week before—Blake said he'd told him. But he continued to partner him with the only recruit that showed a distain for him.

"Thomas, Lucan. You're up," Aidan shouted after the two female recruits had both made it safely to the ground. "The current winning time is a tie between Neah and Drew. If either of you can beat two minutes and seven seconds, you win the codes."

Killian gulped and stepped up to his side of the rock wall. There were no harnesses, just faith in the hidden sensors in the floor and his belt.

"He means when I win the codes, I think Aidan forgets who I'm competing against," Lucan whispered for only Killian to hear. Killian turned away, seething internally, but not letting Lucan see. A desire to beat Lucan overcame him, it was the only thing he wanted. He wanted to win the codes just to prove to Lucan he wasn't a weak nobody. Surprisingly, his mind was calm and locking his grip onto an ice crusted, jagged stone, began his climb.

Killian focused hard on blocking out the swift shuffles of Lucan's climb on the other side of the wall. He imagined Lucan nearing the top while he was only feet from the bottom. Lucan's relentless taunts of his victory shadowed his calm focus. Shaking his head, he determined once more to win the codes to the training center.

As his mind focused on his goal and decided that would be his outcome, an image of the red-rock and fine sand appeared in his mind. He could see himself climbing swiftly up using the perfect crags and crevices in the stone wall. The image was so vivid, but clearly he was climbing the icy glacier. At that moment, the wall shifted— hot red stone, with slippery sand grains, rested under his hands. Killian lost his footing slightly from the surprise. His heart pounded in excitement as he'd just been thinking of the red rock and it had almost appeared on cue.

Continuing upward, he focused hard on finding the right jutting rocks for his footing and grip. He no longer cared where Lucan was, determined he would succeed for himself. Killian's biceps were throbbing, but he didn't stop. As he continued up the slippery sand stone, he quickly found his form and began climbing quicker. In his mind, a new image came into play, the rock wall was shrouded in a thick darkness. If he used his focus enough and kept his head down he could easily see the bulbs from his belt reflect on the black rock and light the way upward.

Killian smiled, having no idea how the premonitions were happening, but he confidently continued to climb the Ignisian stone wall. When the darkness came after the shift, Killian instantly dropped his head to use the glowing bulbs. The anticipation of the impending shadow helped his nerves and he didn't stumble in the least. He was pleased to hear the shuffle of feet and the gasp of recruits when Lucan's wall fell under the blanket of black too.

The small bulbs cast a greenish light against the black stone that illuminated every crevice. He moved swiftly, never lifting his head to see his progress. A whispered chant was filling his ears from below.

No, I'm not hearing this right, he thought. Below him, he heard his name with cheers of encouragement seeping up the rock wall. The recruits were chanting *for him*. Suddenly, Killian felt his head pound against a barrier. Looking up, he realized he'd made it. He was at the top. Without hesitating, he began his descent. Halfway down, the cheers grew louder and more excited. In his mind, he knew the darkness would not last—he'd seen the shift already. He was ready for the freezing rock that cut into his raw skin the remainder of his descent. Jumping from the wall onto the padded floor, he was immediately surrounded by the group of waiting recruits. Sam gave him a mighty slap on his shoulder. The excited girl jumped up and down continually saying, "Did you see that, he went so fast!"

Killian was beaming. His excitement and glory were overshadowed for a moment as he thought about the mind tricks. He'd seen every change in his mind—he felt like he had cheated even if he couldn't help it. Could other recruits do such things? The strange occurrence was something Connor would need to know about.

A loud thud shook him from his thoughts. Lucan had finally descended off the wall, and was fuming. His face boiled as he glared at Killian. Lucan's hateful gaze was shrouded by Aidan's large body stepping in front of him.

"Thomas! Wow, I would never have expected this from you. I mean that in the kindest way. You completed your climb in one minute, fifty-nine seconds!" The group cheered, even though he had beaten them all. "I can honestly say you have surprised me. That isn't easy to do. I have no doubt you have *special* Custodis abilities," he whispered to Killian. Aidan rose and faced the group. "We have our winner! Killian Thomas, you have earned the codes for the training center for one week. You now have unlimited access. Use it wisely! Come to my office and I'll give the codes to you." Killian's stomach ruffled in excitement. He'd never accomplished anything praiseworthy, and for the first time in his life, he didn't feel mediocre. Even Lucan's biting glare couldn't steal this moment from him.

Late that night, Killian heard a knock on his door that startled him awake. He made his way to the large wooden door nervously. It was late, but he assumed it would be Connor to ask if he'd had any strange happenings—which he had.

"Who is it?" he asked abruptly.

"*Death!*" an over exaggerated voice replied, followed by a group of people chuckling. Killian smiled and opened the door finding Blake, Dax, Sophia and Mercedes huddled in the hallway.

"What are you all doing here?" Killian whispered. It was well after midnight, but they all had a playful look in their eyes.

"All we do here is train, sleep, eat, and train some more," Blake said. "A rumor is flying around here that you have been given the codes to the training center!" Killian laughed. Word spread quickly about his victory earlier.

"Come on Killian! Let's go have some fun. It's so serious around here lately," Dax said, giving him a false pouting face.

Mercedes looked at him, flashing an excited smile and small wink. He smiled back at her, thinking it wouldn't be such a bad thing to relax a little. He had never had a real group of friends, but this small crew meant something to him.

Killian laughed and closed the door behind him, walking into a sea of satisfied slaps on his shoulder.

The typical empty hallways seemed even eerier and silent once everyone was sleeping. He found it odd that the office didn't have a guard or watchman at night, only the upper floors had nightly patrols. The cool steel floors of the training hall chilled him, but the excitement of breaking the rules and having fun as a group filled the coldness with a strange warmth.

"You're not going to give us the codes?" Blake asked as Killian slipped over to the door to type the code.

"Sorry...I feel like I finally earned Aidan's respect today and I'm not supposed—"

"Kill, relax. I know you can't give them out," Blake said, punching his shoulder like he used to.

While Killian typed in the code to the door, Sophia bounced up and down. It was evident she was anxious to shoot her bow without anyone scrutinizing her technique. Blake stood patiently waiting and Dax flirted with Mercedes by swatting her hair into her face. She laughed and gave Dax a playful shove. Killian knew Dax was a relentless ladies man, but still felt a pang of jealousy at the banter.

"Okay we're in," he said, happy to split up the flirtatious behavior and let them into the room.

The friends piled in to the room and ran—Dax and Sophia raced of course—to the practice field. Mercedes stood next to Killian. She seemed a little tense but still excited.

"I can't believe we're doing this. We could get into so much trouble."

He laughed at her and noticed two black bands on her wrists holding small but vicious looking knives. She immediately relaxed as she met the target. Before he knew it, he watched as the knives ejected into her open palms and flew through the air as she threw the pair together at a small round target; she was only off from the center by half an inch. Killian was amazed at her accuracy and Blake let out a long whistle when he saw the knives. Mercedes held her hands, palms up once more and instantly the two blades dislodged from the target and landed back onto her bands.

"Wow, you have caught onto the weapon training a lot faster than I did. In fact I think you might be better than me." Blake said.

"That's not true. Andy, our group leader, said you were one of the fastest recruits to pick up combat," she said tossing him an unusually small cross bow with small arrows, as well as a larger bow. Blake laughed and expertly aimed both bows. The arrows soared through the air, around Dax and Sophia, who stood in the way of the target and landed in perfect grouping even closer to the center than Mercedes' knives. Blake smiled proudly. Glancing at Killian he tossed him a spear.

"Come on, aren't you going to throw?"

"Honestly, I don't know how I'll do. You saw, I'm not the best with the weapons. I don't think they like me," Killian answered half joking.

"Oh come on, you just have to *will* it to do what you want, remember?"

Killian licked his lips nervously. Dax and Sophia had stopped their speed shooting game with their bows, to watch.

"Really, I'm pretty bad."

"Come on Kill, you're a Thomas, right? Stop being modest!" Sophia's silver eyes sparkled.

Killian smiled, he wished he was being modest. Why did Sophia have to throw the Thomas name around like it automatically made him a perfect fighter? Killian had been told recently by Blake that most people believed he was going to be the lead recruit mostly because of his name. His father had been the lead recruit, and so had his grandfather all the way back to James Thomas. Killian had shrunk under the pressure but had not let on to his feelings.

He reeled his toned arm behind his head and pressed the button, releasing the hidden points. He had to admit that although he'd only been at the Praetorium for three weeks, he'd been pleased with the change in his physique. The constant training was shaping his muscles so his uniform didn't have to shrink as far to fit his frame.

The spear warmed his palm, he focused on the weapon and where he wanted it to end up. Releasing the spear he saw it speed through the air; it hit the target with a loud, *clap*. The spear pierced deep into the target, tearing some of the material around the puncture site.

Sophia's mouth opened slightly, Dax looked confused, Blake laughed and Mercedes looked at him sympathetically. The spear had pierced the very edge of the Malumian target; if it had been a real Malumian Wolf, it would only have angered the creature making it more vicious.

"What was that?" Blake laughed. "You did better than that the first time you tried—does someone here make you nervous Kill?" Blake stooped over, as his own sarcasm made him laugh harder. Killian glared at him and folded his arms, feeling quite embarrassed.

"I told you," Killian pouted. "I try *to will* the weapons, but it never seems like I get a connection." Mercedes nodded and told Blake to be quiet. Blake stood straight again and wiped a tear from his eye.

"It's okay," Dax said. "Not everyone can have the accuracy and aim like I have with Medusa." Blake rolled forward again laughing as Dax kissed his bow and flexed his bicep.

139

Killian endured the teasing for several minutes before they all grew tired of the joke and made their way to the climbing walls. This, Killian knew he could master, especially after this morning. He wasn't surprised when Sophia beat everyone on the dark climb, but they didn't praise her much since she was from Cimmerian and was used to the dim lighting. Killian out climbed everyone else, which he was proud of. This time, he'd done it without his strange visions. He even came in before Dax, putting him in a sour mood for a while.

The group found themselves after hours of climbing, throwing, even developing their own obstacle courses in the ice pools, collapsed on the grass of the practice field. They laughed and shared stories of their embarrassing moments at the Praetorium and tales of their families. Sophia's father remained in Cimmerian, so she was allowed to visit during one month out of the year. She puffed up with pride saying he was a direct guard of the throne room of Queen Maurelle. Killian was surprised to learn her mother was Sasha, his realm school instructor. Sasha also worked with Mercedes in the Beastian section.

Dax came from a long line of recruits. They had been some of the most effective guardians of the borders of the Hemisphere, because of their skill with weapons, but also their strength.

"Dax, you haven't told them about your softer side," Sophia teased. Dax's tan skin reddened and his flamed eyes brightened in a fierce orange "Don't let him fool you all he's quite a tender heart."

"Zip it Soph, or I'll tell them about the time you thought you were blinded by one of the lights because you missed the target. She actually sent herself to the clinic and wouldn't leave *even after* Shannon cleared her of any blindness. Can't you imagine Sophia just lying there shouting "I'm blind, I'm blind" and Shannon rolling her eyes?" Sophia's mouth hung open, shocked that Dax had told the story.

"Oh, Dax you monster. Mercedes, have you ever wondered why Dax isn't a Beastian? He sure knows a lot about the creatures doesn't he?" Mercedes nodded and looked at Dax, who hid his face knowing Sophia was unstoppable. "He loves the animals, no *adores* them! He has been caught so many times feeding the little garden elves and the Glacien reindeer that are in the stalls around back. Oh Dax, what a softy." She teased him and pushed him over. Everyone laughed because it *was* surprising. Dax by all appearances was intimidating and fierce, to imagine him stroking a reindeer was amusing.

"Killian, I have to admit," Mercedes said. "Oh, maybe I shouldn't say anything."

"No, you can, what is it?"

"Well, I was surprised you said you aren't that skilled at fighting. I would have thought…well, before we came here you were a…" She blushed not sure if she could continue.

"Oh," he mumbled. "No, I didn't really learn anything there." He felt anxious talking about this with her. Admitting his imperfections caused him unease.

"What? What were you?" Dax asked suddenly.

Blake glanced over at Killian, knowing the truth. Mercedes blushed, obviously embarrassed for putting Killian on the spot.

"Well, I—uh..." Killian cleared his throat, preparing to confess his greatest shame. "I was in prison. I was on my work release program when Mercedes and I were brought here."

"Whoa, I have to admit, I never saw you as a criminal," Dax said. There was a strange hint of awe in his voice.

"I met Killian a year before, just by chance. He was very nice. I'm sure he didn't do anything huge," Mercedes spoke up trying to salvage her part in bringing it up. Sophia nodded in agreement with her.

"He wasn't a criminal," Blake said bitterly. Killian smiled at him. Blake was obviously still upset by the unfair sentence Killian had been given. The other three members of the group stared at Killian, silently urging him to say more.

"You want me to tell you why I got locked up don't you?"

"Only if you want to," Mercedes said, trying to hide her curiosity.

It was only natural. Killian and Mercedes had grown closer together over the two weeks she'd been at the Praetorium. He had almost forgotten the position he had been in when they were attacked by the wolves. It was amazing she hadn't asked before now. A tug of uncertainty pulled at him, what if she didn't like what she heard? What if it changed her opinion of him when she heard his cowardly abandonment of Laura? He conceded he would be curious if the roles were reversed. If he wanted to continue getting closer to Mercedes, the truth would come out eventually.

"It's not a happy situation. I...I didn't become a good person in prison. I stopped caring for others, I only looked out for myself. I've tried hard to change since I've been here," he said trying to prepare them for his story.

"You're a good guy, Kill," Blake said softly.

"We would love to hear about it if you want to tell us," Sophia said in a kind voice.

Taking a deep breath, Killian began to tell them about his life before the Praetorium. "I was brought up without parents, as you know. After bouncing around a bit I lived with a family for ten years, until I was eighteen. The lady was nice, but she never stood up for herself to her husband.

"His name was Richard and Laura was his personal punching bag. I was at one point too, until I got bigger than him." Killian glared at an empty space as he drifted back to the horrible memories. Mercedes reached over to him and grabbed onto his hand, sensing this was difficult for him. Killian thought he heard Dax murmur *disgraceful*. Shaking his head, he gave her hand a grateful squeeze before continuing.

"The day I was arrested Blake had just dropped me off." Blake nodded silently as his own memories flowed in accordance with the story. "I walked in on him beating her up so bad I thought he was going to kill her. So being an idiot I stepped in front of her and I hit that man so hard he fell and got pretty banged up on the

142

way down. He was so angry, I thought he was going to grab his gun." He saw Sophia and Dax glance at each other. Killian wondered if they knew what a gun was after his conversation with Blake earlier. "A Terrenian weapon." Both of them nodded their heads, finally understanding. "So, like a coward I just ran. I left her there. I barely made it to Blake's cover house before the police picked me up. Richard lied and told the police I had beaten Laura. He was a business man in the community and I was a quiet, troubled kid with no family; you can guess who they believed."

"Didn't his wife tell them the truth?" Mercedes asked, wiping a tear from her cheek.

Killian gave a melancholy chuckle, Blake snorted in frustration as well. "Nope, she was scared to death of the man so of course she sided with him."

"That's giving her way too much credit Kill," Blake sneered. "It was her moment to get away from him. She stabbed you in the back and sentenced herself to a life of hell."

"Well, who can say the manipulation she'd been through?" Killian answered trying hard to keep the resentment he had long ago buried from boiling up again. "So, I was locked up for a year. I had a week to go when we met." He finished glancing quickly at Mercedes. They sat in silence for a long time, before Mercedes squeezed Killian's hand again and gave him a smile.

"Well, I think you were a hero, Killian, not a coward," Sophia said. "Any of us would've killed the man, but you didn't, so that makes you a stronger man." Killian just smiled at her. Mercedes looked at Sophia like she had taken the words right from her mouth.

"Guys, this has been astronomically fun, but I think we better get back. Aidan is going to be here in an hour, and I would rather Nathaniel and Miller discover us than Aidan," Sophia said. They all agreed and began making their way back to their rooms.

Mercedes left the elevator first since the Beastian floor was beneath the recruit floor. She turned to Killian before leaving.

"Thanks for doing this for us, it was so worth the risk." She stood up on her toes and kissed his cheek, before shyly walking away.

The elevator car immediately filled with whoops and hollers from Blake and Dax with Sophia trying to shut them up, saying how sweet it was. Killian ignored them all; he didn't care what they said. This had been by far the best night of his life.

Chapter 9
The Four Relics

"Thomas, you have to be swift in the attack! My grandmother could see what move you were doing next with her eyes closed!" Aidan shouted from behind Killian. He panted, exhausted from hours of training. The late night escapade was catching up with him, and Lucan was loving it.

Lucan circled him, twirling his knives in his hands, grinning. He reveled in his tenth defeat and seemed to enjoy more and more making Killian end up flat on his back. Killian tossed the spear onto the soft field, frustration coming to the surface. He wanted to wipe the smug look off Lucan's face; it had been the only thing he had seen for hours.

"How do you expect to jump realms if you can't even defend yourself against a fellow recruit?" Killian glared at Aidan, he was beginning to act a lot like Brooks lately. The short lived praise he'd had yesterday had dissipated as soon as he'd come to the training center.

"Now, take one minute recruits and then we are going to go again!" Aidan shouted to the group. "Thomas you need to focus. You of all people should understand mental strength and how important that is in combat," he said more quietly to Killian. Aidan

145

sounded like he was insinuating something, but he didn't press the question.

An involuntary smile spread across his face when the small Beastian group strolled in to work on their own combat training. Mercedes had her long hair pulled into a tight bun on top of her head. She caught Killian's eye and waved at him. He knew there was an unspoken attraction between the two of them. Her group moved over toward the pool, apparently preparing to practice water creature defense. He noted the multiple floating fish-like creatures bobbing in the pool waiting to be studied by the Beasties.

"Ready to lose in front of your girlfriend?" the arrogant voice of Lucan drew Killian out of his peaceful thoughts of Mercedes.

"You know what Lucan..." He trailed off. Killian wanted to let loose his temper and fight back against the relentless torment. Taking a deep breath, he pushed his frustration down inside. "Lucan, I will take great pleasure seeing you fall on your face." He finished cool and collected, returning a similar smug glance.

Killian quickly picked his spear off the ground and pushed the metal bar against Lucan's chest. Lucan stumbled back, surprised at the abrupt attack. Killian immediately began his offensive maneuvers trying with all he had to keep Lucan in the defensive position. Lucan's face was angry; his frustration evident. Pulling out his sleek knives, holding them blades down, he spun around and jutted his shoulder into Killian, knocking him backward.

Killian found his footing and tried to slow his mind. Out of the corner of his eye, he could see Mercedes and a few other Beasties stop to watch the exercise. This did not help his mental focus. As Lucan lunged again, aiming a knife slightly above Killian's shoulder, Killian spun the opposite direction. He ended up behind Lucan where he quickly tried to push the tip of his spear between Lucan's shoulder blades. Lucan turned around just in time and blocked the jab with the blades of his knives. The weapons clinked together, bringing both men face to face. He knew the spectators would assume this was a simple routine workout, Killian knew better. If he could, he had no doubt Lucan would pierce his chest so deep he would die in moments.

Killian twisted his spear so it dislodged from the blades of the knives. He stepped far back from Lucan, allowing himself a few moments to slow his thoughts and strategize his next move. He felt his entire body loosen and relax so deeply he thought he would fall asleep in the center of the field. Opening his heavy eyelids he noted Lucan's shoulders were heaving with deep breaths as he fumed. Out of the corner of his eye, Killian was shocked and unnerved to see a second Lucan had suddenly appeared. It was happening again!

Killian watched as the doppelganger Lucan rushed at a second image of himself. The vision of Lucan slid on the ground, wrapped his legs around the identical image of himself causing him to fall to the ground where Lucan clamored on top of him holding his knives to his neck and chest. The vision of Lucan had won the fight.

Killian's heart raced and the vision faded just as the real Lucan began charging. Killian knew exactly what to do. As Lucan dropped to the ground to take out Killian's footing he moved slightly to the side, out of the line of attack. While Lucan was facing away from him, still sitting on the ground, Killian rushed him from behind, wrapped his arms around Lucan's shoulders and tackled him to the ground. Lucan struggled from underneath Killian, but he quickly straddled him pushing his knees onto Lucan's arms, applying enough pressure to pin him to the ground. He held his spear above Lucan's face until Aidan blew the whistle signifying, if the fight had been real, Lucan would be dead!

Both men rose from the ground panting from the exertion. Lucan's eyes blazed in anger at Killian. An overwhelming wave of furious emotion filled his chest. He was thrilled to have finally beaten Lucan but was uneasy about the vision.

"Alright Thomas, that's more like it!" Aidan shouted from behind. Lucan was already stomping away, and Aidan just watched him go. "Well, Thomas if you thought he didn't like you before I would just watch your back during training from now on." Aidan

147

chuckled, Killian returned the joke with a nervous laugh. "How did you do that? I knew you had combat skills in you, but Thomas...it was almost like you were floating out there. You made weapon fighting seem easy."

"That's cause I taught him everything he knows," Blake's voice came from over by Mercedes. He was standing by the group of Beastian girls, most of them were giggling amongst themselves pointing at Blake. Killian had learned most of the single, female recruits in the Ponderi found Blake quite handsome. Mercedes' eyes were locked on Killian. They were beaming with adoration and pride. Killian would fight Lucan every day if he could see that look each time. He hoped it made up for his disastrous spear throwing last night. But the uneasy feeling of the odd visions crept across his mind dissolving the exuberance of the moment.

"Recruit, what are you doing here? You are supposed to be on the climbing walls." Aidan tried to sound put out with Blake, but everyone knew he was one of Aidan's favorites.

"Well Aidan, I was instructed to bring Killian up to Nathaniel's office. He wanted to talk to him about something." Blake winked at Killian, then winked at the girls standing around Mercedes. Some looked as if they were about to swoon from his attention.

"Well, alright. Thomas, you get back down here as soon as the meeting is over. You need to go again to make sure this wasn't a fluke thing." Aidan said gruffly before he shuffled away with the rest of the recruits.

Killian looked where Mercedes had been standing, she was waving at him while practically being dragged by the other girls to the pool.

"Come on Kill, Nathaniel was pretty anxious to talk with you," Blake said, already halfway to the front entrance. Killian jogged over to Blake and headed to the elevators with him. Once inside the car, Blake gave Killian a hard punch on the shoulder.

"What was that Blake?" Killian asked, rubbing the aching muscle in his arm.

"Where did that *fight* come from?"

"I don't know...I just focused finally I guess."

"Kill, I saw the whole thing. If I didn't already know you I would have thought you were a senior recruit or a trainer!" Killian smiled shyly, reveling in the praise. "I bet Lucan is going to *kill* you now!" Blake said dramatically.

Killian's heart raced at the thought. Although he knew Blake hadn't meant it literally, it was always in the back of Killian's mind that they still hadn't discovered who was behind the attacks on him and Mercedes.

"Well, it was about time for him to get beat. He's been beating me since I got here so I don't feel sorry for him." Killian answered as the elevator dinged open to the glamorous hallway.

"Yeah I guess. Hey, tell me if they assign you a jump. I can't wait to see how it goes for the first time," Blake answered excitedly. Killian looked at him in surprise that he was talking about his jumping into other realms. "What? You're a Custodis. We all know you are getting ready to jump, it's what they do." Blake said with sarcasm while shoving him out of the car.

"Yeah, but...how does everyone find out these things?"

"Kill, I've done my fair share of brown nosing here, but it's given me connections." Blake smiled before he whizzed away behind the wall.

He knocked on Nathaniel's massive door and waited. After no reply, he slowly opened the door. Nathaniel wasn't at his desk. He walked in slowly sweeping the room with his eyes. Nathaniel was sitting at a small wooden desk, one that reminded Killian of a school desk used hundreds of years ago. Nathaniel was writing something furiously on a piece of paper.

"Sir? Blake said you wanted to see me," Killian said clearing his throat. Nathaniel's head shot up. His dark beard was not as neatly trimmed as usual, but his blue suit was just as fine as always.

"Killian, my boy! So good to see you. Forgive me, I did not hear you knock," He said folding the paper and sliding it the slot of the desk. Nathaniel stood and walked toward the overstuffed sofas at the other side of the room. "Please come sit," He said motioning to the matching sofa in front of him. Killian quickly sat across from Nathaniel and waited anxiously for what he had to say.

"Sir, Blake said you needed to see me."

"Yes, I do. It's time to jump, Aidan has cleared you and we have a fresh arrival of blue pebbles for the Ignisian people, so to Ignisia you will go," Nathaniel said quickly, finishing with a coy smile.

"So, I'm just going to Ignisia to check in on them and deliver some pebbles?" Nathaniel paused suddenly appearing uneasy.

"No, Killian. You won't just be checking in on the Ignisians. I've assigned you there from the report Aidan gave to me. He said your ability on the rock wall was amazing. I believe you will be much like your father—a very trusted, valuable recruit. I need my best tomorrow."

"Sir, what's going on?"

"Killian, there have been reports of attacks in Ignisia, specifically in their molten caves. It is incredibly hot inside the caves and Egan, the chief, has sent word that several cave guards have been brutally killed."

"That's terrible. Do you think it's the Trinity?" Nathaniel nodded and paced in front of his desk.

"I don't know if there is a relic in the molten caves, though it would be a marvelous spot to keep one hidden because of the difficulty to survive inside, so it's possible the Trinity is trying to enter the caves. We have to meet with Egan and explain how crucial the situation is now. He may be able to provide insight on the Ignisian relic guardians. He will have to trust you to reveal such a heavy secret."

"I don't know if I can get him to trust me, but I'll try. What do I need to do to jump?"

"First, you will meet with a Beastian in the morning. They will speak with you about any Ignisian creatures you need to prepare for. I would like you to take the remainder of the afternoon and rest. I don't know how long you will be in Ignisia tomorrow, but you most certainly need sleep to be ready. Jumping realms can be taxing."

Killian nodded. "Sir, what if the Trinity have all the relics already? We don't have any, so it's possible."

"Not so, my boy." Nathaniel punched a code in a concealed number pad along the side of his magnificent desk and pulled out a small gold box. "We are in possession of the Terrenian relic, a rare lily seed." Killian gaped. He had never seen an image of the Terrenian relic, it wasn't available in realm school, but it was rather anticlimactic to hear it was a seed.

"*A seed*? That's a relic?" Killian scrunched his eyebrows together as Nathaniel opened the lid, inside was a large glistening seed. It looked smooth with a dark brown outer covering. Its almond shape was perfect, but looked nothing like a flower seed.

"This is no ordinary seed. It is infused with an incredibly strong power, creation and destruction of metals. It may not seem like an important power, but think for a moment how many metallic elements exist in the planet systems of Terrene." Nathaniel paused when Killian's eyes widened as he realized the effects of using such a power.

"James Thomas was to be the realm leader on Terrene. After the venture, Merlin bestowed the relic to him and it was given to the Ponderi. Each Ponderi director is entrusted with the code to access the lily seed. So thanks to your ancestor, we have always had one relic in our vaults all these years. We keep it well hidden, and don't share what it looks like or what it is capable of to anyone." Nathaniel carefully closed the gold box and returned the seed to his drawer. That explained why he hadn't learned about it in Realm School. "Tomorrow morning at eight o'clock, meet me by the front entry way, Killian. I need your strength in Ignisia. We

151

need Egan to hand over any information he has on the whereabouts of the relic. Tell no one, my boy."

"Why can't anyone know?" Nathaniel stood up and began pacing in front of Killian. He had never seen the older man so uneasy before.

"There is unrest in this Hemisphere Killian. The Trinity is subtle, but striking against many of the realms. If any of the relics fall into the wrong hands...you can imagine what could happen." Nathaniel paused before changing the conversation direction. "You feel confident if you happen to meet with Deshuits? Remember they are dangerous and will kill you if they get an opportunity." Killian nodded quickly, noting the man's accent grew thicker as his intensity grew. "Good."

Nathaniel gave Killian a quick pat on the back. He wondered if it was meant to reassure him, but he most certainly did not feel reassured. Nathaniel rose to the doorway and opened it clueing Killian that their meeting was over. "Tomorrow morning then my boy. Take the rest of the day to prepare mentally and physically any way you have to. I want you to meet with Aidan, he will instruct you on the etiquette and customs of Ignisians. And Killian...please be careful."

****

The brilliant greenish sun was setting as Killian approached the entry way he had first entered when he'd arrived at the Praetorium nearly a month earlier. He'd taken the entire afternoon to practice with the spears, even though Nathaniel had told him to rest. Blake had helped him for several hours, promising to keep his jump a secret. Killian was exhausted and his mind was foggy with the unknown. Tomorrow was the day when all his training would become real. Would jumping hurt? Would he meet a Deshuit? Would he even make it back alive? Killian had stopped Dax to ask about Ignisia after a boast session from Aidan about the grandeur of his realm. It was hard to gain information from Ignisians about their realm, since they were the proudest race of people. According to them everything was glorious, everything was perfect, it was the most beautiful, most powerful, grandest of all realms...nothing of great use.

Dax had been nearly as bad as Aidan. He'd gone on forever about the vast beauty and harsh deserts in his home realm. Finally, he'd explained how to find Egan's home. Ignisia's sun, according to Dax, looked like a roaring fire in the sky, full of wild flames, not a perfect circle. The sun always perched directly over the city center where Egan was. The flames serve as a remarkable way to assist lost travelers in the desert in finding the largest, most resourceful city in Ignisia.

Killian's mind wandered to the mission Nathaniel had given him. As far as those he'd spoken with knew, he was delivering the Blue Pebbles, and that was all. He'd kept the relic hunt to himself, even away from Blake. The pressure was beginning to overwhelm him. Nathaniel had made it seem that his winning the contest on the rock wall made him the greatest Custodis of all time—little did he know about his fluke visions. The thought of coming back empty handed caused the blood to rise to his head. Killian placed his head in his hands hoping to slow the dizzy feeling that was overpowering his mind.

"Enjoying yourself?" Another voice filled the entryway. Killian rolled his eyes.

"You should have been a Ponderi spy Connor." Connor smiled and stepped out of the shadows.

"Maybe I am." Connor did a ridiculous ninja move that knocked his glasses off his nose. Killian couldn't help but laugh. "I haven't checked in for a few days, but I wanted to make sure I spoke to you before your jump."

"In case I die?" Killian teased.

"No, smart alec. I feel like I may be close to figuring out what is going on with you. I've been researching a lot, so much in fact Shannon is going to hate you if she finds out my research is for you. She says I'm being *neglectful*," he said with sarcasm. "Anyway, there are a few characteristics that could seal the deal for me."

"Do you want to tell me anymore details about what you think it is?"

"Well, if I'm right...it's something big. I don't think I should even hint to the idea until I'm one hundred percent. But it's old, and very powerful Killian, so have you had any other odd things happen recently?"

"Well," Killian hesitated. If it was as big as Connor was thinking, he wasn't sure he wanted to know. But he did trust Connor, he knew he would do everything he could to help him. "My emotions still are getting more intense. I really think I'm feeling what other people feel."

Connor nodded and scrunched his face. "Perception? Maybe a strong ability to sense other's mannerisms?"

Killian shook his head. "No, it's more than that. I can feel anger, I can feel pain...even if I'm not angry or in pain. But on the other hand, I can feel joy so intense it makes my head spin."

Connor just nodded. "Anything else?" His eyes bore into Killian almost as if he knew there was more.

"Yes, but...Connor how big is this thing you're researching? I admit it's kind of freaking me out."

"Killian, I told you I don't want to say anything more than I have to in case I'm wrong, now what else has happened?"

"Fine," Killian huffed. "Today when I was training with Lucan...I...I saw things happen before they actually happened. I knew what moves Lucan was going to make...that's how I beat him in training today." Killian hung his head. He didn't know why he felt guilty about these visions, but everyone was so impressed with him. It was unfortunate they were impressed with a phony. He wasn't skilled, he just knew what to do beforehand.

Connor stared at the wall for several moments, every so often pushing his glasses back to the bridge of his nose.

"Has it happened more than once?" he finally asked.

"Yes," Killian answered sheepishly. "I won the rock climb because of it. It's not because I've improved, I just knew exactly where to place my feet." Killian stood up and leaned against the enormous glass window. "Connor, what am I going to do? Nathaniel is sending me to Ignisia tomorrow because he thinks I'm a talented recruit. I didn't do anything…I just…cheated. I'm probably going to die tomorrow." Killian gulped at the enormity of his words.

He heard Connor stand behind him. "You're not going to die. You have more skill than you know. If I'm right Killian, you will have the ability to get home safely tomorrow. I might need to take a blood sample when you return if that's alright."

Killian nodded, still feeling depressed. "Sure. Aidan already took some to prove I was a Custodis." He didn't feel up to admitting Aidan saw something strange in the sample.

"Perfect. I'll take that specimen and study the particulates. I'll get started right away and I should have an answer by the time you return." Connor grabbed Killian's shoulders like a big brother would do and looked him in the eyes. "Killian, don't worry. You will make it back tomorrow. I want you to focus on being calm and trusting your instincts. Ignisia is a rough place, but I know you have talent and are strong. You will make it back, alright?" Killian smirked. As much as he hated to admit it, Connor had made him feel better.

"Good," Connor slapped him on the shoulder. "Now go and get some rest. I'll meet up with you when you get back. Good luck, Kill." Connor silently disappeared back to the shadowed hallway. Killian smiled, Blake was the only one who called him Kill, but he admitted he didn't mind Connor using the nickname, it was almost like another good friend.

***

Morning came quickly. Once he'd dressed and made his way to the wall to summon the elevator, his stomach began twisting and churning in knots. Within moments, the elevator doors opened to the front entry way. Nathaniel stood in a fitted

155

navy suit, his dark hair combed back, much neater than the frazzled look he had yesterday.

"Ah, Killian," he said turning around when the elevator dinged, "very prompt, thank you." Nathaniel held Killian's spear rod in his hands and a brown knapsack that he assumed held the pebbles. Next to him was the same, tall young man that had delivered Mercedes after the imp attack. His snow white hair was pulled low, in a short ponytail and his wind burned cheeks flushed. Killian glanced over his chiseled, blemish free features and felt a pang of disappointment thinking Mercedes' savior was a beastie too. He walked over to them. Nathaniel handed over the weapon and sack. "You remember Speron, right? He will take a few moments to explain some of the Ignisian creatures to look out for."

"Hello Killian," Speron whispered, as he bent low at his waist in a typical Glacien greeting. Rising, he pulled out a holographic bulb. Speron pressed the small black button at the end of the bulb bursting a hideous image into the space above them. The creature was a terrifying black fanged frog-like creature. "First, be aware of the *átorhach* that hide under small rocks and dark caves. Their skin is poisonous and will cause seizures, but their fangs will kill you in minutes." Speron pressed the small button again, changing the hologram image. Floating flaming balls bobbed across the room; they reminded Killian of flames on a thin candle, but without a wick. "These are fire wisps. They seem harmless, but do not follow them. The wisps can cause even the most skilled outdoorsman to find themselves lost in the most unforgiving Ignisian desert. They are hypnotizing and reach into your mind, hoping to lead you to your death. In the deep deserts, you can expect to die from the elements within two days."

"Is that all?" Killian asked nervously.

"One more, but I seriously doubt you will ever see this, it's just regulation to mention it. The Draykan," Speron pushed the button again and a frightening creature flashed into the air. It had a black, curved beak and a red feathered head matching an eagle, but a scaled body with enormous clawed wings like a mythical dragon. "Ignisia only has one Draykan to our knowledge, and they use it typically against invasions from enemies. This is why I say you

156

won't ever come in contact with it. It is relentless against its prey. Its jaws can crush a large man in an instant. Recruit Thomas, please take care with the creatures of Ignisia. Most are friendly desert creatures, but these that I've explained to you will kill you." Speron bowed his head slightly as he packed up his holograph strip and packed it into a cloth case. "Good luck recruit," he said as he walked away.

"Don't worry too much my boy. Even on Terrene you have ferocious creatures that you never see. The odds of running into these deadly creatures are slim, but we need our recruits to be prepared." Nathaniel pulled out a small device from his pocket and typed on the buttons for a moment. "I just need to find the jump site," he said frustrated as he tapped the screen. "Forgive me I always forget the location, I have to refer to the guide from time to time. Ah, it is right out here. Follow me, please." Killian and Nathaniel went through the front doors, into the crisp morning.

"Now my boy, simply stand over there on the stone circle, yes just to the left of me." Killian saw a small stone circle overgrown with plants and grass. "Now, put on this wrist band." Nathaniel handed him a gray wrist band that had three symbols encircling the band. The top was shaped like a messy "Y", the second a straight, vertical line, and the third and upside down "U" with horizontal line through the center. "The top symbol is Glaciem, the middle for Ignisia, and the bottom for Cimmerian. You need to really focus and be clear in your thinking if you want a smooth jump. Crossing the barriers is an unusual feeling and you need to keep in mind it's unclear where you will land once you arrive. The engineers have tried meticulously to arrange the jump track as close to the main cities in realms as possible, but it isn't always perfect. Are you ready?"

"I...I think so," Killian answered adjusting the spear on his back that Nathaniel had given him. He had attached the sack of pebbles to his belt and it swung surprisingly light at his side.

"You'll do fine, Egan is expecting you. Good luck my boy."

Killian walked onto the stone circle, he was nervous but tried to relax his body. As his mind went blank and his muscles relaxed he felt the stone beneath him heat up, the warmth rushing up his legs and making its way to his head. He peeked at the stone, it was radiating with white light. His whole body was warm and relaxed when he felt his body being pulled, but it was as if he was stuck on the ground resisting the force. He knew it was time. Opening his eyes, he looked directly at Nathaniel, who stood in front of him shielding his eyes from the bright stone. Firmly he firmly pressed against the middle symbol. The band mimicked the heat from the stone and instantly the pulling sensation ripped him away from the Praetorium.

Killian was twisted and turned in all directions. He was swirling through a fast tunnel that made him feel he was in the center of a tornado. He could hardly breathe as he shot forward into oblivion with no end. He had no control over his limbs as his hand twisted and slammed into his eye. His heart pounded as he gulped in small breaths of air against the incredible speed he was traveling at. How was he supposed to land going this fast? He knew he would be crushed against the ground annihilating every bone in his body. Down the swirling vortex a hot wind hit his face; the wind was mixed with sand that whipped against his skin like needles. An unseen rope tugged against his feet, slowing him down. He burst through a thick gel-like barrier and splashed into a warm, shallow pool.

He surfaced sputtering and coughing the swallows of water he had inhaled upon impact. He squinted against the brightness and was overwhelmed by the warm air and the aromatic smells of desert flowers. The pool he had landed in was surrounded by majestic, crimson rocks, some like sandstone, others translucent ruby-like stones. Clear, bright, turquoise water rippled at his feet filled with small red fish continually mistaking his boots for food. Adobe style buildings cast a desert skyline in the distance along a red hillside; that was where he needed to go—the large, wild fire blazing above the town gave away the realm's city center. He smiled, thrilled with the experience of traveling through the endless tunnel and through the barrier. He had successfully jumped. He had arrived in Ignisia.

Chapter 10
Ignisia

Killian stepped out of the warm pool and climbed up one of the ruby rocks. The rock flowed with a warmth that traveled through his palm and up his arm. He stayed low on the vibrant stone, defensively checking his surroundings in case threats were nearby. A vast, open desert lined the path that would lead him to the city. Meager cover and protection surrounded causing beads of sweat to drip into his eyes. Lacking shelter was both good and bad; fewer places for him to seek cover, but also fewer places for unwanted creatures or Deshuits to hide. Behind his head, he heard a soft whisper in an incoherent language. Turning he saw a small, floating flame. He was instantly intrigued and wanted to touch it. As he reached out for the bobbing flame, it grew brighter and more hypnotic.

Something in the back of his mind warned him to leave the sweet flame alone, but why? It was harmless and fascinating. The flame moved away from the warm pond and continued whispering to him, urging him to follow. Killian's heart beat against his chest, he shouldn't follow this fire. Suddenly he remembered a name, a warning about something...a fire wisp. Killian backed away slowly and with effort. An energy from the strange wisp pulled him forward toward the empty desert, but inside he felt something stronger fight back.

"Leave me alone!" he shouted at the small floating flame. Instantly the wisp burst into a firework of sparks and disappeared.

He pulled the spear from his strap and held it tight in his hand, after meeting the wisp so soon after jumping, he wanted to be ready for anything. Before jumping off the rock, he relaxed his body just as Connor had instructed. Now was the time to be focused more than ever – his life just might depend on it. Killian scanned the surrounding boulders. Behind the stones was a small colony of tiny, double-headed, blue and white lizards. Speron had never mentioned lizards so he believed the creatures were not a threat. Killian slid from the large ruby stone and began his trek across the desert.

The sand was silky in texture but hot. Killian could feel the heat through his thin boots so he had to move quickly to avoid the discomfort of burning feet. He retained a mental image of the small, inviting Oasis he'd landed in while continuing to move forward. The wind blew the red sand around him as he pulled the hood on the back of his shirt over his head to protect his skin against the pin-pricks of whipping sand.

Up ahead, he could see several red stones jutting up through the sand that leaned against one another, forming a small cave. He felt uneasy about stopping at such a shielded area where danger could be hiding, but the small grains of sand were relentless against his raw skin. Jogging toward the cave he tried his best to peer into the black abyss. However the dim cave hid everything from his vision.

Upon arriving at the heated stones, the wind was blowing so vigorously that Killian gratefully threw himself into the unknown cavern. He leaned against the wall and brushed off the layer of sand plastered to his skin. After he had composed himself, he pulled out a small glow stick made of glass and the rod from his back. Pushing a small button the stick glowed a peaceful white light and he took in his surroundings. The white light lit the small shelter, casting eerie shadows on the bumpy stones. With the new light that had entered the cave, Killian strained his eyes attempting to make sure the cave was clear of a threat. A short way down the cavity, he could see an opening. The rocks had formed a tunnel and opened out the other side, close to the desert city. Gripping his spear tight in his palm, he quickly paced himself into a jog through the cave.

Killian kept his eyes focused ahead of him while trying to sense danger all around him. The white light glimmered against the sporadic translucent ruby stones, uncovering much of the hidden crevices in the rocky tunnel. Killian skidded to a stop at a hidden trench that spanned across the desert floor. He cursed under his breath, realizing the crack was too wide to jump over. Frustrated at the stall in his journey, he sheathed the spear in his leather strap. He tied the light stick onto a small leather string hanging from his shoulder so the light would continue to shine and quickly tested all the climbing training he'd done over the last few weeks.

The climb was relatively easy; he only slipped once, but quickly caught himself. Crouching low, and holding tightly onto the crag in the rock, he knew the ruby, sandstone would not hold his weight for long; the fine grains were slipping and sliding underneath him. Before he lost his grip on the rock, Killian grappled for his spear. In haste, he stabbed the soft red, rock before pressing the button launching the lower half of the spear against the stone. The force propelled him off the unreliable stone and safely on the other side of the deep cut in the cave. He took a deep breath and calmed himself enough to bring his thoughts into focus as the adrenaline seeped out of his body.

The uneventful tunnel would soon be behind him. Closing the spear back to the compact rod, he sheathed it again safe on his back and jogged the soft sand path toward the opening. As the sunlight caressed his face, Killian was struck with a shooting pain spanning his entire head. Vertigo overwhelmed him as his legs gave out, tumbling him to the sand.

Warm blood flowed into his eyes. Killian tried standing but fell back to the ground. He grappled for his spear knowing he was under attack by an unseen opponent. When his hand grasped the end of his spear trying to pull it off his strap, the side of his face seared in pain from a booted kick. He floated back and forth from consciousness to nothing. Killian rolled away, his eyes full of his own blood from the blow on his head.

He heard a malicious laugh fill the tunnel. Finally, pulling through the hot pain in his skull, he wiped the blood from his eyes and stood waiting for the attacker to come again. In an instant he held the rod of his spear in his hand, his fingers wavering over the button ready to release the sharp points. Nothingness surrounded him; his light stick revealed nothing ahead or behind him. Taking the pause in attack to focus and prepare, Killian frantically searched for the culprit. Laughing filled the tunnel again, he saw a swift, dark movement fill his peripheral vision, but he was too slow to react before he felt a rod slam between his shoulder blades.

He fell to the ground, twisting onto his back, trying to see who was behind the attacks. Nothing. The attacker had once again fallen back into their perfect hiding spot in the shadows.

"You coward! You can't face me! You attack me from behind then run away!" Killian shouted, his annoyance and frustration overpowering him. Scrambling to his feet, he ran toward the opening. Lunging for the bright, open sphere to escape the dark tunnel, two cloaked figures stepped from the shadows and blocked his way. Giving one quick glance over his shoulder he could see a small swarm of black, cloaked people coming into view behind him, trapping him inside the tunnel. Freedom would come only by overpowering the two figures in front. Putting his head down, he sprinted forward with all he had. The two in front unmasked gleaming, gold blades that looked like long shards of glass from beneath their cloaks. They defensively held the weapons prepared to fatally pierce Killian before they allowed him to leave the tunnel.

Killian thought quickly, trying to focus his mind on what he needed to do next. As he charged the two figures, he saw himself split and an identical version of himself ran in front. Another vision of one of the cloaked figures charged his vision self. He saw himself use the spear once more to push off the ground and land on his feet on a large jutting boulder forming the wall. His doppelganger pushed hard with his feet on the stone

162

before landing on the outside of the tunnel, behind the confused, shocked images of the vicious people. They stared in amazement as Killian succeeded in his impressive leap through the tunnel. Just as soon as it had appeared the vision faded and Killian was brought back to the present situation of barreling toward two armed, faceless people.

He smiled, thankful his mental trick was at it again in his time of need. Putting his faith in the mental strategy, Killian ran with all his might. A moment before the blade, of the now pursuing cloaked figure cleaved his neck, he pushed the button on his spear. The strong steel threw him into the air high enough to launch over the jagged blade. His feet briefly hit the stone before he pushed, using all his energy, against the rock wall. His momentum launched him over the heads of the daunting attackers, causing them to fall on the ground, and he landed awkwardly at the mouth of the tunnel. He gave one glance over his shoulder. The first attacker had picked themselves off the hot sand, but now the swarm from within the tunnel had joined their two brothers who had blocked the entrance. Killian quickly turned out of sight from the tunnel and climbed on top of the rocks that formed the shelter. Now his combat training was going to prove itself. He knew there was no way to make it to the city with these pursuers on his tail so he needed to eliminate as much of the threat as he could.

On top of the jagged tunnel, he held his spear in one hand, waiting for his target to exit. The first cloaked figure ran out into the warm sun of the red desert. He stood below Killian looking back and forth, trying to find his missing mark. Killian took a deep breath before leaping from his perch and landed directly in front of the cloaked man. The man drew his jagged, gold blade and angrily slashed the air, narrowly missing Killian's torso. Killian dodged and thrust the closed steel rod toward the man's chest. Clenching his jaw, he shut his eyes and pushed the top part of the button, releasing the upper point on his spear. He gulped as he felt the point hit something solid, but he couldn't open his eyes. Gurgles and gasps forced him to look at what damage he'd caused with his weapon. Killian felt sick and swallowed bile back down his throat as he saw the point of his spear nestled deep in the throat of the cloaked man. The man's hood had fallen back and blood flowed freely from the open wound. The man's face was painted a dirty gray and his pale blue eyes looked at Killian as he slowly lowered to his knees, frantically grappling at his throat until no more sounds came out. Killian's hands were shaking as he pressed the button returning his bloodied spear back into the shaft. The man landed face first onto the sand, immediately staining the bright, fiery red to a deep burgundy.

Disbelief overwhelmed him as he realized he'd just killed another human being. But the swish of a deadly blade brought him back to the present situation. Killian again used the spear to launch himself into the air, landing on a second man's shoulders who had failed in his attempt to cut Killian. They both fell hard, spraying grains of sand into the air. Unraveling himself from the cloaked man he flung into direct combat with his pursuer.

Killian ran toward the person and thrust his pointed spear deep in his upper thigh. A high, shrill scream pierced the air. The hood fell from a young but rigidly toned woman.

"What? You're a girl," he dumbly remarked. Her teeth glimmered in a wicked sneer. The white twisted braid on her head stood out against the ash colored paint on her face. From what he'd learned in realm school, dark paint tagged her as a Deshuit in an instant. Pulling his spear from her leg, and despite her injury, she yanked her long gold blade from her hip and lunged for him. Reacting, Killian clipped the side of her head with one end of his spear. The blow was harder than expected, she instantly fell to the ground unconscious at his feet.

In his mind, he sensed the others surrounding him. He knew they would attack in a group. Killian lunged to the side trying to avoid their pursuit, but he tripped on another attacking Deshuit. He landed hard but quickly coiled around in the sand, trying to get away from the approaching killers.

Before he found his footing, a Deshuit pounced onto his back, dragging him back into the soft sand. The Deshuit wrapped his legs around Killian's midsection, pinning him to the ground. He unmasked his face, revealing crude, black paint and began grappling for Killian's spear.

Killian held on to his weapon with every ounce of energy he had. The Deshuit had successfully removed one of his hands from his spear. Killian swung his empty fist and hit the man square in the head. The man groaned and toppled to the ground and Killian scrambled to his feet and grabbed the spear, pointing it at the man in the sand.

The Deshuit's short brown hair was covered in red dust. He swung his face toward Killian, an immense sensation overcame him. Loathing and disdain. The uncomfortable sensation released from the Deshuit seeped into Killian's heart, threatening to overtake any sense of control he'd won. The man was older than the woman, but still had a handsome young face. After focusing on the markings of the dark paint, Killian recognized symbols representing each realm.

Killian held the spear over his chest, surprised by how anxious he was to thrust it deep in the man's heart to ease the discomfort of the Deshuit's hate. The thought scared him. His hands trembled against the cold metal, it was the only thing standing between him and sure death from this vicious enemy. Without taking his eyes off the fallen man, he felt the other Deshuits halt their pursuit. They now stood in a circle watching the stalled confrontation between the two men unfold. Killian assumed the man on the ground must be important to them and they didn't want to risk his death by attacking, or he probably would be dead by now.

The man's eyes widened as he studied Killian's face, his hate fading from his countenance as well as fading from Killian's mind and heart. Killian wondered, as the feeling left him, if other people were perceptive enough to tune into emotions around them or was something wrong with him? The Deshuit curled his lips up into a smug smile.

"You shouldn't have come here this day, your life may have ended," the man on the ground growled at Killian.

"I'm not here for trouble. I have a very important task I am trying to do, something that will even protect *your* lives." He spat

165

back, continuing to hold the spear over him. The man just stared at Killian. He felt like he was reading his thoughts.

"You are a skilled fighter. One might say it appears you know what's going to happen before it does." The man smirked up at Killian. Killian's heart raced. Was the Deshuit insinuating he knew about his trick?

"I just want to pass in peace," Killian explained, knowing Deshuits did not allow recruits to *pass in peace*.

After a long pause, another Deshuit approached the fallen man. The figure was hooded, but one could easily tell a woman was beneath the cloak. Killian clenched the spear tighter, anticipating the duo to attack him together, but the woman simply knelt beside her Deshuit brother.

"It's him." Killian thought that had been what the hidden woman had said. He tried to brush off the thought that this vicious clan knew who he was. The thought frightened him more as he wondered if they knew him, would they attack people close to him? The man gave her a curt nod and slowly stood. Killian pointed the spear closer to his chest, but the Deshuit held up a hand. Killian took that as a sign he was not seeking to hurt him...at the moment.

"Then pass," the Deshuit whispered standing upright. The shadowed woman stayed nearby. "But I warn you to use this rare opportunity with wisdom."

The others surrounding them sheathed their blades and slowly dissipated back into the tunnel, except for the woman and man he'd pinned. Killian watched them in bewilderment. The man whom he'd pinned on the ground looked back at him before re-entering the tunnel.

"Be careful who you trust. I fear you may have enemies nearby," the man said sincerely as a sad look crossed his face. "I hope you find what you seek, Killian Thomas." With that, the man returned his black hood to its place covering his skull, and disappeared into the darkness of the tunnel. The woman with the hidden face stared at him. Killian could only make out her chin and full lips beneath her hood. He met her hidden gaze before she turned and joined her fellow Deshuits. He could have sworn she smiled at him—not viciously, but almost a smile of reassurance as if she were concerned for him.

Killian stared at the dark opening, stunned and feeling sick. The Deshuit knew his name. He had never heard of Deshuits allowing a Ponderi recruit to wander unharmed. Either the Deshuits died, or the recruit died—at least that was what Aidan had told him. Everyone in the Praetorium iterated often that Deshuits hated the Ponderi. They were bloodthirsty and wild. Yet, they had let him go. Why would he know his name and why would he let him live? His stomach lurched when he turned and saw the cloaked, Deshuit corpse on the ground. The man's face was covered by the thick hood that had fallen over his head when he fell to the sand, hiding his lifeless eyes. Killian was grateful for that blessing. He couldn't fathom seeing the face of his victim. The reality of what he had done overcame him and he emptied his stomach on the sand beneath his feet.

Killian sat, holding his head in his hands for several hours, trying to justify killing another person. Finally, as the bright reddish-green flames faded, he stood. The sky would soon be dark, and the fire in the sky was the one sure guide to Egan. He had allowed himself to believe, if he had not killed the man, he would be dead. It was an unfortunate, necessary evil. A shiver raced through his body as if shaking away the deeds that had transpired in the tunnel. Taking a deep breath, he made his way toward the adobe city.

The entrance to the city was marked by a large sandstone archway. The houses and buildings were beautifully crafted from the same red rock and ruby stones he'd seen surrounding the pool of water. They all had markings of desert flowers and odd looking lizards and birds. The streets were full of Ignisians laughing, buying, eating; everything that people in his world did as well. The bright, colorful hair and clothing distracted him for several moments. It appeared that Ignisians prided themselves on their eccentric attire. The more radiant, the more piercings, the more colors, the better. He thought Fia had dressed over the top; throughout the town square he observed a man with a mostly

167

shaved head, only allowing a few blue, orange, red and white spikes of hair.

One woman had ruby red jewels pierced into her skin along her brow, cheek bones, and jaw line. Killian winced as he looked upon her face. It must have been an incredibly painful procedure.

Killian glanced down at his uncovered hands. His skin looked pale as snow compared to the brown skin of Ignisia. Their bare arms and necks shimmered in the bright sun with flecks of gold. Aidan had boasted once that Ignisian's skin was ingrained with tiny, shimmering reflectors to limit their absorption of the harsh sky flames. Aidan had puffed up with pride explaining while others from different realms *may visit* Ignisia, their skin would eventually shrivel and warp if they stayed permanently. Ignisia was the only realm that could not house permanent immigrants from other realms, much to their pride.

Killian walked into a large building in the center of the street. From what he had learned through Aidan's realm instruction, this would be where Egan, the chief, resided. The building reflected the warm sunlight on the outside, becoming a glistening, desert jewel in the town square. On the inside, the sun was absorbed through their walls, making the temperature rise in the building so the risk of a cold evening was eliminated. Killian knew Ignisians hated any hint of cold and did all they could to avoid it.

The building was not as grand as the Praetorium. However, it had its own sense of beauty. Large ruby lanterns hung along the long hallway with beautiful blue, white and purple flames. It cast a stunning glow across the floor. The plants were spiky barbed cacti with fragrant pink flowers. Their scent was so inviting, he exerted all his energy to continue his trek down the hall.

Killian stopped at the end of the hallway and knocked on the large black door in front of him. Moments later a woman with red and blue tipped hair and earrings in her lips and nose opened the door.

"Yes? What do you need recruit?" she asked, while stiffly crossed her fist over her chest. The woman obviously was not interested in greeting him with the typical feminine kiss.

"I'm here to speak with Egan," Killian answered simply. He tried to focus on the woman and what she was feeling. He absorbed a fleeting piece of her annoyance of him being at the door before opening it wide and ushering him in.

"I must ask the reason for your visit with Egan so late in the day," she said briskly.

"I found myself quite...delayed or I would have arrived earlier. I am here simply to report time sensitive information from the Praetorium. I'm afraid that is all I can say." The woman nodded and pressed a small button on the wall next to her. An even larger black door swung open and a man with a bright yellow beard and spiky white hair walked out.

"What is it, Eva?"

"A recruit here with information from the Praetorium sir," she answered respectfully. Egan turned and eyed Killian up and down. Killian immediately sensed *his* annoyance as well, but also intrigue to his purpose.

Egan's bronze skin was taut and stretched over the rippling, toned muscles throughout his body. His ears were pierced with bright red jewels as well as his eyebrows. A flaming tattoo covered his entire bare chest and the same glowing flame necklace as Aidan lay over his heart. Egan had surprising eyes, different from any other Ingnisians Killian had met. Instead of the deep brown eyes he had blue eyes with sputtering white flames behind them. He also noted his skin was not as tan as his countrymen.

"Yes, I received a notice you'd be arriving. Though I expected you earlier." Egan said roughly. His large fist pounded his bulging chest as he sternly greeted him.

"I need to speak with you about some information from the Praetorium," Killian repeated again, ignoring Egan's annoyed tone. Egan just stared at him. Killian could feel the reluctance the leader emitted. "With all due respect sir, I have not had the easiest time getting here. I would very much like to speak with you without resistance." Killian was surprised at his own bluntness, but the stress of his encounter with the Deshuits was still lingering. Ever since he'd arrived, he'd been met with contention. Even people wandering the streets turned up their pierced noses as he walked by; no kisses, no fist greeting.

Egan glared at him. A wave of frustration at a younger inferior speaking to him in that manner overcame Killian. The sensitivity to other's emotions could be helpful at times and he knew he needed to ease up or Egan would dismiss him.

"Come in recruit, but make it quick. Eva, please bring in some palm juice for us." Egan turned into his office and Killian followed.

Once inside Killian immediately cooled down. The office was strangely not as warm as the other parts of the building. Egan certainly was a different Ignisian. He motioned for Killian to sit on a chair made out of a black rock resembling hardened lava, but was surprised to find the seat rather comfortable.

"Sir," Killian began. "Forgive me for coming so late, but I am simply here trying to deliver the pebbles." Killian unlatched the knapsack from his belt and placed it on Egan's magnificent desk. Egan gave him a stiff smile.

"The people of Ignisia will thank you for these. Our water has been getting a little gritty." Egan chuckled.

"I wanted to check on your people's circumstances. Is there anything they need?" Killian stammered. He had said the words so weak, and Egan's glare made him shrink in his rock chair.

"You want to know how the Ignisian people are faring? Recruit, I thank you for the pebbles, but they should have come weeks ago. The Ponderi seems more concerned about other things as of late and my people are suffering because of their inattention." Egan's face was turning a deep shade of red. "What is bringing about concern now? And to make it worse they send *a boy* to check on us." Egan was fuming, Killian didn't need to sense his emotion to know what he felt. He didn't know what to say.

170

"I'm sorry."

Egan seemed taken aback by this reply. "You're sorry? I just insulted the Ponderi, and you say...I'm sorry?" Egan gawked at him. "What's your name recruit?"

"Killian Thomas." Egan's eyes widened. He nodded his head but remained silent. "I have to be honest, Egan, I'm not here just to deliver the blue pebbles. I need to speak with you about the relics and the recent attacks in your caves."

"I must admit recruit Thomas, I'm rather surprised you've been given such sensitive information. Why is the Ponderi asking such questions?"

"Well…Nathaniel believes…the Ponderi believes possible Trinity members are the ones behind the attacks." Killian paused trying to focus on Egan's emotions. He wanted to tread carefully. He still had difficulty trusting others he didn't know, and just because Egan was a chief didn't exclude him as a Trinity suspect. Killian felt a small wave of surprise and anxiety pass over him. He knew it was Egan's. To him this made clear the Chief was unaware of who was attacking his people. "Sir, the Trinity is suspected of stealing the Cimmerian relic. They may be trying to get the Ignisian relic. They wish to destroy Terrene, sir. Please, we need your help in telling us who the Ignisian guardians are so we can remove the relic from Ignisia and return it to the Praetorium for the time being." Killian finished quickly, hoping to convey the urgency of the situation.

Egan stood from his large desk and looked out his rustic window at the dying sky flames. "Recruit Thomas, I believe what you say is true." He turned back and looked at Killian. "I can sense you are valiant and seek the relics honorably. I'm afraid telling you who the guardian is may prove difficult." Inwardly Killian's heart sunk. He'd hoped Egan would simply tell him. He should have known this mission would be more difficult than anticipated.

"It's not because I don't want to. If it's true and the Trinity is murdering my people, I assure you I will do everything in my power to stop them." Egan looked down at the ground just as a knock came to the door. Eva brought in a tray with a pitcher and glasses brimming with a mud-colored liquid.

"Ah, thank you Eva, just what I needed." She smiled back at Egan, set the tray down and left the room. Egan took a big gulp of the drink and made a satisfied noise. "Try it, it doesn't look appetizing, but it is delicious." Taking a long drink, Egan's disturbed demeanor returned. "You see recruit, I've been sworn under a powerful oath to never reveal my relationship with the particular guardian. The guardian doesn't even know who they really are. You can imagine how upsetting it would be for them if they learned their charge."

"Yes, I can imagine," Killian said stoically remembering the relic he never knew about. "The relics also are at a greater risk of getting lost when the individual isn't aware of the importance of the object. Egan please, I understand you are an honorable man and wish to keep your word, but don't you see...an entire realm will be destroyed— billions of innocent people." Killian felt himself getting emotional as he thought of Earth and the people who lived each day unaware of the threat against them.

Egan didn't speak for a moment. Wiping his forehead, he leaned on his forearms and looked at Killian. "I'm afraid to put the guardian in danger, they...mean a great deal to me." Egan seemed nervous. Killian could see beads of steaming sweat dripping down his brow. "The...guardian...is my..." Egan stammered, but didn't finish. His eyes suddenly rolled back into his head and his body began seizing.

"Egan, what is it? Egan, what's wrong?" Killian panicked when white, foaming saliva slowly, frothed over Egan's lips. "Help! Eva, HELP!" He yelled rushing over to Egan. He was choking and gasping. Eva burst through the door and gasped as she looked at the state of her Chief.

She pressed another button on the wall behind Egan's desk and within seconds a hoard of men rushed in and pushed Killian aside. The men grabbed convulsing Egan and together carried him away. Killian hoped they would give him medical attention. Eva stood next to him sobbing and shaken. Killian stepped toward her, hoping to comfort her when she turned on him, flaming eyes full of rage!

"WHAT DID YOU DO TO HIM?" She screamed. "YOU TRIED TO KILL HIM!"

"No, Eva, *no*. We were just talking and something happened." Killian was panicking. He was going to be blamed for this...what if Egan died? He was going to cause an all-out realm war!

"It's you isn't it? You are the one behind the deaths! GUARDS!" She screamed at the door. Killian could hear rushing feet down the hall. He wasn't going to get the chance to explain himself, so instantly he ran out the large doorway just as the outer office was filling with several bright uniformed guards.

Killian dropped his shoulder and plowed into the stomach of one of the guards. Both men fell to the ground, but quickly Killian jumped up and ran down the lantern lit hallway. At the front entrance of the building another man stood in his way preventing him from escaping. Killian pulled his spear off his strap, holding it in both hands, rushed the guard with all his might. The guard tried to dodge the steel pole coming toward him, but Killian successfully plowed him to the ground and continued down the bustling street.

A loud siren sounded from the building behind him and the people in the street plummeted to the ground. He gawked at the odd behavior for a moment wondering what they were doing. It became clear in seconds how easily he was now spotted by the guards with all the townspeople flung on the street taking cover.

Killian turned and sprinted toward the open desert. His stomach lurched when he heard heavy wings behind him. Above him in the sky was a large, scaled bird. It appeared to be half eagle and half dragon; it was unlike anything he'd ever seen.

The Draykan!

The bird had an enormous chain around its neck with blood red feathers tacked to metallic scales. Its black beak opened as it

173

let out a terrifying screech and the flaming eyes spotted Killian quickly.

The creature dove from the sky, talons open and Killian lunged for his life into the nearest shop. The blood curdling screech of the bird's frustration for missing his prey made his ears ring. Killian gasped for breath. He needed to get back out into the street before he could jump out of Ignisia!

Taking a deep breath he sprinted out into the street but he didn't know where to go. Was he supposed to jump from another jumping stone? No one had told him, he'd just expected Egan to help him get back to the Praetorium. He could hear the flapping again of ferocious wings. Taking a risk, he tried to focus all his energy on the Praetorium and safety. Luckily the warmth spread throughout his body along with the welcome pulling sensation. The breeze from the nearing wings blew against his face. The warmth wasn't spreading fast enough.

In a desperate attempt, Killian flattened himself against the sandy earth, narrowly avoiding the deadly talons. The creak of the metal scales sent shivers down his spine. The bird was recoiling his pursuit once again.

Killian abandoned the open street and dove into the same shop. His ears were filled with cries of the flattened people on the street and agonizing screams from the monstrous bird. If he didn't jump from the building, he wouldn't jump at all. He would be framed for attempted murder—or worse, killed by the demon bird.

"Get out of here," a woman's voice suddenly hissed above the shrieks from the Draykan. He turned his head and was shocked to see the dark painted face of a petite Deshuit woman crouched by one of the wooden tables.

"I…I can't! I can't get to my jumping location." The monster pawed and gnashed at the window to the shop. Killian heard shattering glass and he knew the beast would be in within minutes.

"Killian," she shouted. "You can; you have it inside of you, I can only buy you a few seconds now LEAVE!" The Deshuit woman dashed out the door of the shop. He could hear her holler at the beast, and for a moment the pounding feet plundered toward her shouts.

Pushing a stone stool away from him, he stood firm on the glistening, volcanic rock that made up the floor. He thought of the Praetorium, hoping it would be enough. Bringing the soft, silk sheets on his bed into focus, the open entry way of the Praetorium and the shining emerald eyes of Mercedes, the warm sensation filled his feet again, though the band on his wrist did not follow as before.

The dining area of the restaurant he'd taken shelter in began to swirl. A magnificent, powerful wind tumbled dishes and goblets on the tables. Killian's shoulders and neck burned as his blood heated from the power. The space in front of his eyes rippled and shimmered, in the street the red sand was swirling and frothing around the building in response to the blustery wind, concealing his location in the shop. Unseen matter was suspended in front of him. What was happening? The boiling power within, urged him toward the swirling mass and somehow he knew the tunnel suspended before him would take him home. But where had it come from? A ferocious scream filled his ears as the gruesome head of the black beaked eagle was plowing through the glass windows again. The monster was trying to reach Killian, and would succeed in seconds. He knew it was time and swiftly stepped toward the tunnel that had seemingly appeared from his own thoughts.

The matter frothed and swirled upon his decision. Killian made eye contact with the blood shot eyes of the metallic bird and yelled, "GO!" as loud as he could. In a violent fury, he was pulled out of the diner and into the whirling tornado, leaving the freakish deadly bird behind.

Chapter 11
Accused

The thick, suffocating tunnel pressed against Killian's lungs until he was sure he would never breathe again. Suddenly a white flash of hot wind brushed against his face and he landed hard on a soft, silky carpet that was welcome after the strenuous journey from Ignisia. His heart pounded furiously, and his muscles pulsed with adrenaline. Somehow he knew he was no longer in danger, but he still jumped when a deep voice sounded behind him.

"Killian?" Nathaniel peered over his magnificent desk. "What are you doing here?"

Killian gasped short, jagged breaths, taking comfort in seeing the Ponderi leader. But soon the frightening shrieks of the Draykan, the hidden Deshuit woman, and the unbelievable portal that had appeared from thin air, crushed down on his shoulders pushing away any comfort.

"Connor," he gasped, "I need...to speak...with Connor."

Nathaniel squinted his eyes until his attention was diverted to a soft beeping coming from a screen that had appeared atop the polished marble surface of his desk. Nathaniel's eyes widened as he read the message and quickly brought his gaze back to Killian.

Killian knew what the message had said by the shadow crossing Nathaniel's dark eyes.

"Killian, what happened?" The older man moved from behind the desk and grabbed tight to both his shoulders. "Did you do something to Egan?"

Killian shook his head, continually gasping trying to find his breath as his body began shaking from shock. "I need to speak with Connor," he repeated. He couldn't move passed the thought of telling Connor about the Draykan, what the woman had told him, and how he believed he created a portal from nothing.

Nathaniel stood, releasing his breath in exasperation. "Killian, this isn't good." Though he seemed frustrated Killian heard him page for Miller and Connor to come as soon as possible to his office.

Killian knelt on the ground of the grand room, shaking as his body temperature dropped. Somewhere he heard Nathaniel shuffling about the room, but he couldn't raise his head to see what he was doing.

"Killian, here drink this." Nathaniel's voice was foggy, but he could see the man bend down next to him. "Come on, my boy. It will help."

Finally, Killian saw a steaming mug of liquid. It smelled strongly of peppermint and chamomile. Killian grabbed the mug gratefully and held its warmth close to him. Nathaniel wrapped his arms around his trembling shoulders and slowly lifted him from the ground, leading him to one of the soft, white sofas.

Nathaniel paced near the magnificent window for what seemed like hours before Miller and Connor frantically burst into the room. Slowly, Killian craned his neck and met the gray eyes of Miller. The old man stared on in disbelief switching his gaze between Nathaniel and Killian. Connor nervously pushed his thick glasses up his nose, clutching a folder full of papers close to his chest.

"Nathaniel, what's going on? Fia is frantic," Miller said in a hushed voice. "She said Killian *killed* her uncle." Somewhere in the back of his mind it registered that Egan was Fia's uncle.

"I didn't hurt him!" Killian said desperately. Painful memories of being falsely accused filled his heart. He felt dizzy and buried his head in his hands.

"Connor," Nathaniel said, ignoring his Regent and Killian, "why is Killian so insistent on speaking with you?" Nathaniel's voice wasn't angry, but incredibly firm and direct. Killian lifted his head and watched as Connor shifted uncomfortably under his gaze.

"Sir, after Mr. Thomas initially arrived and admitted to some…abnormalities, I took the liberty to research if there was anything more powerful in his relic that may have passed on to him." Connor, Killian was sure, had tried to answer with confidence but the words came out shaky and soft.

Nathaniel and Miller both stared for several tense moments at their engineer. Killian's heart wrenched. He didn't want Connor to get in trouble because of him; the man had only tried to help him and was one person he truly trusted.

"Well," Nathaniel finally asked, opening his hands, "did you find anything?"

Connor shifted again, glancing briefly down at his folder of papers. He didn't speak; he only nodded slowly.

"Connor, please," Nathaniel said briskly, "enlighten us."

Miller ruffled at Nathaniel's tense tone, but locked his eyes again with Killian. He couldn't get a read on the old man. Was he angry, or distressed? Before any overwhelming feelings filled his mind he heard Connor clear his throat.

"With all due respect, sir… I am certain my findings fall under Hemisphere Council, according to protocol."

Killian didn't understand what Connor meant by *Hemisphere Council*, but Miller gasped behind him and Nathaniel's lips parted slightly as his jaw dropped.

"You're sure, Connor?" Miller asked.

"Yes, sir. The findings will need to be brought to the attention of all the leaders. Especially after the accusations against Mr. Thomas presently."

Miller's face dropped and his lips pursed. Nathaniel moved swiftly behind his desk and began typing on a keyboard that had appeared at his touch of the surface.

"I didn't *do anything*! Why don't you believe me?" Killian was slightly embarrassed at the sound of his desperation. He watched as Miller squared his shoulders and turned to Nathaniel.

"Nathaniel, I'm going to excuse myself for the time being." His voice was dry and absent of emotion. "Please inform me when the leaders arrive."

"Of course." Nathaniel waved Miller off without looking up. Killian bristled as he watched Miller walk by him without acknowledging him. His stomach pulsed in anger. Miller certainly believed he was guilty. It was happening again, he would be sent away for something he didn't do.

"What leaders are you talking about?" Killian asked bitterly, interrupting Nathaniel's furious typing.

The older man glanced up and paused for a moment. "Killian the realm leaders are part of the Hemisphere Council. We have not met in nearly a century. If Connor says something strange was in your relic that requires the Council, we must take this serious." Nathaniel straightened and looked at Killian with fierceness. "I must also follow protocol with these accusations.

179

Killian until the council arrives I will have to confine you to your room so we can learn what happened in Ignisia."

Killian stood in anger, but he couldn't bring himself to speak.

"I'll have Connor take you down," Nathaniel said, nodding at Connor who appeared more relaxed. Killian shuffled toward the doorway. Before leaving the room he turned back to Nathaniel.

"I didn't do anything to Egan."

Nathaniel sighed and sympathy filled his eyes. "I believe you, my boy. But try to understand we must follow protocol and find out what happened. We aren't sure if Egan is alive or dead. Please have patience. If you have nothing to hide, then you have nothing to fear."

When the swift elevator doors opened to his floor he was met with several hushed groups of members speaking amongst themselves. When they saw Killian all voices stopped. Killian's face flushed with embarrassment. How could rumors have spread so quickly?

"Killian!" Dax's deep voice boomed along the hallway. His friend's face looked torn between anger, and sadness. "Is it true? Did you kill my chief?"

"Easy Dax," Blake appeared next to him. He winked at Killian, but he too looked curious. "Just relax until we know more okay."

"I want to hear it from him," Dax huffed, never breaking eye contact with Killian. "Lucan informed the recruits Egan was attacked and killed by you, Killian. Is it true?"

Killian's anger spilled over and he couldn't stay silent. "If you want to believe Lucan, go right ahead Dax. Maybe you don't know me as well as you thought you did." Turning toward his door he met a pair of tear-glistened emerald eyes.

180

"Mercedes," he breathed out. He hadn't seen her, but she'd seen his outburst and the strain of what he'd said was written all over her face. "Mercedes…I didn't…" he couldn't finish and he refused to see an accusatory look on her face if she believed him capable of such things. He had killed a person earlier, the thought still made him sick. The anguish of his friends thinking he could possibly kill voluntarily was too much to bear.

Placing his hand on his door he quickly stepped inside, Connor following close behind closing the door on all the prying faces.

"Killian," Connor whispered, "are you going to be okay?"

Killian leaned against his bed frame holding tight to one of the posts and shook his head.

"Connor, I didn't hurt Egan. How can everyone think that?"

"I'm sure they don't think you did anything—"

"You heard Dax! My own friends think I'm guilty!" Killian plopped onto his face in the soft billowing comforter over his mattress.

Connor cleared his throat awkwardly. "Killian we'll get everything straightened out when the council arrives."

"I have to go on trial again for something I didn't do." He rolled onto his back and covered his eyes with his hands. "Why didn't you tell me your research was so big?"

"I did Killian, I just didn't know it was…this big. Until today I just wanted to wait to tell you my theories until I knew for sure, but today I found a report of someone having *identical* abilities to you."

"I opened a portal, Connor. Does that change anything? That's how I made it back. Unless the jump site can move."

181

Connor shook his head. "The jump sites are a specific place Custodis are required to jump from. It is connected to your bracelet. There is no way the site would move to where you were."

"Well, does that change anything about your theory?"

Connor shook his head. "I wish it did Killian, but you being able to bring yourself home—it only solidifies it more in my mind."

"Just tell me what it is!"

"I can't, I'm bound by protocol. You will learn everything with the council. Until then, I'm sorry you'll have to stay in your room. There will be a guardian placed in the hallway for your protection."

Killian sighed in defeat. He was sure the guardian was there so *he* wouldn't leave his room. Connor turned to leave, but Killian remembered one final question.

"Wait, who is on the council? I don't understand when they say leaders."

Connor gave him a small smile. "Killian, be ready to meet the Empress of Glaciem and Queen of Cimmerian."

Chapter 12
Infinium

Lavender sunlight warmed Killian's face and the comforting sensation dulled the bitterness burdening his heart. For two days he'd rested on his massive bed staring blankly at his ceiling; two days of wondering what was happening beyond his cherry wood door and if his royal judges had arrived. Drifting his gaze toward the shimmering window, his attention was brought to his rumbling stomach. Meals were prompt and the radiant sunlight signaled breakfast would be arriving any moment.

As if reading his mind a loud knock sounded at his door. Standing in the empty hallway a plump chef held a steaming tray of endless breakfast foods—more than he could ever eat in one sitting. The pink-cheeked man smiled kindly, and bowed his head before passing the tray to Killian. Without a word, the man turned and left. If circumstances were different Killian would have laughed about the punctuality and dependability of the strange, happy chef. But it grated against his nerves that the plump man had been his only interaction. He'd heard nothing. No one had checked in on him, not even Mercedes. Though his room was grand and large, he was feeling like a caged animal. He was back in prison, just with a nicer bed. Sighing in frustration Killian uncovered his steaming breakfast and was lost in endless streams of syrup and seasoned meats.

Several hours later another knock sounded. Killian sauntered to the door, passed the cold breakfast tray still full of uneaten towers of pancakes and bagels. Glancing at the purplish-green morning sun, he wondered why the chef was early.

Blake stared back at Killian after opening the door. Killian eyes widened. It hadn't been so long since they'd seen one another, but he was still taken back by his friend's face.

"Wow, you look awful." Blake scrunched his nose. Killian rolled his eyes. He knew he should've been grateful to see a friendly face, but the seed of annoyance pushed aside any friendly greeting he could've mustered. Granting Blake a small grunt, he turned back into the room and tried to close the door.

"Hold on a minute Kill. Geez when did you get so touchy?" Blake said with sarcasm, sticking his foot in the door. Killian just stared, hoping to portray how put out he was for the false accusations and his lock-up. "I'm here to take you up. The royals are here."

Killian's heart stopped. He knew the realm leaders had been summoned. Hearing the word *royal*, painted a different picture. Two, powerful women, who had never met him, were coming to be his judge and jury, and quite possibly the executioner.

"Breathe Kill," Blake laughed.

"Easy for you to say," he answered hoarsely.

"Come on," Blake tugged at his arm. "They're expecting you. The Empress is not a woman you want to keep waiting."

Killian gulped, gave himself one last look in the mirror on his wall before he stepped before his judges. His face was darkened from not shaving, but his hair was still short enough he

184

could pass it off as neat. Slowly he followed Blake toward the open elevator car.

"Blake, does everyone think I killed Egan?" he asked as they shot through the walls.

Blake shuffled a bit before answering. "There are some...firm believers of your guilt that are stirring the pot."

He didn't have to say the name, Killian knew it was Lucan. Blake turned toward him as they stepped into the long hallway of the upper floors. "Killian, don't worry. I know you didn't do anything, your name will be cleared."

"I wish I could say the same for the others," he mumbled as they approached the door.

"If you mean Dax, take it easy on him. He's really been wrestling with the last thing you said. He wants to believe you, but it's his chief Kill. Ignisians practically worship Egan. Mercedes, because I know that's who you really care about, believes you. We've just been ordered not to communicate with you. I was specifically asked by Nathaniel to come get you since we have the longest history."

Blake would never know, but hearing Mercedes believed he wasn't capable of hurting Egan lifted an invisible weight off his shoulders. Knowing at least two people were behind him gave him the energy needed to face those behind the door.

The furniture in the room had been rearranged. The comfortable, inviting white sofas were missing and only a large wooden chair sat in the middle. Against the magnificent window was a long, extraordinarily intricate wooden table with four people seated behind. Next to Miller and Nathaniel he met the frosty eyes of a white-haired woman cloaked from her shoulders to the floor in billowing white robes. Draped over one shoulder was light blue and gold sash tied in an impossible knot around her waist. Her icy expression caused Killian to shrink until he locked eyes with the woman sitting next to her.

185

He recognized Maurelle immediately from the image he'd seen in realm school. The hologram did not do her justice. Her long ebony hair was streaked with glittering silver strands and rested in a lose braid over her bare shoulder. Her deep black gown was glittered with purple diamonds that matched her dark purple lips. But her silver eyes stopped his breath. Maurelle didn't wear protective glasses like other Cimmerians so their unique color pulled him in. They peered deep inside him, but were not accusatory and seemed to smile at him. Her pale face stood out against her dark dress. Killian was quite sure he had never set eyes on a woman with such a unique, elegant beauty.

"Thank you Blake," Nathaniel said, shifting Killian's gaze away from Maurelle and back to his friend. Blake gave him a quick wink and left the room. "Killian, please have a seat." Nathaniel pointed to the single chair. Killian obeyed, feeling every eye in the room pour into him. Standing in the corner was Connor, he hadn't seen him earlier. Next to him was a dark haired woman with the same silver eyes and Maurelle. She stood in the shadows obviously avoiding the harsh light and smiled softly at Killian.

"This council has been called to address accusations against Killian Thomas," Nathaniel said formally. "As well as addressing concerns brought by Connor, one of our engineers. His discoveries involve realm security so the council has been requested to hear the findings." Nathaniel scanned the other three people seated next to him before continuing. "First order to be addressed to all those present, Egan has been stabilized. He is alive, but still quite ill and unable to speak." Killian breathed out a sigh of relief. He was pleased to hear Egan had survived the attack.

The Empress's face grew colder at the mention of Egan and she glared harder at him.

"We will begin by allowing Connor to present his case of findings." Nathaniel leaned back in his chair and all eyes watched Connor stalk into the center of the room. He clutched tight to the same folder of papers Killian had seen two days earlier.

"Thank you," he whispered. "Council members, for the purpose of my case I've been given permission to disclose the Thomas family has been the Cimmerian relic guardian since their creation."

The empress huffed. "Please do not tell us zis is about za relics." Her accent was thick, one like Killian had never heard. It was as if she was both Swedish and Russian, but neither accent was dominant. "Zay are dangerous, and people have been killed for zem before. Ve should leave zem alone."

"Understood, Your Highness, but there is a greater issue involving the Cimmerian relic," Connor answered with more confidence. "Killian was named guardian of the relic when he was a young child. I was witness to the transfer which my mentor performed. There was something strange about the relic, almost as if there was another power added upon the magic Merlin had infused in the gold charm. My mentor presented it to a magical expert who also agreed there was something strange about the relic."

"Excuse me," Maurelle finally spoke. Her voice was smooth, almost poetic and her brilliant eyes shimmered in the light. "I'm very curious Connor, how magic could be added upon a sealed magical object. I knew Merlin, and he never added magic to an object without first sealing it so nothing could be tampered."

"That is why, at the time, we were confused. The expert herself sensed something was strange about the relic, but didn't know what. Killian was eventually sent to Terrene and was bonded to the relic. When he arrived back here, he said there was damage to the charm after years of use. But what struck me were his subtle abilities."

"Vat kind of abilities?" Gwyniera asked in a tense tone.

"Killian has unique dreams, lifelike dreams. He's been able to see things moments ahead of when they actually happen. He has a strong sense of other people's emotions, and after he returned from Ignisia he insisted he opened a portal."

"I did!" Killian blurted out. He met Maurelle's sparkling eyes and felt instant embarrassment for his outburst. Connor turned around and raised his eyebrows, as if signaling Killian to stay quiet.

"I'm not accusing you, I'm setting up a history for the leaders," he huffed under his breath before continuing his speech. "Sorry, Majesties. As I was saying, after some of his earlier reports I've been researching anything with similar abilities. I am one hundred percent confident I've reached a solid conclusion about what was infused within the relic." The council sat on edge as Connor paused; Killian guessed it really was for dramatic effect knowing Connor. "I believe Killian has an ancient scientific formula inside him called Infinium."

The word meant nothing to Killian, but it meant something to the council. Miller gasped, Nathaniel slowly raised off his seat, Maurelle covered her mouth and Gwyniera began a loud tirade.

"*Zat is not possible*," she cried. "It vas destroyed at za end of za venture."

"Empress, I assure you *it is* Infinium. It was created again and infused into the relic before Killian took guardianship."

"Connor, you're sure?" Nathaniel asked.

"Yes, sir. Dalia has also verified my findings. She has more experience with Infinium than anyone." Connor pointed at the Cimmerian woman standing against the wall.

"He is speaking the truth," she said in a similar poetic voice like Maurelle.

"Dalia," Maurelle said desperately to her Cimmerian companion, "what does this mean?"

"Zis all goes back to you Maurelle, and Cimmerian's cursed magic," the Empress seethed.

"Empress, please," Miller cried. Killian's eyes shifted between the two women. He was shocked the Empress had been so brash. The Empress was the first harsh Glacien he'd met; nothing like the other calm, quiet people.

"No, she is free to express her concerns," Maurelle responded, holding up a pale hand. "Empress, this has no more to do with my father and the Terrene Venture than you and I do. I know that is who you are truly accusing, not me. My father was many things, you frequently remind me, but he was not the creator of Infinium on the Venture. If you recall what Connor told us, the formula was recreated and infused into the relic."

The empress looked as if she wanted to say something more, but she held her tongue and sat down, crossing her arms.

"Yes," Connor said. "It was recreated. This is not the original formula. We know the original Infinium disappeared and allowed the power to corrupt his mind. I'm going to allow Dalia to explain what this means. I would like to add a final note. Dalia has been involved in this relic for years, she was also the magical expert consulted by my mentor. Her opinion solidifies my findings more than I ever would be able." Nathaniel raised his eyebrows and nodded.

"Wait!" Killian cried. "This Infinium…is it the power that ended the venture?"

No one spoke for a moment, but Maurelle nodded her head. "Killian, I was told as a young girl the power was a mutation and planted the seeds of the other abnormal creations developed during the Venture conflicts. But I suppose Infinium was the beginning of the end during the Venture."

Killian ran a hand through his short hair. He remembered the story of the council at Stonehenge. He knew a strong power had corrupted the people and had caused violence between the races. Now Connor was saying it was inside him.

Connor stepped back and the tall, Cimmerian woman stepped out of the shadows. She placed a pair of thin glasses over her eyes as the light increased. Killian could see she was older than Maurelle, which meant she could be over one thousand years old.

"Infinium was created to open the dormant areas of the brain. It was designed to give the host the power of every realm. Killian's experiences point strongly toward dormant Infinium. The power has not activated inside his mind, or we would know it. But he is experiencing side effects of the strong chemical surges from the formula. This is why he has premonitions, or can feel emotions. If the power was close to activation, it would be quite possible to summon elements in the Hemisphere and open a portal if his life was threatened."

"But Dalia, how is it possible Infinium transferred from the relic to Killian?" Miller asked with a twinge of emotion in his voice.

"I don't know who created the formula a second time, but they would have to have a great understanding of the living magic inside the relic. As my Queen said, Merlin sealed all the relics, but Infinium is not magic, it is man-made and connects to a living force. It is strong enough to bypass magical barriers in weak life forces. Each of the four relics has large amounts of Merlin's magic, which is a life force of its own. This is how it crossed the barrier on the Cimmerian relic and bonded to Merlin's magic."

However, a human, or a living creature has a stronger life force than bottled magic. When Killian's relic was damaged I am certain the bottled Infinium latched onto the stronger life force when it had a chance, which is him. The relic still holds all Merlin's magic, his magic is bonded with the charm. Infinium would be free to escape. I don't know why it was created, but I can assume its creator planned to use it at a later date and didn't anticipate it escaping and latching to Killian."

"Is there any way to date its creation?" Nathaniel asked briskly. "Perhaps we could learn who developed the new Infinium if we knew how old it was."

"I have no way of knowing the age of Killian's Infinium," Dalia whispered simply.

"Perhaps zis boy is za one who created it," Gwyniera sneered.

"Empress," Nathaniel began, "as Connor said, the relic had a strong power pull when it was transferred to Killian as a toddler, insinuating Infinium was already in the relic during the transfer. A young child is not capable of creating such an ability." Gwyniera pushed her nose in the air, but Killian smiled at the older man.

"More importantly, what does this mean for our friend Killian?" Maurelle sang. Killian's stomach twisted. The queen addressed him like an equal, yet he felt so much less than her.

"Killian will be fine, if he can learn to stay calm, and keep Infinium dormant. If it activates, he will need training to control the power. The current side effects will be nothing compared to the strength of active Infinium," Dalia answered.

"It is of realm security because of the strength of the power," Connor continued. "Each leader needed to be made aware of the potential power inside Mr. Thomas. We are fortunate that Killian is not a power hungry, lunatic. But even so if Infinium were to activate and join with his cells chemically, he would in theory have the powers of all four realms. Having such a power cannot be concealed from the races."

"Can I say something?" Killian asked.

"No Killian," Nathaniel answered kindly. "We understand it's difficult to hear us talk as if you are not here, but the accused does not deliberate with us. You will have your moment to speak."

Killian frowned. He'd already asked a question and Maurelle had answered it, but he obeyed and stared blankly at the pearly white carpet.

"And we appreciate you informing us of the potential threat," Maurelle said sweetly to Connor.

"Ha, perhaps ve should not take such a risk vith him. Are ve not also here because he is accused of trying to kill a leader?"

Killian closed his eyes; with the distressing talk of the strange ability he'd forgotten the accusations against him.

"Yes, Empress," Nathaniel said. "In order to see the truth without objection or alteration the queen will be extracting the memory."

"Vat! You vant magic to be used ven you have tried so diligently for years to keep it controlled." Fear of magic was easily detectable to Killian underneath Gwyniera's tone.

"It has always been the Ponderi's position when it is a matter of extreme importance, magic may be used in a controlled environment," Miller instructed. "I can think of no one with more control of magic than Queen Maurelle."

"Gwyniera, I don't understand all your protests," Maurelle said sweetly as she floated toward Killian. "Haven't you missed me at all? It's been so many years since we've gotten together my dear empress." Gwyniera's pale skin flushed at the jab and Dalia smirked at the floor.

Killian liked Maurelle, she helped him feel calm which he would expect more from a Glacien empress, but the frosty woman was becoming more difficult to deal with each time she opened her mouth.

"Killian this won't hurt," Maurelle said putting one hand on each side of his face. "Don't worry it will be over soon."

She winked at him. Killian closed his eyes. Maurelle smelled like tropical flowers, she had a warmth radiating from her that made him think he would do anything she ever asked of him. He felt a twinge of guilt thinking such things about the Queen when moments before he came in the room he'd felt similar things toward Mercedes.

As soon as her warm palms touched his skin the images from the last few days flashed across his mind as if rewinding an old tape. Eventually he saw the red deserts of Ignisia, Egan's office, the horrifying Draykan. The moment he dreaded the most soared across his memory: his spear impaling the attacking Deshuit.

After only a few seconds Maurelle removed her hands and held them up in front of her face. In between her palms a projected image of all the memories played out for the council to see. The screams of the Deshuit plagued his mind, he saw Connor lower his gaze and Miller look faint when the man fell to the sand choking on his own blood.

The council watched closely as they scrutinized the dialogue with Egan. Killian felt a shiver as the Draykan shot from the sky searching for him until he produced the billowing, earthy portal that took him home. The extraction was impressive, more than the Supraserum. With each shifting scene, the color altered over Killian. Sometimes he had a reddish tint, when he killed the Deshuit he had a green cast to his skin. Other times he was blue.

"Interesting, indeed," Nathaniel said as he scratched his chin. He focused on Killian before continuing. "Killian before the council deliberates on the extraction, is there anything you'd like to say?"

Nervously he cleared his throat. This was his only opportunity to give the truth. "I didn't hurt Egan. I don't know who did. Ignisia was a horrible experience…you saw what I did to the Deshuit." He lowered his eyes, ashamed to meet anyone's gaze. "I've been accused of hurting others before. I didn't do it then, and

I didn't do it now. I don't know what you're going to examine closer in that memory, but you'll see I didn't do anything wrong. If I somehow have this awful power in my brain, I am going to need help with it. I don't know what it's capable of, but sending me away or locking me up, or whatever you plan to do with me isn't going to solve the problem of Infinium." He paused for a moment. "That's all I have to say."

"Thank you, my boy. I'm going to excuse you, Dalia and Connor so we may come to our decision. Thank you."

Killian stood and left the room with the other two. Connor patted his shoulder, but said nothing. What could he say?

"Killian," Dalia whispered after Connor had blazed away in the elevator. "Would you mind if we spoke for a while. There are things I need to tell you about Infinium. Things I only want *you* to hear."

Chapter 13
The Ultimatum

Killian and Dalia walked out the main doors of the Praetorium. The lawn was a small wilderness full of forest shrubs, and large foreign plants he'd never seen. He stood next to a flowering bush full of rose-like flowers, but instead of thorns on the stems each petal had needle sharp pins sticking out of their edges.

"So, what did you want to tell me?" he asked. It was intriguing the woman wanted to speak with him alone.

"You need to understand how dangerous Infinium can be, not just to others but to you."

"How do you know so much about Infinium?" he asked softly touching one of the barbs on the petals. The flower immediately rolled itself up into a tight bulb at the sensation.

"I was the original Infinium's guardian." Killian's eyes widened at the confession.

"The man who created it? You protected him?"

Dalia nodded. "In a way I protected him from himself. His name was Axel and I have seen the beauty of his creation, but also the danger. As I said in the meeting the formula is dormant in your body. It will only activate if it feels like it is close to death."

Killian scrunched his face. "Why do you keep referring to it like it's living?"

"In a way Infinium is alive, it requires your body to survive. And if threatened it will activate by connecting with you at a cellular level. An Infinium bond will completely alter your genetic makeup. This is how it strengthens you, it makes you greater than you are. But don't be foolish in assuming it is for you. Infinium will activate to save itself." Killian didn't respond, but turned and shifted his gaze to the green and blue painted moon now lighting the sky.

"We don't have much time to speak alone Killian, and I need you to believe me that having Infinium is a blessing and a curse. It is powerful Killian, and truly can give you the talents of all the realms. This can give you power to do good, but also can feed on your natural greed. It did so with Axel."

"What do you mean?"

"Axel became obsessed with the power and kept pushing his strengths until he was lost in his mind. He was dangerous and allowed Infinium to further his power hunt. He created the formula with good intentions; so others could be equal to Master Claec, but at the end of the venture Axel had become just as power hungry as his enemy. Infinium destroyed his mind. I protected him, but one day he had disappeared during the night. He was so weak, I can't imagine he lived much longer." Dalia paused, Killian thought he saw glistening tears coat her eyes.

"Dalia, is that going to happen? I didn't want Infinium...I...I didn't ask for it." Killian was panicking as he imagined himself maddening with power over time.

"If you allow it. If Infinium ever activated, and you disciplined yourself you could have more amazing power than most people in the Hemisphere. There's more Killian. I fear if the Trinity ever discovered you have Infinium it will be a great prize for them. They would have a valuable weapon to use in their relic search."

"But it's already latched to me, how would they get it?"

Dalia shifted uncomfortably, also moving her gaze to the brilliant moon. "They would have to drain much of your blood. But it has to be a very precise procedure. Your heart must beat long enough to keep Infinium alive. If you die, before enough of the formula was drained in your blood it would die as well."

"So you're saying an evil society might want to drain me alive? Great." He felt sick as he lowered himself to the soft grass. Dalia kneeled next to him.

"Killian, I will do anything to protect you from the Trinity, so will the leaders. I must warn you to keep this information close to you. I didn't even want the council to know, not that they aren't trustworthy, but the fewer people that know the better chance you have the Trinity will never learn of Infinium."

"You can't protect me if the council decides to lock me away, can you?" He looked at the dark, damp grass embarrassed at his brisk tone.

"You won't be locked away. It was simple to see your innocence in the extraction. Deliberating is just protocol."

"How can you tell I'm innocent?"

"Didn't you see the shifting colors? It signifies your mood during each encounter. When Egan was poisoned, you genuinely felt surprise, panic and sympathy for the Chief. If you had poisoned him your mood would different." Dalia spoke so matter-of-factly it actually calmed his nerves. "It's just like Infinium in a way," she continued. "Magic extraction can also tap into emotions."

As Dalia finished they heard the Empress's harsh cry of anger coming from the entry of the building. Flashing Dalia a confused look they both darted toward the doors.

The council had adjourned and were standing in the entryway, but also next to them were Blake and Mercedes.

"Vat is she doing here?" Gwyniera shrieked pointing at Mercedes.

"Your Highness, Miss Forino is one of our beasties. We don't understand why you're so upset," Miller pleaded.

"Gwyniera, calm yourself," Maurelle chided. "can't you see you're upsetting the poor girl." Mercedes locked eyes with Killian as he entered. The bright emerald color was soaked in tears. Blake glanced at the queen, then Killian. He had his arm wrapped around Mercedes protectively as Killian stepped toward them.

The empress looked like she was going to explode in anger. Turning to Nathaniel she seethed once more. "I have never been more insulted." The empress stalked away with a fierce glare back at Mercedes.

"What was that?" she sobbed. Killian went to her side, though they hadn't spoken in several days he needed to help her.

"Don't think on it," Maurelle said in her calming voice. "Gwyniera isn't as young as she once was, she probably is mistaking you for another acquaintance." Mercedes chuckled at Maurelle's jab toward the empress.

"Thank you Your Highness," she said. Her hand slowly crept to Killian's without breaking eye contact with the queen. Her touch sent Killian's stomach into a twirl after days locked away from her.

"Killian," Nathaniel's agitated voice broke through the crowd. "We were on our way down to find you before Miss Forino was accosted. The council, including the Empress," he added with emphasis, "has come to the conclusion you in no way harmed Egan. This is good and bad news. Good news that you have been cleared of any wrong doing, but bad that we still have a villain roaming the Hemisphere." Nathaniel paused looking thoughtful. "We appreciate your patience during this my boy. While you rejoin your friends and fellow recruits for Peridus training Miller and

Dalia will be traveling to Ignisia to extract memories from Egan's closest subjects. Hopefully we can find the culprit soon."

"We should let you get some rest," Maurelle said, hinting to the others to leave Killian in peace.

After everyone had left, only Mercedes and Blake remained with him.

"So, do you want to tell us what happened now, or later?" Blake asked. Mercedes held his hand tighter.

"I don't know if I have energy for anything else tonight. All I'll say is I'm glad it's over. I appreciate both of you for never doubting me." He locked eyes with Mercedes. She wiped her face of her stray tears and smiled at him.

"I would never believe the rumors going around. I know you better than that."

"Okay guys, I'll leave if you want me to," Blake said backing away.

"   Shut up," Killian laughed. "We're coming too."

***

The next morning the halls were bustling with excitement as recruits, beasties, analysts, engineers—every Ponderi member made their way to the training center. Killian shuffled behind a giddy group of young girls until the long chestnut hair of Mercedes flashed into view. Running up behind her he playfully wrapped his arms around her shoulders. The other girls widened their eyes when they saw Killian.

Mercedes scowled at them. "Stop it, you guys heard the announcement. Lucan spread the rumors before he knew the truth."

"Sorry," a blonde beastie squeaked. "We know he didn't do anything it's just hard to wipe two days of talk out. Sorry Killian."

Killian waved his hand as if it was nothing, but inside he was angry.

"How are you?" Mercedes whispered close to his face. His stomach tightened, all he wanted was to be closer to her and make up for two days of being apart.

He brushed a strand of hair off her face. "I'm fine," he cupped her cheek. "You were the first person I wanted to see before everything happened…the thought of you helped me get back safe from Ignisia Mercedes. I'll tell you everything as soon as we get a moment." Killian put his forehead against hers. All this time he felt consumed with emotion, now when he wanted to express his feelings, he couldn't find the words.

"Killian," a small, but deep voice broke through their moment. Dax stood behind him looking down at the ground. "I wanted to tell you I'm sorry for ever thinking you were capable of hurting my Chief. I was not true to those I should trust with my life. I hope I can earn your forgiveness."

"Dax," Killian said slapping his steaming shoulder. "it's alright. I know people were saying things. It would be hard to know what to believe especially when the council was brought in and I was locked up."

"That's no excuse. You wouldn't turn on me."

"Forget it, okay. It's alright." Dax nodded, but Killian suspected it wasn't enough for him.

"Thomas! Hurry up you need to get into the training center!" Aidan's voice boomed across the commotion. He briskly waved his arms several people ahead of them.

Mercedes chuckled. "Aidan has been anxiously waiting for you to get back when you were locked in your room we all thought he was going to explode. He expects you to be his shining star during Peridus."

Killian followed her toward the training center. "I bet Lucan loves that." Mercedes laughed and held his hand again.

The athletic field was packed with people. In the center, a large raised platform rose above the crowd. Nathaniel, Aidan, Gwyniera and Maurelle stood in the center.

"Welcome!" Nathaniel boomed. His voice was loud like he was speaking into a microphone, but Killian couldn't see any device he was speaking into. "This week marks the beginning of the preparation for the Peridus!" Enormous cheers broke out as Nathaniel chuckled.

"We know you're all excited and ready to get going, but first we want to make you aware of some remarkable guests that will be joining us. You all know the Peridus is something to look forward to each year, and a brilliant way to unite us together while showing off our individual, valuable skills. Joining us this week is Empress Gwyniera of Glaciem." The Empress stood regally and hundreds of Glacien members fell to their knees. Applause welcomed the Empress from the other members. "And of course, we'd like to welcome Queen Maurelle of Cimmerian." The Cimmerian members mimicked the Glaciens as they bowed low to their Queen. "Your Majesties, we welcome you to our celebration." The two women nodded and smiled at the crowd before taking a seat in two remarkable pearl colored wing-backed chairs on the platform.

"Now, as many of you know Peridus was created to promote our best selves. It reveals our elite, and we generously reward the recruits who have worked hard training, developing, and serving the Hemisphere. We are honored to have realm royalty joining us this year." Nathaniel paused as the applause and cheers overpowered his voice.

"Except he isn't telling them why they are really here is he Killian?" Sophia had shouldered her way through the crowd and stood behind Dax, smiling mischievously. Blake had followed and was laughing behind her.

"Hey guys," he answered pleased to see his friends. "You really think everyone really believes the leaders are here for the games and not for the council?"

Dax nodded vigorously. "They knew about the council, but think they were coming for the games anyway. The council just brought them here earlier. The only reason *we* know the truth is because we know you. Nathaniel has done some amazing Lucan disaster clean-up the last twenty-four hours."

Nathaniel's voice drowned Dax out as he bellowed to the crowd. "As always, the top three competitors will be rewarded for their hard work, but the goal should always be first place. The winning competitor of the Peridus will be promoted to leadership in their field, as well as unlimited access to research labs, the athletic fields and honors from every realm leader!" The crowd rumbled with excitement and cheers.

"Wow," Blake said smiling, "I wouldn't mind having unlimited access to the field."

"Yeah, you can forget it Blake. You're going against me so I wouldn't plan on winning," Dax said smugly. Everyone laughed as Blake gave Dax a hard punch in the shoulder.

"Today marks day one of your training and preparation. The games will begin in four days. There will be four different levels, those members who earn enough points to continue will progress. The member with the most points after the fourth level, which will take place in the simulation room, will be our Peridus winner! The levels are designed to bring out your strengths during adversity. You can expect yourself to be tested both physically and mentally. Not everyone is required to participate. You may electronically join Peridus over by Aidan today."

"The simulation room—that's supposed to be really intense," Mercedes whispered to him.

Killian nodded. "That's what Aidan told me when I first came here."

"Today, for those wishing to join the Peridus, you will begin with your regular groups. Aidan will oversee the recruit training here, Cora will take Beasties to their stations, and Luther will handle analysts and engineers. Tomorrow everyone will have free reign to work on any skill you think you may be weak. Have fun and work hard." Nathaniel finished as the crowd disassembled and moved quickly to Aidan who stood with a translucent tablet in his hand. One by one recruits that wished to participate in Peridus placed their palms on the tablet until it beeped cheerfully. Killian truly didn't want to participate in Peridus, he would rather observe, but the scowl from Aidan as he pointed to the line urged him quickly along to the tablet.

Mercedes gripped Killian's hand after she had entered her name. The beasties were leaving the training center to their hall, but she looked longingly at him. "Honestly I could care less about the games right now. I feel like we'll never get a free moment." She looked at the ground shyly.

Killian pulled her into his chest. "I know what you mean. When this is all over we're taking an entire day, just you and me." Mercedes smiled and gave him a quick kiss on the cheek and turned out of the training center with the rest of the Beastians.

"Well gentlemen, let the games begin," Blake teased, wrapping his arms around Dax and Killian's shoulders.

"Hello, Killian." Their heads flipped around and saw Maurelle standing behind them. Sophia bowed low at the sight of her Queen. Maurelle had changed from her brilliant gown and was dressed in a tight black pantsuit that hugged her athletic form perfectly. Her billowing hair was braided on the sides and pulled up into an impressive up-do that looked complicated to Killian. His friends quickly bent at the waist to show respect to the queen, and Killian awkwardly followed. Maurelle was breathtaking and regal, that was certain, yet she was playful and humble—conversing with others as equals.

"Your Majesty, it's great to see you again," Killian said quietly. Maurelle smiled at him and walked toward Blake. She ran a hand over his sleek cross bow. Blake looked nervous around the Queen, but Killian noted the slight curve of his lips at the Queen's attention.

"Likewise Killian," she said, "I had hoped you all would allow me to practice here with you…the Peridus is such an interesting process. I thought it would be fun to unwind for the next few days, would you mind if I joined?"

"Of course you can Your Majesty," Blake blurted with a small bow again. Maurelle smiled at him and followed behind as he led them toward the center of the athletic field.

Killian released an uncomfortable burst of breath. The others knew he lacked good skill, but the queen didn't. She'd seemed slightly impressed last night after learning he had a power locked away inside his mind, but surely she would be disappointed at his awful skill with weaponry.

Maurelle stepped in front of a target, still holding Blake's bow. She closed her stunning silver eyes and pulled the trigger. The sleek arrow stuck in the center perfectly. Sophia clapped in awe behind them. Maurelle beamed, revealing her perfect teeth.

"Wow, I thought I was the best shooter. You've humbled me, Your Majesty." Blake almost drooled.

"It helps when you've been alive for nearly seven hundred years, darling," she said teasing him and patting his cheek. A low chuckle passed through the group.

"Killian, are you ever going to throw your spear?" Maurelle asked after each person had taken a turn shooting or throwing their weapons.

"Uh...well I'm not very good to be honest, Your Highness."

Maurelle sauntered over to him and put her hands over his, clasping his steel spear with him. His stomach jolted at her touch. Her hands were soft and silky, but firm under her grip.

"You don't have to be skilled with Infinium," Maurelle whispered. "You can control elements, see what may come, surely you can will your spear to hit a target." She winked at him and stepped out of the way.

"What is she talking about?" Dax whispered to Sophia, who shrugged.

Killian took a deep breath and held his spear tight in his hands. He wasn't sure how to control this power when it was dormant, but if Maurelle thought there was some way it was possible he would try. Gripping the cool metal he reeled his arm behind his head, and thrust the spear into the air as hard as he could, all the while urging the deadly point to land where he desired. Almost as if controlled by a magnetic force, for the first time since his arrival at the Praetorium Killian saw his weapon pierce the cloth target, right alongside Maurelle's arrow.

There was a shroud of silence encompassing the group until Sophia shrieked in excitement.

"Wow, Kill...you are just full of surprises lately," Blake said. Killian beamed and glanced back at Sophia and Dax. Dax was reluctantly handing Sophia a large red crystal—they called it an *Igcuso.* Killian frowned. Dax was a relentless bettor during training, often waging against certain recruits, and Killian had quickly learned that single crystal was the equivalent of fifty dollars.

"You bet against me, Dax? Come on, was I that bad?" Dax's flamed eyes spurred to life and gave off a subtle steam as he flushed with embarrassment.

"Well, do you want me to make you feel better, or would you rather I be honest?" He smiled sheepishly. Killian rolled his eyes, feeling his own cheeks get hot.

"Well, no matter what you were before, I have a feeling you will no longer lack skill with your spear." Maurelle beamed at Killian.

"How did that happen? I've never been able to throw like that."

Maurelle put her pale hand on his arm. "Infinium is powerful Killian. You have the ability to control and manipulate objects around you, the spear responded."

"Wait what is this Infinium thing you keep talking about?" Dax asked, frustration coming out in his tone. Sophia shoved Dax as he spoke so informal to Maurelle.

"Show some respect Dax," she snarled.

Maurelle smiled. "Please, it's refreshing to have people speak to me less formally. I...suppose it allows me to just be normal for a while. So please, all of you, at least for the time being, I would appreciate it if we could all just speak to each other like—"

"Friends?" Blake chimed in. Maurelle nodded excitedly. "We'd be happy to have you train with us, Your Highness."

"And to answer your question, I will let Killian tell you what Infinium is when he's ready." Maurelle smiled at Dax. "It looks like I will have to excuse myself from your training, the athletic director appears to need all of you."

They turned and looked as Aidan was storming toward them; his tan skin was red and flushed.

"Recruits I need you over at the pools now." He turned his attention to Maurelle. "Majesty." He nodded his head, showing as much respect as he was able. Maurelle just laughed.

"Perhaps I will join you later," she said walking toward Nathaniel, who was still on the platform

"Recruits, you three are some of my top competitors," Aidan said, a hint of anxiety behind his voice. He moved in closer so no one else could hear. "You are not to let me down against Luther and Cora, understand?" Killian still had difficulty reading Aidan, he wasn't sure if he should salute him, or say nothing. Dax stood at attention and Blake slapped Aidan on his steaming shoulders.

"Of course bud. We won't let you down...look who you're talking to. Just up the wager, I know you have going on with the other departments, and give us a cut." He signaled to all three of them. Aidan pursed his lips but didn't continue his rant. He gave the three of them a curt nod and walked toward the pools.

Blake was chuckling and shaking his head. "That guy, he's going to totally lose his cool someday."

206

The pools were steaming as the freezing temperatures meshed with the warmer air when they stepped inside the glass walled room. Ice floated on top, more than Killian had ever seen before. Ivy and Aidan ran around handing each recruit a light belt they were to tie around their waist. The mood was light and full of excitement as recruits prepared for the drills. Killian glanced up and met the eyes of Lucan. He glared fiercely back at Killian. Last time they'd been near one another was when Killian had beaten him on the rock walls. Instead of cowering away from Lucan's gaze, Killian smirked and gave him a wink which caused daggers to shoot from Lucan's eyes.

"If the pools are selected for the Peridus, they will set up as a relay. You have two partners that are responsible for finding a token in the pool," Aidan began. "Each partner must start at a different end of the pool and the second cannot begin their turn until the first has found their token and tagged them. You can see the pools are not meant to be comfortable. I warn you, many of you, even Glaciens may not be able to bear the temperatures during the real competition." Everyone stared at Aidan with wide eyes, the excitement had dulled and some recruits subconsciously backed away from the pool. "Now, everyone find a practice partner, pick your team color, and we will begin."

Dax decided to pair up with Sophia, they both wore red banners for their team color. Blake had immediately tagged Killian and they wrapped gold cloth around their arms for their team. Both Sophia and Dax pouted before teaming with each other since Maurelle had hinted something was different about Killian and both wanted to be on his team.

Killian was selected as first partner. Lining up along the edge of the frosty pool he had a wave of frozen air hit him and suck his breath out of his lungs while his stomach churned like a rogue wave. Lucan had ended up next to him and never took his gaze from the water. Killian's anger boiled standing next to him. Lucan had, for no reason, tried to destroy his reputation.

"Recruits!" Aidan yelled, "find your token and tag your partner before you must exit the pool for hypothermia. We have internal body sensors marked on you so you cannot go further than safety permits…don't even try it. Now, take your positions. Ready, set, GO!" Killian took a deep breath and dove into the freezing water. He felt instant pain as the water encased him like hundreds of knives. He gulped water and lost his breath. Opening his eyes, around him he saw Lucan's dark hair diving lower and lower. With new resolve, Killian focused and began searching for the token he needed before he could tag Blake.

The water was crushing as he dove deeper. The pools were abnormally deep. His skin was numb and the stabbing feeling was lightening. Inside the pools, there were trenches and caves replicating the deep water of the Glacien sea where the blue pebbles were harvested. Killian's chest was burning, so he surfaced and took a deep breath. He was surrounded by many other recruits filling their lungs. He didn't see Lucan but knew he would stop at nothing to win this competition so he was sure to surface as little as he could. Killian gulped a large breath of air before diving back toward the caves. He figured if they were going to hide a token the caves would be the spot to do it.

He pushed himself further, his chest burned again, longing for oxygen and his head pounded against the pressure. Killian focused on his task, and soon the burning eased slightly. A glimmer caught his eye; tucked deep in one of the crevices he saw a gold blinking light. Smiling inwardly, he tucked his arms tight to his sides and quickly darted through the water so he could surface and tag Blake. The token released easily, all it was, was a simple blinking flashlight connected to a silver chain. Killian strung the light around his neck and made his way toward the surface.

A bright blue light flashed out of the corner of his eye as well as a swift blinking yellow. Looking down he saw Lucan's form floating near one of the rocks. The sensors on his belt were blinking the yellow and his blue token's chain was caught on the stone. The yellow meant his body temperature was dropping too quickly.

Immediately Killian swam back toward Lucan, who was weakly struggling against the tether. Killian put his hand on Lucan's shoulder and grasped the chain around his neck. He began seeing spots as his lungs bulged and pulsed searching for air. He noted his belt began blinking yellow as well. Far up on the surface he could see white suits lining the edges, obviously the medics preparing for a rescue. Killian's heart pounded as Lucan's body went limp next to him and eerily bobbed around.

Killian tugged on the chain around Lucan's neck and snapped the metal quickly. He wasn't going to make it, his lungs were drowning, and his vision was fading. He needed to get up to the surface and felt burning through his body with every heartbeat urging the water around him to assist him. From behind Killian felt a push, urging them to the surface. He held tight to Lucan's arm and glanced as a wave of frothing water burst through the pool like a geyser. Within seconds, both Killian and Lucan broke the surface.

Killian gulped for air and choked up water at the same time. The sides of the pool were full of energy as medics dove in after the two men. A burly Glacien grabbed Killian by his collar and quickly pulled him to the side and out of the pool.

A young woman with long auburn hair brought a soft towel and wrapped it around his shoulders. Next to him, he finally heard Lucan sputtering and coughing up water. Killian looked over at him with relief. Lucan met his eyes and Killian was overwhelmed with a sense of confusion and remorse.

"Kill! Kill, what happened?" Blake shouted kneeling down next to him.

"I saw Lucan down there…he was stuck." His voice was hoarse and choppy. Slowly he handed Blake the blinking, gold token and pushed his shoulder. "Tag." His eyes were bright, but his countenance was dark as the intensity of the exercise overwhelmed him. Blake laughed and patted his back.

"Eh, I think the contest is over at the pools. One little emergency on the first round and Aidan falls into a fit." Blake's eyes were smiling as he pointed to a pacing Aidan, who repeatedly grabbed his head in frustration. Killian laughed and turned to Lucan.

"Hey, are you doing okay?" He didn't like Lucan; he was angry at him. But he was still genuinely concerned about him. They were both recruits, both Custodis, and he hoped at some point they could work together to find the relics and stop the Trinity.

Lucan didn't say anything. He just nodded and looked at the ground. Taking that as the best answer Lucan would ever give him, Killian stood hugging his towel close to him and followed Blake toward the door.

"Thanks...Thomas," Lucan's quiet voice said behind him. Killian turned around and looked at him. He still was glaring, and Killian still had no idea why Lucan hated him so much, but he would take what he could get.

"Sure thing, I know you would do the same for me." He smirked and walked away.

"Well, that was an interesting start to the first day," Blake said as they entered the climbing walls.

"Yeah, you can say that." Killian leaned against one of the walls breathing deep as he caught his breath. "Does everyone *have* to participate in the Peridus?"

Blake looked at him incredulously. "Come on Kill, they won't let anyone die." Blake leaned in closer and lowered his voice to a whisper. "We're going to be up against a lot more than Peridus games when we are all facing the Trinity, better get used to it."

"There you guys are," Sophia shouted, interrupting their discussion. She trotted over to them with Dax close behind her. "Killian, how are you? That was really brave what you did for Lucan, but you didn't have to go back, the dive medics were ready to go get him."

Killian shrugged. "I didn't know that. All I saw was Lucan passing out; I couldn't just leave him there," he answered exasperated.

"We have a free hour to work on whatever we want. Feel up for a climb?" Dax's eyes brightened as he grasped a jagged ruby rock on one wall.

"Mind if I join?" Mercedes called out as she crossed the field toward the walls. She looked water-logged Killian up and down curiously. "Have fun in the pools?"

He rolled his eyes and smiled. "Don't ask. Let's just climb."

Though premonitions didn't come, Killian was still impressed with his climbing skills. The rocks frequently shifted to different terrains, but he rarely slipped. Dax had set a personal goal to beat Killian, but for the fourth time Killian pounced onto the soft, pliable mat beneath the rocks seconds before a steaming Dax dropped.

"Killian, you are quite impressive on the rock walls." Maurelle stood behind them, along with Gwyniera, who stood aloof with her nose in the air. Instantly Sophia fell to her knee again, with Blake as well. Dax bowed his head like Killian and Mercedes.

"Your Majesty, Empress. It's good to see you both. How are you enjoying observing the training?" He saw Mercedes shift nervously next to him. He was reminded of the empress's outburst the night before. She seemed more calm next to Mercedes, but never met her eye.

"I find it fascinating. I haven't been to a Peridus tournament for centuries. The Ponderi has certainly accelerated in their training techniques." Maurelle explained. "Gwyniera has found the Beastians quite interesting. The Empress was enraptured at their knowledge of creatures."

"Oh," Mercedes said turning toward the Empress. "I'm a Beastie, I would love to show you around if you'd like, Your Majesty."

The Empress puffed up her chest and looked Mercedes up and down. Her eyes were tormented with rage, misery, and confusion. "I'd rather not," She said quietly. The Empress quickly turned on her heel and walked away from the group.

211

"Why does she hate me? Or is she like that to everyone?" Mercedes asked to no one in particular, but her voice quivered, threatening to give way to her emotions. Killian hugged her shoulders against him, hoping to help her feel better.

"I wouldn't worry about it, my dear." Maurelle patted her shoulder. "Gwyniera is a complicated ruler. She is just and fair, but I've never met a woman with more icy layers."

"It's hard to believe such a hard woman rules over such a peaceful land," Dax said loudly.

Maurelle nodded. "Yes, it is. Well, I must be going now, I just wanted to say hello before I left for the evening. Nathaniel wishes to meet with us several times through the rest of the day until Miller and Dalia return. Hopefully, I will see you all tomorrow."

The excitement of the games had distracted him from Dalia's conversation and the dangers of the power inside him. Infinium was a part of him. Someday it might activate and he would have more power than he could imagine, power the Trinity wanted. He had a choice to use Infinium to find the relics, or ignore his potential and risk the Trinity finding them first.

The relics and Infinium had given Killian an ultimatum: Fight, and *possibly* live, or die along with everyone he loved.

Chapter 14
The Warning

The rest of the training days flew by. Killian spent most of his time practicing fighting with his spear as well as finding time to work with the Beasties and engineers. He had never been to the middle floor where the engineers worked on gadgets and projects. Connor came in often since he was a Bio engineer and helped Killian understand better how to think of ways to use his environment to help him out of an emergency.

"Are you happy you joined?" Blake asked him during an outdoor training on a large rope platform.

"If you would've asked me the first day, I would've said no," he answered. "But I have to admit it is fascinating learning about all the different departments."

Analysts tracked any strange realm activity by using crystal satellite stones developed by Glaciens that pulse images across the track systems. They also had to understand every cultural difference, every language dialect and every tradition in each realm. Engineers had been the ones who spent countless years developing a jumping portal for Custodis to cross through. Even the chefs were specially trained to understand the differences in the realm food and are not promoted to the dietary staff until they master each delicacy from each unique realm.

The wonderful part about the Ponderi is everyone was celebrated for their strengths. Some engineers or beasties could have been Custodis, but found their strengths in other departments.

Killian wasn't sure if he was in the right department, but if he was honest with himself, he wasn't confident in his abilities in *any* of the different areas in the Praetorium. Although he wasn't drawn to the creatures and didn't find it that intriguing, he often filled his hours with the Beastians, shadowing Mercedes as she excitedly told him every little detail about many of the creatures of the realms. They practiced defense together on shaped targets and bonded with the Ponderi creatures in the stables and fenced areas behind the Praetorium.

On the final training day Blake, Dax, and Sophia had agreed to train with the Beastians with him, deciding they didn't know what kind of creatures the Peridus would bring so any skill would be beneficial.

"Recruits, please stand by your Beastian companion. The Peridus begins tomorrow and this will be your last opportunity to train with the holographs in a controlled environment," soft-spoken Cora directed. Her white hair was long and braided around her head creating a headband from her own hair. Though she never appeared anxious, Mercedes had told Killian the Peridus games were making her edgy. Cora wasn't worried about the actual recruits, she was more concerned for the real creatures they would face during the competition.

"Mind if we partner up?" Mercedes said, rubbing shoulders with Killian.

"I'd prefer it that way."

"No fair. I called Mercedes yesterday," Sophia pouted from behind them.

"Chill Soph, Mercedes isn't attracted to you like Killian," Dax teased loudly making sure they all could hear him, along with a few others.

Mercedes' face flushed a deep red before she turned around and smacked Dax's shoulder. "Watch yourself Daxy, remember this is my level of expertise. I may set Cimmerian leeches on you during the games."

Dax laughed, but his eyes shadowed. She turned her head around and looked straight ahead. Killian bit back a laugh as she saw Mercedes smile, listening to Dax whisper to Sophia, "you don't think she would do that do you?"

Killian recognized Speron, the Beastie that had given him the crash course of Ignisian creatures. He was tapping Sophia on the shoulder asking if she would like to partner with him. She gave him a sweet smile and linked her arm with the Glacien. Dax frowned and light wisps of steam floated from his skin. Blake came up next to him and put his arm around his shoulders as Speron led Sophia away.

"You know buddy, she's never going to figure it out if you don't tell her."

"What? What are you talking about?" Dax stumbled. "Why do I care if Soph goes with that white-haired wimp?"

"Hey, I didn't say anything about Sophia. I was just talking about Cora not knowing you don't have a partner," Blake teased. Dax's skin got redder from embarrassment after stumbling into the trap.

"Are you recruits ready?" Cora asked, stepping up to them. "Recruit," she said turning to Dax, "where is your Beastian companion?"

"I don't have one yet, ma'am."

Cora looked agitated, as much as a Glacien could, and snapped her fingers to a young brown haired Beastie, motioning for her to come with Dax. The girl looked about twelve or thirteen and Dax didn't seem pleased. "I'm pairing you up with Izz." Cora floated away and began opening doors, allowing partners into the rooms to train against controlled creatures.

"Great, I get to babysit," Dax mumbled under his breath. Mercedes raised her eyebrows.

"I wouldn't underestimate Izz," she said turning around.

"Oh, no," Izz answered in a sweet, young voice, "I am really relieved I get to be with him. He seems so much stronger than other partners I've had. Sometimes the creatures are quite frightening." Izz turned and faced Dax. "Thank you for being willing to be my partner." Izz turned forward again with an innocent smile on her face. Dax looked at her with scrunched eyebrows but didn't answer her.

"Looks like it's our turn," Mercedes said and tugged on Killian's arm. He linked his fingers in hers and stepped into the dark room. As Cora closed the door, he immediately heard rattles and creaks.

"What are we supposed to be doing in here?" he whispered.

"Shh," she answered. "I think it's a Massu." Mercedes took a deep breath through her nose and unbuckled two knives from her waist, placing them on the magnetic wristbands. "Come on this way, we need to stay away from the darkest point of the room, so avoid corners."

Killian unstrapped his spear, mimicking Mercedes. "What's a Massu?"

Mercedes came close to his face and whispered. "Think of a jaguar, but ten times larger, with teeth like a shark."

"What?"

Mercedes didn't answer because a low growl filled the room. A large padded foot escaped the shadows and a massive, bulky figure stood in front of them. Mercedes was right. The cat was huge with enormous talon-like claws. Its teeth filled its mouth in three serrated rows. The cat roared and thick life-like saliva sprayed across the room.

"Stay ready," Mercedes instructed. She clutched her knives tight and stepped against the wall. Killian followed her, but also

216

felt he should protect her somehow. Slowly he stepped out in front of her just as the enormous paw swung toward them.

"KILLIAN!" Mercedes screamed and pushed him out of the way before the deadly claws struck him. Mercedes sliced her knives ferociously across the thick fur of the Massu. A painful shriek sounded from deep in its throat. Dropping his mouth in surprise at her instincts, he watched as she sliced, jabbed, and chopped skillfully with her daggers at the giant cat.

"Mercedes get out of the way," Killian yelled at her and stumbled toward her, but stopped as he heard her hum an eerie tune. The cat swatted its paws at her again, Killian swung his open spear, but Mercedes beat him by slicing the daggers deep in the paw. The cat shrieked, but Mercedes kept humming. After a few moments, the swats became weaker and less vicious. Mercedes hummed louder and before long the Massu slunk on to the ground and took heaving breaths as it slipped into a deep sleep. The large cat blurred and faded away until the room was empty.

"Where did it go?" Killian asked in a shrill voice. "Why were you humming?"

"It was just a hologram," Mercedes said returning her knives to the bands.

"What?" Killian's heart was beating against his chest. The adrenaline was leaving his body. He felt the breath, he saw the cat bleed when Mercedes cut him, how could it be a hologram? "Why were you so worried about it hitting me then?"

"You would've felt pain. Cora told us yesterday the animals were designed by the engineers to be as life-like as possible. If it had struck, your brain would've registered it as something painful." She sauntered up to him again and wrapped her arms around his neck. "I didn't want you to get hurt. Even if it wasn't real."

Killian's head was spinning, her face was inches from him. Killian raised his hand to her cheek and brushed her hair back. "Well, I'm not too thrilled with the idea of you getting hurt either." Slowly he pulled her face toward his and leaned down closer to her.

"Recruit Thomas, Beastian Forino?" Cora's voice sounded from the door. Her pale face stood out against the dimness in the room. Mercedes stepped back away from Killian and licked her lips nervously.

"Yes, we're here. We're coming out." Mercedes gave Killian a shy smile and walked toward the door after Cora.

Stepping into the hall they heard Dax's loud voice ranting about something that had happened.

"...Then she picked off the little demon things with this amazing dart gun!" Dax was standing in front of Speron and Sophia and kept pointing at Izz, who had a smug smile and leaned against the door with arms crossed.

"Dax," Mercedes called out, "how did your training go with Izz?"

"Oh, this girl," he exclaimed pointing to Izz, "she can fight with me any day! I've never met someone so quick and with spot on aim! Our holograms were freakish little elves. They bit me so hard!" He gave Izz a high five, who still remained silent, and showed his hand that had no bite since it had only been a pseudo bite from a hologram.

"You haven't seen anyone with such straight aim *except me*," Sophia chimed in.

Dax shook his head. "I don't know Soph, I think Izz could give you a run for your money." Dax turned before he could see the deep scowl cross Sophia's face.

"Sorry to break this up, but Nathaniel has instructed everyone retire early tonight in order to be rested for the Peridus," Cora said softly. "You all did remarkably well. I have instructed my Beasties to give each member from a different department a manual on creatures you may come in contact tomorrow so you can better prepare. You won't always have a Beastian nearby during Peridus."

"You guys feel like something sweet before turning in?" Sophia asked after the Beasties had handed out the manuals. Blake and Dax heartily nodded, Mercedes and Killian followed along, shyly glancing at one another and thinking of their almost kiss.

The friends finished up large bowls of sweet ice from the Glaciem ice quarries and were making their way out of the dim dining hall into the brightly lit steel hallway when they heard angry voices.

"I *will* stay out of your way, I assure you, but I have every right to be here," a deep growling voice echoed.

"I have always been disgusted vith your disrespect...you...you renegade!"

"That sounds like the Empress and...Egan," Killian whispered. They turned the corner and sure enough found the pale—for an Ignisian—Egan and the Empress standing close to one another, obviously furious to be in one another's presence.

"When are you going to *understand* Gwyniera? I was willing to change myself...to give up everything for—"

"Quiet you fool," Gwyniera angrily pointed to their gawkers standing by the wall.

"Chief Egan," Dax said stepping forward, and crossing a fist over his chest in a salute, "it is an honor, sir. I'm glad to see you are doing well."

Egan's blue flaming eyes acknowledged Dax and he gave him a curt nod, but then they fell on someone else. Egan stumbled backward slightly as he peered at Mercedes. He glanced back and forth between her and the Empress, with his mouth falling open.

"Pfft." The Empress sneered at Egan before stomping away out of sight.

"Are you alright sir?" Dax asked, confused by his Chief's behavior.

"I...I must be going...I will see...you all tomorrow at Peridus." Egan rushed the opposite direction, glancing once more at Mercedes before disappearing behind a wall.

"What was that?" Blake asked.

"Mercedes do you know Egan?" Sophia tapped her shoulder softly

"What? Why are you asking me, he was looking at all of us," she said defensively, "right Killian?"

Killian bit his bottom lip. "I'm sorry, but I think he *was* looking at you." He wished he hadn't spoke as Mercedes' eyes fell to the floor. "Hey, don't worry. Remember Maurelle said not to let the Empress get to you. Maybe Egan isn't used to seeing people from Terrene."

"You're Terrenian and so is Blake," she argued quietly.

"Well, true, but he's already met me and both our families have been part of the Ponderi forever." It didn't seem to appease Mercedes. "I don't know Mercedes, but don't let it bother you okay." He tilted her face toward him and smiled at her.

"Yeah, you can't take anything Ignisians do to heart," Sophia chimed in playfully.

"Come again?" Dax snorted.

"You heard me."

"That's it, Soph," he snarled, though his voice was friendly. "Tomorrow I am going to *destroy you*." He began walking pompously away from the group. "I had better get some rest, not that I'll need it."

"Are you kidding me? Daxton Ari Flint, I am going to bring those steamy little tears out of your eyes tomorrow just..." Their voices faded behind an elevator as they left to their rooms, arguing together.

"Those two need to just hook it up and be done with all this passive aggressive competition," Blake laughed. Mercedes even chuckled a little.

"Well, Kill are you coming? Des is on her floor already and we really should get some sleep." Killian turned and mouthed the nickname 'Des' to Mercedes, who rolled her eyes and waved as he and Blake entered the car and sped away to the recruit floor.

Once he arrived at his door, he had a sudden wave of exhaustion pile over him. Through the last three days of training, he had worked harder and learned more about every department in the Ponderi than he had in the entire two months he'd lived at the Praetorium.

He dragged his feet around his room, throwing his clothes in a messy heap on the floor. He figured the laundry fairies—at least that was their nickname to him—wouldn't appreciate the mess, but he was too tired to care. He pulled on a pair of baggy sweat pants and forwent the shirt. As he turned from his enormous closet, he stopped dead in his tracks.

A hooded figure in a deep blue robe was hunched over the large mahogany desk next to his open window. Killian's heart raced with fear but surprisingly felt only a sense of urgency as the figure slowly raised their shadowed head. Killian stood motionless in the doorway of his closet and could feel the eyes from the darkness pouring into him.

The mysterious figure raised a black gloved hand and tossed a white envelope onto his bed. Killian glanced quickly at the letter. With his attention off them, the figure darted through the window and disappeared into the greenish-orange night.

Killian collapsed against the doorframe as the fear fled from his body. He rushed over to the mysterious envelope wondering if it was wise to open the parcel. He thought to the emotions in the room, apart from his surprise and fear, he hadn't felt anything malicious. Still he wondered why the person would need to hide their face?

After several thoughtful moments, he tore open the thin paper and read a short, frightening message.

They know about Infinium. Peridus will bring enemies, be safe.

Chapter 15
The Peridus

The next morning, Killian's heart pounded and small beads of sweat fell from his head as he stepped into the training center. All around him Ponderi members were jolting with excitement at the opportunity to compete in the Peridus. Others, who had chosen not to participate, lined great steel bleachers that had been set up through the night, clapping and cheering for all the members below on the field. Killian glanced around the room, feeling anxious and jolted at every touch as people piled into the tight space. He couldn't shake the unnerving message from the night before.

The three realm leaders sat on the side of the athletic field that had huge gray curtains hiding something on the opposite side of the field. Egan still looked pale and uncomfortable, Maurelle sat in the center, thoroughly excited, and Gwyniera had her body turned away from Egan's direction, deliberately avoiding him. Killian knew there was something between the two leaders that he desperately wanted to find out, but also why they both had such opposite reactions around Mercedes in particular.

"Today is an exciting day!" Nathaniel announced across the athletic field after everyone was settled into hundreds of steel seats on the grass. "Those who have chosen to participate will be tested beyond your strength, but three of you will be named our winners. And one will gain the highest honor in the Ponderi and become a leader in their field, as well as access to many areas in the Praetorium currently off limits.

"The Peridus course will test you mentally, physically, and emotionally so do not take it lightly." Nathaniel smiled, obviously pleased with his coy explanation. "Everyone please make your way to the center of the field for the competition."

Killian followed the rest of the crowd, scanning for his friends. He smiled as he saw Dax, Sophia, Blake, and Mercedes huddled close together, also scanning the crowd for him; quickly he moved toward them.

"Killian, there you are," Mercedes said brightly. Her hair was pulled into a large ponytail full of intricate braids and loose curls, Killian thought she looked stunning but noticed she frowned as she scanned his face. "Are you alright?"

"Yeah, I'm fine," he answered. "I'll admit I'm a little nervous about today, but I'm fine." He didn't want to tell her about the note his mysterious visitor had left. She didn't need to worry about him while she was competing.

"Competitors," Nathaniel's voice sounded again, "turn your attention to the side of the field." As he spoke, the large curtains were sucked underneath the floor revealing enormous sets of obstacles. Killian gaped at the large ropes, the short steel beams and huge covered buildings concealing what was inside. The course appeared impossible to complete and a sinking feeling grew in Killian's stomach.

"If you fail at any point through the course you will be disqualified. You will be awarded points by several things: ability to progress through the course, speed and skill during each obstacle, and leadership. Do not waste time, or you may find you are unable to finish the course." The room was silent as the crowd and competing members contemplated what he meant. "Everyone line up at the starting point," Nathaniel directed. The long line of competing members followed his instruction. The murmurs had ceased as each member prepared mentally for the task. The initial task was a long line of ropes hanging next to one another. He assumed the idea was to swing between each rope without falling.

Killian wiped his sweaty palms on his pants, anxiously looking over his shoulder for any sign of a suspicious person. All he saw were the three realms leaders and Miller on their raised seats across the steel platform on the other side of the field. The crowd was booming as members cheered and chanted for their favorite competitors.

"On your marks…get set…GO!" Nathaniel shouted through his invisible microphone. A wave of energy passed through the field competitors. Ahead of him he saw hordes of members leaping for the thick ropes, several competitors fell onto the soft gel mats below after the first jump. Many slammed their fists in frustration and cursed for being disqualified so quickly. All too soon Killian was up on the steel platform standing behind Mercedes, waiting for his turn to take the plunge on the course.

Mercedes leapt gracefully off the platform and grasped the first rope with ease. She wrapped her dangling legs tight around the rope and released her hands. Killian sucked in his breath in disbelief as he watched Mercedes travel the length of the ropes like a Chinese acrobat, using both her legs and arms in a mystical, graceful way. When she landed on the other side, she smiled and gestured for Killian to follow her before she pranced energetically around a corner and out of his sight.

Taking a deep breath Killian reached for the first rope and swung from the platform, his muscles tensed and he easily dangled for a moment. Glancing at the spectators he saw every one of the leaders watching him close. With the extra pressure he swiftly made his way along the ropes, not near as impressive as Mercedes had done. His muscles ached, but on the last three ropes he swung much easier and leapt onto the other side without much trouble. Behind him, the pounding of boots on steel made him feel anxious as the fellow competitors were racing against the time.

He quickly rounded the corner until he crashed into the back of a stalled recruit. A large group had formed at the next stage in the course. He craned his neck searching for Mercedes and

225

thankfully found her standing next to Blake, Dax, and Sophia. They were huddled together pointing and discussing something. Killian slowly sauntered over to them and observed the obstacle.

Steaming water from the frigid temperatures spanned a large covered space in the course. On the other side of the pool three grand, marble staircases emerged from the icy water. The upper half of the grand stairs led upward until it disappeared behind a long thick, black curtain. The lower half was submerged deep into the pool. The only way to reach the staircases and continue on was to swim. There was no escaping the frigid pools.

"What do we do?" he asked his friends.

"We have to cross obviously," Sophia snapped. Killian chuckled. He didn't take her moods personally—Sophia wasn't one to handle stress well.

"I got that, I'm just trying to understand the three staircases, I thought you had to partner with someone on the pool. At least that's what we did during training."

"They've switched it on us, they want us to figure it out on our own," Blake added. "My guess is we need to pick *the right* staircase."

"Well, we're wasting time," Dax growled as he strapped his bow to his back. Killian reached his arm back to make sure his spear was tightly bound to him. "I say let's jump in as a group and figure it out as we go."

"The water is freezing," Killian argued. "We need to be organized. If there is ever a time to dive deep, I can be the diver. Mercedes, you are the quickest thinker you work on figuring out if it matters which staircase we take, you three," he said pointing to Dax, Sophia, and Blake. "You can fight off any surprises we might find in the water. If we wait too long in there, our body temperature will lower too much and they'll disqualify us." The rest of the group nodded their approval to his plan and stepped to the edge of the water. Other members had already jumped in and made their way to the staircase.

Killian winced as he observed a small girl from the engineering department clinging to the side, too frozen to move. Another engineer was trying to coax her to let go, but the girl wouldn't budge. Yellow flashing bulbs shone from her belt. He knew her body temperature was getting dangerously low, she would be disqualified in minutes. He turned his attention away from the poor girl unable to help her, took a deep breath, and plunged into the freezing pool.

The water struck him to his core and knocked the breath from his lungs. He hurriedly glanced around and found his friends huddled and temporarily stalled as their bodies adjusted to the shocking water. Within a few moments, he saw Blake point toward the bottom of the pool where dim, blinking lights were. Killian nodded and pointed to his chest and dove deeper. His head pounded and his lungs screamed for air, but he kept propelling through the water anxious to get out of the pool. When he reached the bottom, he saw the gold blinking lights were attached to silver, old-fashioned keys that were tied to a long bar fastened to the bottom of the pool. His lungs were burning and he knew he had to surface soon. Reaching toward a key he was angrily pushed out of the way. A tall, dark competitor shoved him and wrapped the key he'd been aiming for around his wrist. Killian pushed through an anxious crowd of competitors ignoring the poor behavior from the other member. Finally, he weakly grabbed a key and pushed his foot off the bar holding the keys and darted toward the surface.

The air was warm as his head broke through the glassy water. Filling his lungs with refreshing air, he scanned the frantic pool that was now filled with competitors anxiously trying to get out. He saw Dax's bright head along with Sophia at one of the staircases. Quickly he swam over to them, now upon closer inspection he could see the staircases were blocked by tall, metal fences. The metal was not typical Ponderi steel, but opposite; it was distressed with pockets of rust dotting the thick bars.

"Sophia, Dax," He shouted just as he saw Mercedes and Blake surface again.

"Killian," Dax responded, "the gate, toward the bottom is locked. There are three separate gates."

Killian bobbed right next to the group and held up the key. "These keys were at the bottom, do you think it will fit into the right gate?"

"That would be too easy to figure out which gate was the right one," Sophia said shaking her head. "I bet the keys will open any gate, but you take a risk of picking the wrong staircase."

"I don't think there is a wrong one," Mercedes chimed in. "Look some people have already gone through on the other two staircases."

She was right, competitors were spreading two gates open and several were running up the stairs before disappearing through the thick, black curtain. Killian watched and waited. The pool area was suddenly filled with shouts and screams from behind the curtain. Some competitors that had begun their trek up the marble staircase stopped and ran back toward the pool, not daring to run into the unknown.

Mercedes' mouth hung open in surprise. "It sounds like both of those gates are horrible, if there is a correct gate, we might be at the right one."

"Or they are all horrible," Dax seethed. "Guys we need to get going, look at the water…" Dax trailed off as they whipped their heads around. The water was lowering; something was draining the pool.

"Quick, Kill give me the key!" Blake shouted. "We need to get out of the pool or we're done."

Killian anxiously tossed Blake the key and he dove beneath the water. Dax swam to the gate and Killian followed so they would be ready whenever Blake surfaced again. Behind the two girls, other competitors huddled close anxious for Blake to surface again and for the gates to set them free from the freezing water and the whirlpool that was forming in the center of the pool. Although the leaders would keep the competitors safe, the daunting drain that was emptying the pool was intimidating. Especially since Killian had no idea what happened to competitors that didn't complete the Peridus, what if that is what his unknown enemies wanted, for him to get sucked away from the open and be left alone away from the protection of his friends and the leaders.

As soon as Blake's head broke through the water it pulled him from his wandering thoughts. Killian and Dax pulled and swam hard against the bars and opened the impressive, yet ancient-looking gate. The group swam, quickly followed by others, until their feet hit the smooth, slick marble steps.

Turning around they watched as the water level continued to lower. Competitors dotted the clear, blue pool trying to swim through the gate, but quickly the current grew too powerful and angrily pulled them out and away from their escape. It was horrifying to see them pulled under water through the giant whirlpool and out of sight. He shook his head from his place on the marble stairs as the others pounded up the steps. Killian's eyes widened as the water drained completely, but no competitors were left on the dry floor of the pool. The Peridus was revealing the Ponderi's vicious and horrifying sense of competing.

There was no time to stew any longer on the Ponderi and their methods. If he and his friends wanted to finish, they had to keep going or they would be in the same predicament.

"Hurry, up here," Mercedes shouted. The group darted up the slick stairway until they crossed through a dark curtain, hiding them from the spectators. Beneath the shroud, it was silent. They couldn't hear anything that was going on beyond the black tent which made it all the more unsettling. There were three other young girls with them, but they made no move to take the lead. Instead, they followed Killian and his friends, still shaking from the water...or perhaps nerves he didn't know.

"STOP!" Dax's voice bellowed through the dark room. Killian could barely make out his thick arm grabbing onto Sophia's shoulder. Sophia wrenched off the protective glasses she always wore, realizing she wouldn't need them in the dark. They both were looking down at the stairs where an entire marble slab was glowing in an eerie green color under Sophia's boot. Almost on cue with the glowing step, a hideous screech surrounded them.

"Weapons," Blake hissed. All of them grappled for their weapons. The three younger competitors screamed and tried to run from the awful noise. Mercedes breathed heavily as she stepped closer to him, anxiously waiting for the attack that was sure to come.

A shriek and the sound of wings filled the air overhead. In a whirl, two black wings passed above them and pounced upon the three fleeing competitors. The girls cried and screamed, begging for help, but all Killian could do was watch in horror as the winged creature carried them off into the darkness.

"Keep going, it might come back!" Dax commanded. They listened and darted up the steps, yet almost immediately the flapping wings filled the dark stair way again.

"Not this time!" He heard Sophia shout behind him and release one of her long steel arrows. A bone-chilling cry sounded and a hideous, winged creature fell with a solid thud from above them. Its face was horrifying with hundreds of beady eyes dotting a black, leathery face. It had a small black hole for a mouth and strong insect-like limbs attached to a solid black torso. The wings were ratty, but impressively thick and heavy.

When the creature hit the marble, it immediately disintegrated into nothing.

"Aranide!" Mercedes shouted. Lowering her voice, Killian was sure he was the only one who heard the rest. "They aren't supposed to be real, why would they be in Peridus? Don't let them take you." She shouted again at the group.

"Why…what are they?" Sophia's voice was frantic.

"They are like leeches, slowly draining your blood through your chest, directly over your heart."

"It isn't real guys, remember that," Blake said though his voice wavered. The creatures appeared real in every sense, even the wind from their wings, and the stench of their breath. "The stairs are rigged and signal attacks. I'm guessing it'll get worse as we get closer to the top, but we have to keep going. Sophia's stair had a small gold circle on it, watch for that mark or anything like it. Keep a sharp eye. Soph, you're the only one that can see in the dark, you have to help guide us. "

They quickly began the trek up the stairs again, fervently watching for any strange symbols on the staircase.

"Dax, your foot," Sophia cried moments later.

Killian could almost see Dax roll his bright, flaming eyes as he cursed, frustrated as he lifted his booted foot and revealed a subtle gold circle. Roars and screeches sang out behind them. It wasn't just one Aranide, it sounded like a flock. Hearing the low rumbling growl with the high pitched Aranide screeches, Killian knew the horrible leeches were joined by other creatures all too familiar to him.

"Malumians," he whispered, releasing both points on his spear. "And they aren't alone. It sounds like those winged freaks are with them."

They sprinted up the stairs, ignoring any sign of the cursed golden circles. Ghostly glows filled the dim, never-ending stairwell as they set off trap after trap. The wings and growls were added upon by patters of hoofed feet and deep roars of strange, deadly creatures.

"Mercedes!" Blake cried. "Help us know how to kill all these things."

Mercedes was swatting her hair against ugly, deformed rabbit-like creatures that were attempting to gnaw on her ankle and elbow joints. "These...are...Geyser elves. Their...fangs are...like needles...not dangerous just...*annoying*!" She bellowed giving a group of the elves a hard, swift kick, sending them screaming across the stairwell until they disintegrated into nothing. "Most of these are creatures that aren't supposed to be real. They are mythical," she explained as they continued up the stairs. "I heard Malumians and more Aranide. I think we have a few harpies, maybe some Pans by the hoof sounds—basically poisonous satyrs. Just keep running, they are dangerous and take skill and tricky shots to kill. Try not to engage anything, it will take too much time. Only attack if you have to!" She was breathless from shouting her instructions as they ran.

Glancing over his shoulder, Killian's heart sunk as he saw the blood red eyes of a pack of Malumians pounding up after him. Grasping tight to his spear he stopped and faced the vicious creatures, ignoring the horrid wings that flew above them. Though Mercedes advised them not to engage the creatures, there was no way to outrun everything. Maybe he would be able to buy his friends some time, even if he was disqualified.

Focusing on his targets he threw the spear as hard as he could, watching the sharp point lodge itself deep into the crown of the scabbed-headed leader. The wolf immediately disintegrated and the spear flew back to him. When the sleek rod was safe in his grip he turned and followed the others. Whistles of arrows sailed through the air passed his face, Sophia, Dax, and Blake had followed his lead and attacked the airborne Aranides. The distorted creatures burst into dust with each arrow, but the Malumians still pursued and the wings kept coming. Mercedes threw her blades at the wolves over her shoulders without even looking behind her; the knives hit two wolves square in the head, killing all the pursuing Malumians. He saw odd creatures slink from the darkness. Small, porcelain faces of young women built into small hawk-like bodies shrieked and aimed for their heads. Mercedes threw her daggers piercing both bird-women in the hearts. After they had disappeared, the hoof sounds began making their way back down the staircase away from the group. Hopefully, it meant the Pans were fleeing.

Low flapping sounds whirred over Killian's head.

"Everyone get down!" Blake screamed. On instinct Killian dropped to the stairs, relief flooding through him when Mercedes dropped next to him, but a high pitched scream chilled him.

"SOPHIA!" Dax's heart-wrenching cry filled the air. Looking up Killian saw one of the horrible Aranide wrapping its terrifying limbs around Sophia's torso and carrying her up into the pure blackness of the curtain until they could no longer see her.

His heart pounded in his chest. He was the one that was supposed to be taken, now Sophia was gone.

"No," Mercedes cried. Heavy sobs heaved through her body. "I don't want to go any further, this is horrible." She cried turning into Killian's shoulder.

"We're almost done," he comforted. "Look, there is light up ahead. Sophia, I'm sure, is fine." He said the words, but something warned him that the frightening creatures hadn't been after Sophia. He didn't know where the Aranide had taken her, but he had to believe she was fine if he was going to continue.

"Dez, Kill, hurry something's happening. We have to keep going!" Blake and Dax were sprinting up the last remaining stairs toward the brightness. Killian grasped tightly to Mercedes' hand and pulled her up with him. They ran two stairs at a time until they made it to the top of the horrifying stairwell.

At the top, they could see a line of large steel doors, but behind them the floor was separating them from the doors. Something told him this was the final task, and all they needed to do was get across.

"Hurry, we have to go now!" Killian shouted at Mercedes. He held her hand tightly and they sprinted to the splitting floor. The gap was large and presented a real risk of them falling into the crevice. At the same time, they both pushed off the smooth marble and soared through the air.

The air was knocked out of him when he slammed against the side of the open floor, his legs dangling over the gaping hole. Mercedes screamed. She hadn't made it all the way and now dangled from his hand over a wide, endless black space.

"Killian, Killian!" she screamed frantically trying to grip him tighter. "Don't...don't let me go."

"Hang on, I've got you," He said trying desperately to pull himself up. He could feel Mercedes slipping. "Hang on Mercedes." His heart pounded as he watched competitors from the other two stairwells leaping and falling short of the wall and disappearing down the deep crevice.

"Killian, I'm slipping!" Before he could do anything, her smooth hand slipped from his own.

"No, Mercedes!" He watched as she sped toward the blackness, screaming until she disappeared from his gaze. Killian wanted to let go and fall after her, but two hands reached under his arms and pulled him over the edge.

"Mercedes fell!" he cried into Blake's face. "Let me go."

"Kill, no," Blake said firmly. "We need to keep going! She's going to be okay, come on we're almost done."

Blake dragged Killian with Dax's help toward the steel doors. He looked around at the small group of remaining competitors. There was Lucan, Sam that he'd met on the rock walls, a boxy looking girl with blonde hair and a permanent scowl on her face, and small Ann who had cried for him during his first knife fight with Lucan.

As he gasped for breath trying to get his emotions in check, the doors opened wide and a robotic female voice spoke to them.

"Finalists will enter the simulation through their own door. Please step forward now."

Killian stood straight, desperate to end this mad, horrifying tournament and find Mercedes and Sophia. Taking a shaky step, he walked through one of the dim doorways into a dark room. The door behind him slammed shut and he was alone.

Chapter 16
The Simulation

Silence encircled Killian and it was deafening. His hands were clammy and his heart beat furiously in his chest. Stepping across a high threshold thick, warm, syrupy fluid poured from somewhere above him. Killian choked and coughed as the bitter liquid flowed into his mouth and down his throat. He wiped his eyes as it began burning, but with every clean swipe of his hand a new rush of liquid replaced it.

The syrup was tacky and rank. After a moment, a quiet beep sounded through the room followed by the robotic voice. "Subject assessment complete. Please step forward."

Fast, furious puffs of air covered Killian's body from all directions. He felt the wisps tousle his hair and clothing. Just as soon as the puffs had begun they ended, and the sticky liquid was gone with them. He held his hand close to his face. It was amazing. Not even a small amount of residue was left on his skin.

Bringing his gaze to the empty room, he quickly grabbed the rod behind his back. Holding the closed spear brought him a small sense of security since he had no idea what to expect in the simulator. With each step, the room lightened until it glowed with a soft ghostly light. It was eerie and empty apart from the surrounding walls covered in enormous mirrors; from every direction he saw his reflection. As far as he could tell he was completely alone, but in the same moment a loud scream filled the room. Behind him, he saw two figures in the mirrors. His jaw clenched as a familiar voice rang into his ears screaming his name.

Laura held her hands over her face defensively as Richard hit her. He shook his head, clenching his eyes shut, inwardly wishing for the screams to stop. This wasn't real, he couldn't face this again.

Richard's wicked laugh echoed off the walls. "Looking to be a hero?" His contorted expression looked despicable in the dim lighting as he laughed at Killian's shocked expression and wiped a thin trail of Laura's blood on his pants.

The words stung him; it was the same disgusting scene he'd lived through during their last encounter. Laura's sobs churned his stomach as he glanced down at her. Her nose was bleeding, her thin wire framed glasses rested bent on her nose and her eyes pleaded for help.

"Stop him, Killian, please help me."

Richard's swift hand flew across her cheek loudly, silencing her pleas. Killian jumped at the sound and without thinking he released both ends of his spear and stepped in front of Laura.

"Enough," he seethed at Richard.

Throwing his head back, Richard laughed loudly. "You are really going to step in front of this *disgusting whore*? I thought you were smarter than that. Would she do the same for you, boy?" His brown eyes turned black as his gleeful smile twisted into a malicious sneer. "Remember what she did?"

Richard stepped directly in front of his face and shoved him hard. His skin burned from the blow; it seemed real and it unnerved every sense of him. He didn't know what to make of it, this was supposed to be simulated; he didn't expect to feel the touch. Richard's words tore through him. Even if he was a despicable person, he was right about Laura. She had thrown him to the darkness of the world for trying to help her and protect her. She had sworn to defend him as a mother would her child, yet she failed. She chose to live in fear of Richard rather than stand for the truth and Killian's life was forever changed because of it.

He began lowering his spear as he considered what Richard was saying. The man chuckled.

"That's right boy, you don't owe her anything. Just leave it alone."

Killian glared up at the man he had hated for most of his life. Somewhere in the back of his mind he knew Richard wasn't with him—it wasn't real. Yet, the man standing before him had the same ugly demeanor, the same rage pulsing through his veins as the Richard he had always known.

"No, Richard," he shouted gripping his spear tighter than before, the anger and bitterness couldn't be bridled. He was standing before a shadow from his past, and now was the time to face it. "No matter what happened before, you are done hurting her. You are nothing but a spineless, worthless man, and you have no control over me anymore."

He pointed his spear at the man, and as he stood his ground the image of Laura faded. She was gone; Killian faltered for a moment and took his attention from Richard and immediately a strong hand met his jaw and sent him reeling to the floor. His spear flew across the sleek steel beyond his reach. Richard's heavy footsteps walked toward his head and he heard the cock of a gun. Killian's breath caught in his throat. What would happen if he was killed in the simulator, would it just end? Would he actually die?

"You should have stayed out of it, boy. I'll never stop, you see. I'll *always* have control over you. *You're weak.*" Richard's voice was barely above a whisper.

Killian breathed deeply, feeling the gun against his temple. His mind whirred trying to devise a way out of the situation. Racking his brain and his memories, he thought of Richard, *he* was weak and hid behind the threat of his words and weapon. Killian wanted to destroy the man; he wanted to wipe him from existence and never see him again. His mind drifted to memories as a small child of drunken Richard. He remembered wearing long sleeves to cover the deep bruises from his strong hands. He remembered the screaming, the missed school days while cuts and bruises healed, no one defended him or protected him. This man stole his childhood and it brought a fresh, emotional wave of fury over him.

In a split decision, Killian rolled away from Richard toward his spear. He heard the loud crack of the gun firing but kept running. Finally reaching the steel rod he held the spear in his hand angrily. Richard approached him laughing and pointing his gun at Killian's face.

"You really think you stand a chance against me with your little toy?"

Killian took a step toward Richard and sneered as he thrust the sleek rod into his upper thigh, then he ripped it angrily out of the simulated Richard's skin. The blow caused the man to stumble and cry out in pain as he covered his wound with his hand. The gun fell and quickly Killian kicked it away.

Richard lay on his back, panting in exertion and holding his bleeding leg, chuckling maniacally. Killian tried to resist the urge but swiftly kicked Richard hard in the ribs. He felt a sick crushing of bone against the sole of his boot. Richard laughed harder.

"Are you going to kill me, boy? Do it, maybe you can finally be *worth* something!" Richard spat.

Killian squeezed his eyes shut trying to block him out. *Remember it's a test, don't listen to him.*

"Come on…do it! You believe I deserve it. I probably do," he said nonchalantly.

Killian wanted to silence him with his spear but the man was defenseless against him. He *did* deserve it, Killian truly believed that, but the glint of joy in his eye caused him to waiver. What kind of person would he become if he gave in to the frightening urge to harm Richard? The shadow of Richard was a lunatic and taunted him—trying to get him to lower himself to his level.

238

Killian looked down at his spear, then back at Richard. His black eyes had lost the wild joy and now they stared at Killian with intrigue and wonder on how he would act. Killian pursed his lips and pushed the button on his spear, returning the points to the hollow rod.

"No, Richard. I'm not like you. You aren't worth it."

Immediately the image of Richard's sneering face faded. His twisted face screamed curses and shouts at Killian. He spewed horrid names that made his stomach twist from painful memories. After a few moments the shouts and chaos stopped. The room was empty again. Killian kneeled in the center of the room as emotion came over him. His body trembled as he struggled to keep Richard's voice and words from his mind. He felt angry, not at Richard and Laura, but at the simulation and Ponderi. He couldn't understand why it would be necessary to bring up such difficult memories he'd desperately wished to push away.

Behind him a wall rose, revealing a large doorway. Nathaniel's silhouette stood before him.

"Well done my boy," he said clapping his hands together. "Well done."

Killian glared up at Nathaniel. He respected the man, but he couldn't help but feel angry he'd allowed such a simulation to take place. He wiped a stray tear from his face, embarrassed the older man may see his emotion.

"Is the simulation over? Or are you part of it?" he asked.

Nathaniel chuckled. "No, I'm not a simulation. It's over, and you passed with flying colors. Killian my boy, you demonstrated such restraint, *such control* in a perilous, emotional situation. You are the first to successfully complete the simulation, but the judges are still deliberating on the final scores for the entire competition. I've come to take you to a waiting room while they score the remaining competitors." Nathaniel paused and smiled kindly at Killian. "Killian, never in my years have I witnessed such strength. I am very impressed my boy, very impressed." Nathaniel placed his hand on his shoulder and looked at him with sincerity in his twinkling gray eyes.

Nathaniel directed Killian out the large door and into the hallway. Through the walls, he could hear the rumble of the crowd. His hands were shaking and he suddenly felt exhausted. Nathaniel grabbed tight to his elbow, sensing his weakness as they walked in front of a plain, steel door.

"Step inside, Killian," Nathaniel directed. "I'll get you something to drink, you must be exhausted."

Killian just nodded and obeyed. Inside the room, there were no windows, only tall lamps standing in each corner casting white light around the cool room. The furniture was sharp, angled and modern with no cushions on the chairs, only cool steel. Nathaniel opened up a large steel cabinet door and took out a glass pitcher of water with a small mug. He handed Killian the drink, which he gulped down. The water soothed his scratchy, dry throat; he hadn't realized how thirsty he was. Killian wasn't even aware of the time, but by the way his body was aching and fading he was sure the Peridus had taken several hours.

"Feel better?" Nathaniel asked.

He nodded. "Yes, thank you, sir."

"Good." Nathaniel walked around and sat in the chair alongside him.

Killian's eyes scanned the dull room then drifted back to Nathaniel, who was looking at him with a slight smile painted on his face. Killian shrunk under his gaze.

"Sir, aren't you one of the judges? You said they were deliberating."

"After seeing the rigorous course, I felt I may be needed to assist the finalists after the simulation, so I opted out of the judge's seat this year."

Killian nodded slowly. "Do you need to go get the others now?"

240

Nathaniel cleared his throat and then sat down next to him on a small steel stool, ignoring the question.

"I'm curious, Killian…why did you let that despicable man in your simulation live? You had a chance to take out your fury on a simulated version of your enemy. Yet, you didn't take it."

Killian was surprised by the question. He took another gulp of the water and set the mug down on the steel table in front of him. "I…I don't know what you mean sir? Why *would* I kill Richard?"

Nathaniel smirked, his gray eyes twinkling again. "Why? Killian, the man nearly murdered you *and* his wife, then allowed you to go to jail for a crime you never committed. And the woman," Nathaniel threw his hands in the air dramatically, "she sat by while he did it, and *you defended* her simulation still. I am curious as to why you would protect such a person. Not many people would show that type of restraint, or submission depending on how you look at it." Nathaniel stood and began pacing in front of Killian.

"Is there anything wrong with what I did in my simulation?"

"No, Killian," Nathaniel said, his face showed disappointment. "There was nothing extraordinary about the simulation whatsoever, except for one thing. Your simulations were solid, most are just holograms, but your images were physically there with you, making it more lifelike and more intense. I can only assume it was a side effect of Infinium."

Nathaniel said the words with a surprising bitterness. Killian wasn't sure if he was disappointed the simulator had acted differently for him, or upset that it had been the *only* strange aspect to his simulation. It did solve his question as to why Richard had been able to physically touch him. He glanced at Nathaniel, who was scowling at the ground, not paying him any attention.

"Is everything alright sir?" His heart was beating faster again. Something seemed off about the older man. Nathaniel pursed his lips and smirked at Killian.

"I was hoping to witness the full potential of Infinium, but you allowed your inferior weaknesses to dull the power."

Killian gulped and stood from his chair, slowly he backed away from his mentor and friend. "Weakness? I don't understand."

"You're *weak*, my boy. Instead of destroying —no, obliterating your abusers when you had a chance, you allowed them to manipulate you and use you again. You have more power in your veins than any living being in the Hemisphere, yet you cowered like a frightened child when Richard raised his voice to you. Since the simulation produced physical manifestations, I truly wasn't sure if the simulation would be able to terminate you or not. I thought for a moment you would allow him to kill you. But you backed away and somehow it ended your simulation, which helped me since I didn't want you to die in that room, my boy. Even still, it was disappointing you did not accept the fight."

"Nathaniel I…think we should be getting back. I think Sophia and Mercedes may have been injured during the Peridus, I'd like to see them."

"No Killian. I think we shall stay right here," Nathaniel said hungrily as he unsheathed a vicious dagger Killian hadn't noticed before from behind his back. "I'm sorry my boy. I didn't want it to be this way, but after discovering what Infinium is capable of and witnessing the tedious display of your simulation…I believe you truly don't have what it takes to use the power and in these perilous times Infinium needs to be harnessed by someone with more strength. I'm doing you a favor my boy, the odds are against you. You wouldn't be strong enough to withstand Infinium mentally."

"Nathaniel stop, you don't know everything about Infinium…you can't—"

"Shut up!" he shouted. "I know *everything*. Your little friend, Dalia, spilled it all to me."

Killian breathed harder. Dalia wouldn't betray him would she?

"Of course she didn't do it willingly," Nathaniel continued.

Killian gulped with the realization that Nathaniel must have done something to her. Nathaniel laughed and lunged toward him. Killian felt as if his feet had stones tied to them; he couldn't move. The dagger cleanly swiped along the side of his neck as he tried to dodge the attack at the last minute. Killian cried out in pain and fear and fell to his knees. Immediately he saw dark red blood pouring over his shoulder and down his arm from the large wound on his neck.

"You might as well stop resisting, my boy."

"It was you," Killian gasped, fruitlessly covering the gushing cut with his palm. "You stole the relic, didn't you? You're a member of the Trinity."

Killian reached for his spear, but Nathaniel's hand reached the rod first. The older man plucked his weapon from his leather strap and threw it across the room.

"Do you think if I had stolen the relic you would still be alive? The bond would have killed you. No, I sent the Malumians so you *would be brought* here. I needed you here so you would find the relic; the bond would lead you right to it eventually. I had no idea I would receive the added bonus of Infinium. I should have followed my instinct and killed you when we discovered your grandmother's hideaway. You would've been much easier to kill as a child before you absorbed it. I had always planned on killing you later on, Ignisia was my best opportunity, but it too failed."

"I don't understand," Killian panted. His heart beat against his chest like a wild drum.

"I created the rumor a Trinity spy was jumping to Ignisia, hoping to alert the Deshuits. Then of course, I had Eva arrange her own plan on how to kill you if the Deshuits didn't. It was a little theatrical with the poison juice, but no matter it failed and here we are."

Killian's mind was swimming, either from blood loss or shock he wasn't sure.

"Can you imagine how frustrated I was for delaying your death after learning the Relic was missing?" Nathaniel hissed.

"Especially after I had told the Architect of the Trinity we should've acted years ago. Now it's lost." Nathaniel's tone came out as if Killian should feel sorry for the man for missing his window of opportunity.

Skillfully he swung the dagger again, this time across Killian's stomach. The man moved so quickly with his weapon, Killian had no time to defend himself. He held his hand over his bleeding abdomen. Fear crippled him. Nathaniel had been the one person he thought he would always be able to trust, and he was trying to kill him. The man had skills Killian was sure he couldn't even imagine, there was a reason he was the Ponderi director, and he didn't know how he could out fight him.

"It will be less painful if you just let me drain Infinium from you."

"It's too hard to do...you won't be able to...get it all," Killian gasped as his open wounds seared against one another with every movement.

"My dear boy, you really believe I haven't done my homework," Nathaniel chuckled and lunged again. This time, Killian moved swift enough and missed the dagger. He darted for the door they'd entered but found no handle on the inside. "It's no use, my boy. It only opens with my touch."

Killian turned around. Fear combined with fierce betrayal filled his body. He was angry and wanted to fight back, but he knew Nathaniel was intentionally draining him slowly, with every minute his blood was seeping out. He wanted as many openings as possible to drain his blood to obtain Infinium. He decided the best way to fight back would be to stall him, until he could find a way out of the room.

"You took me from my grandmother...did you kill my parents?" Killian panted trying to keep the man focused elsewhere.

Nathaniel scowled at him and repositioned his long dagger in his other hand. "I wish I could say I had. If I had killed them, I *would have* the Relic. Your parents were our finest relic hunters. When they discovered the relic, Rhetta had Dalia inspected it after it was found. Your grandmother told me Dalia believed there was something more powerful inside the relic. After that, I knew I had to get it. Originally I had intended to only kill your father since he was the guardian. Your parents were faster than me and transferred the guardianship to you before I had a chance." Nathaniel swiped the dagger again, slicing open Killian's shoulder; he'd dodged too slow again. He cried out in pain and frustration. He was losing blood and feeling the effects. Soon he wouldn't be able to move at all—he would be too weak.

"Then your parents went and blew themselves up and your wretched grandmother ran with you and the relic."

"Well…then…it's your fault you don't have it. You…let me and my grandmother live."

"Killian," he said wildly swinging the dagger, nicking Killian's wrist as he held it up to protect his face. "When you are trying to covertly steal something, you can't just go around killing women and children. Miller was far too close to you…watching you and making sure you were protected. Trust me I tried to have Rhetta executed, but Miller and other council members in the Praetorium overturned my vote and banished her instead. I should never have let your family be involved in your protection, Miller only got in the way." Nathaniel glared in anger at the memory. .

"But…" Killian began, circling the furniture avoiding Nathaniel. Suddenly he heard faint pounding on the walls outside the room. Nathaniel seemed to hear it too and immediately pounced on Killian, pinning him hard against the wall. He dug his sharp point into the other side of Killian's neck. Killian's eyes were blurring against the burning pain. He could feel the warm blood seeping out of his neck and down his other arm. He looked at his gray shirt, it was soaked in hot, fresh blood. "If…you kill me…you won't…fi…find the relic," he whispered close to Nathaniel's face.

Nathaniel swung his hand hard across Killian's jaw, causing him to spit blood. Pulling a clump of Killian's short, mud-colored hair Nathaniel pushed his bearded face close to Killian's. "I won't need you to find the relic once I have Infinium."

He released his hair harshly and Killian landed hard on the steel floor. He could feel himself fading into unconsciousness, slowly drifting. Nathaniel held a small glass jar next to his neck as he began collecting his flowing blood by painfully pressing along the gashes.

Killian's mind drifted to different thoughts. He pictured Mercedes, he hoped she would miss him…he smiled even if it was a selfish thought. He thought of Blake, Dax, and Sophia. They were his truest friends and hoped they wouldn't see him after Nathaniel was finished, he imagined it would be gruesome. Something inside him burned, part of him had resigned to death, but there was a strange desire inside that urged him to fight…to survive.

The burning was becoming unbearable as he watched Nathaniel straddle across his mid-section and raise the blood-stained dagger over his throat. He heard shouts from beyond the walls, but he knew his rescuers would be too late. Nathaniel was being careful not do damage the heart so it would continue pumping blood even after death for a few seconds. Killian moaned in agony as the fiery sensation filled his veins; he felt he may die from the burning if Nathaniel didn't finish the job soon. The back of his neck bubbled and seared. Killian closed his eyes trying to be calm before he was murdered, and also to block out the pain that had moved to his skin.

"I'm sorry, my boy," Nathaniel said greedily. Everything seemed to slow down; Killian convinced himself he could hear each ragged breath as Nathaniel shamelessly aimed to take his life. He could almost hear the whistle of the dagger flying through the air toward his exposed throat. This was it.

"What…is…hap…" Nathaniel's voice came out with a struggle. Killian dared crack his eyes open slightly. He saw Nathaniel's dagger inches away from his neck, but it had stopped. Opening his eyes wider to see what had blocked it, his breath stopped—*he* had been the one that had halted the attack. His blood soaked arms were holding tight to Nathaniel's wrists. Nathaniel quivered in exertion as he fought against Killian's sudden strength.

Yet, with all Nathaniel's exertion, Killian felt no pressure, as if holding Nathaniel at bay took no effort.

Fight back!

Something inside him, a voice clearly not his own, urged him to defend himself. With all his strength, Killian pushed back against Nathaniel. The older man exploded off his body and landed in a sick position a great distance across the room. Killian couldn't believe what he'd just done. He heard Nathaniel groan and try to move his twisted leg, but it was bent in the opposite direction, clearly broken. The older man looked at Killian in bewilderment. His eyes widened as Killian pursued him. In a final effort, Nathaniel raised his arm with his dagger and threw the weapon as hard as he could, and with great accuracy.

Somehow, something told him that he could stop the dagger if he wanted. He didn't have to die here. He knew Nathaniel was using his personal bond with the weapon to hit him with a direct shot, but Killian knew beyond reason that somehow he could overpower even Nathaniel's bond with his weapon.

"Stop," Killian shouted at the dagger. He felt ridiculous but knew he could control it. He wanted to see the dagger disappear, it was too much of threat to him and had done too much damage already. As if on cue the sleek, red-tinted dagger burst in midair into fine silver dust and flurried across the sleek floor. Killian turned on Nathaniel and darted over to him. The older man's eyes were filled with fear for the first time since he'd taken him from the simulator.

Killian wrapped his abnormally strong hand around Nathaniel's neck and pinned him against the wall. He glared furiously at the man that had tried to kill him. With each heaving breath, he pressed harder against Nathaniel's throat slowly feeling his tendons and muscles strain against the pressure. Killian's neck prickled with heat again, but it wasn't painful this time, it was comforting and felt natural.

"Are you…going…to kill me now? I'm not…the only enemy…here," Nathaniel gasped in a hoarse whisper, but still found energy to give him a malicious grin.

247

Killian's scowl softened. He loosened his grip on Nathaniel's neck. What was he doing? He didn't want to kill the man. He remembered how it felt to take a life; and the thought of experiencing the torment of killing again outweighed his anger and fury. And the threat of others in the Praetorium that could harm him caused his head to pound. He needed Nathaniel alive—for answers. Nathaniel crumpled to the cool floor when Killian released his grasp. The older man gasped anxiously for air just as the door burst open in a furious blast of light.

Maurelle, Blake, and Egan stood in the destroyed doorway. Maurelle's stunned expression rested upon a crumpled Nathaniel, but Blake and Egan were gawking at Killian and his multiple wounds. As if their attention to his injuries triggered his own weakness he suddenly felt faint from his blood loss. He stumbled and reached for a nearby chair to steady himself.

The trio rushed over to him, Egan and Blake steadying Killian and Maurelle inspecting Nathaniel.

"Killian, stay awake man," Blake pleaded as Killian's head rolled to one side. "Kill, what happened? Come on buddy stay awake."

"Nathaniel...tried....to...Infinium," Killian said weakly as all the burning energy he'd had fighting against Nathaniel seeped out of him with the flowing blood from his wounds. He noticed through his half-open eyes Blake looked back at Maurelle as her silver eyes blazed in anger. He hoped from her expression they understood what he had tried to tell them.

Egan and Blake dragged Killian into the hallway. Curious Ponderi members were crowding around them, trying to figure out what had happened. He heard a girl scream as Killian made his way in front of the spectators. He could imagine what he looked like with blood pouring from every inch of his body and his mouth from the blow to the jaw.

"Blake, Egan...what happened?" He heard Miller's faint voice, desperately trying to gain information.

"Nathaniel," Egan's burly voice answered. "Tried to take the boy's power. We assume that is what happened at least." Miller said nothing more. Killian closed his eyes, all he wanted to do was sleep, but Blake kept pushing his head up, desperate to keep his friend awake.

"Killian! Killian!" His eyes snapped open at the familiar voice. Mercedes was shrieking above the loud surrounding crowd. He glanced toward the sound and saw her pushing her way viciously through the crowd. Killian stood straighter, feeling the comforting, tingle of the once painful burn pulsing in his veins and helping him gain strength. He just wanted to see Mercedes, the last image he had was her falling through a black hole. He used what little energy he had and gently pushed Blake and Egan off him and stumbled toward her.

"Mercedes," he gasped hoarsely. In a short moment, he felt Mercedes pull him against her and help balance him with her body. He felt her sobs as she cried.

"Killian, what happened...are you alri—" She didn't have time to finish. Killian took her face between his hands and furiously pushed his lips onto hers. He held her close to him, feeding off her energy and breathing in every inch of her. She strengthened him. And though he knew he needed help soon, he never wanted to let her go. Finally, he felt his feet giving out from underneath him. Mercedes pulled away and slowly lowered him to the ground, stroking his face. He smiled up at her, she had splotches of his own blood on her lips and cheeks, with fresh tears carving defined streaks along her skin.

Egan and Blake joined next to him. His eyes were fading to darkness and all the murmurs and shouts blurred together until everything faded to black.

Chapter 17

Secrets of the Praetorium

Pale pink light caressed Killian's face. He squinted against the brightness and tried to sit up, but soon wished he hadn't. The side of his neck and abdomen screamed against tightly sutured skin. Slowly he lifted the scratchy clinic gown and peered over the wound on his middle. The scar was jagged, pink and hideous.

"You lost a lot of blood with your wounds," Shannon's kind voice filled the room as she walked in holding a small cup of water. Embarrassed he quickly covered himself up. Shannon chuckled and placed the water on his bedside table. "I don't know how you stayed conscious as long as you did. Nathaniel is an expert weapon handler and knows exactly where to cut to drain blood the fastest." She gave Killian a sympathetic look. "Honestly you almost didn't survive, even with Infinium, your blood loss was frightening. Both sides of your Carotid artery were cut. Any deeper he would have severed them and you would have bled out in a minute. Maurelle had to bond some of her powerful energy to you. It was unconventional, but I'm glad she did it. You were taken off IV's yesterday since your vitals stabilized beautifully." She sat down and raised the gown to inspect the stomach wound again.

"Maurelle did what?"

Shannon frowned as she pushed and prodded the hideous scar. Eventually she brushed her fingers on the back of his neck, pushing and prodding and gawking for some reason before she answered his question.

"You've learned about Cimmerian magic, the Queen holds some of the most powerful energy in the Hemisphere, so she shared some with you. It was very taxing on her. Be sure and thank her when you get a chance." Killian smiled as Shannon's motherly tone took over. "The abdomen scar will get better with time. It was so deep the suture light had to be used several different times. I was afraid I would have to do needle and thread stitches. It's been such a long time, you would probably look like a patched up monster."

"How long have I been sleeping?"

"About seventeen hours. You blacked out shortly after leaving the training center, but you arrived at the clinic just in time." She glanced at her impressive rose gold watch before continuing. "I think you'll be clear to leave here in a couple hours. Can I get you anything before I report to the others on your condition?"

"Uh…" he stammered, embarrassed. "Can you let Mercedes…and my friends know I'm okay?"

Shannon smiled. "Yes, of course. You will need to go meet with Miller and the visiting leaders after you're discharged here. So please don't run off looking for anyone else," she glowered sternly at him, knowing exactly what he was thinking and where he wanted to go. "I mean it Killian. The leaders must speak with you about the incident."

"Okay, okay," he said holding up his hands. "I promise I'll go right upstairs when you clear me."

"Alright, good. Now remember, things happened in that room; events that may have lasting effects…so don't stress too much okay." She looked into his eyes warily. Killian just nodded, not sure what she was saying.

Just as Shannon had promised, two hours later he was dressed in fresh clothes and painfully making his way to the upper floor. With each step, his skin stretched and pulled shooting referred pain all over his torso. Shannon had patched up his shoulders and neck to help cover the ugly gashes though they weren't as painful as his stomach. The throbbing in his jaw where Nathaniel had hit him didn't help either.

Killian made it to the brilliant cherry door and sauntered in to the huge room. The leaders were all anxiously perched in their own seats. Dalia was included in the group too and Killian met her eye with a forceful gaze. She looked exhausted and ragged, which reminded him Nathaniel had done something to her to gain information. He wanted to speak with her and hear what had happened, but it would have to wait.

"Killian," Miller said in a hoarse voice. "Come in, please sit down." Miller held onto his arm as if he needed help sitting on the white overstuffed chair. The old man's face was tired and sad. Killian felt sorry for the man, he too had experienced a great betrayal. Everyone in the Praetorium had explained that Nathaniel and Miller had been close friends for nearly fifty years.

"How are you feeling?" Maurelle's smooth voice asked in a hushed tone, breaking him from his thoughts.

Killian turned and tried his best to smile at the queen. "Much better, Your Highness, just a little sore. Shannon told me what you did to help me, thank you." Maurelle beamed her perfect teeth and gave him a small nod in return.

"Dalia," he whispered across Maurelle to the shaken woman. Dalia turned slowly and gave him a weak smile. "Are you alright?"

She nodded slowly. "Forgive me for being weak, Killian."

Maurelle leaned in toward Killian's ear and whispered to him. "The wretched man burned her with bright lights, nearly blinding her." Killian gulped as he noticed on closer inspection burn marks all along Dalia's temples and eyebrows.

"After what you've been through, Killian," Miller began, interrupting his dialogue with the Queen. "We are thankful you are here with us." Killian choked back emotion and looked at the floor.

"Do you need me to tell you what happened?" He didn't know why the question slipped out, but found he was quite anxious about being asked to relive the experience. There was too much he couldn't explain. He still had no idea how he overpowered Nathaniel but was suspicious that Infinium had something to do with it.

"No," Miller gave the soft reply. "Maurelle extracted the memory for us while you were unconscious. We hope you don't mind the invasion, but we had to know how to proceed with Nathaniel."

"Thanks," he said again to Maurelle.

Miller stood and began pacing in front of the group. "Nathaniel isn't talking. I admit I never saw this coming, he was always so concerned for your safety and well-being." Miller turned and looked at Killian directly in the eye. "Killian I promise, if I'd had any inkling Nathaniel was seeking Infinium for himself I would never..."

Miller trailed off, his voice catching on emotion. Killian smiled. During his time in the Praetorium, it had been Nathaniel that had shown him more of a fatherly affection, it was refreshing to know Miller cared for him too. He still wondered about his relationship with his family though and hoped to get answers soon.

"I know sir," he told the man. "No one saw this coming. It isn't your fault."

"Vell, I vould like to know vat za next plan of action is," Gwyniera's harsh voice filled the room. "Nazaniel is a traitor, true, but zat also means za Trinity is desperate for za relics. How vill ve find zem first?"

"The Empress is right, the relics must be our first priority," Maurelle agreed. "Killian is the Cimmerian relic guardian, which should be the easiest to find. And by easy I mean very difficult, but the others without the bond of a guardian are impossibly difficult to locate."

Miller glanced at Killian, a glimmer of hesitation crossed his face. "Killian, we as a council have been working to figure out a plan of action for the relics, I'm afraid not all of us agree."

"I thought we needed to search for the relics. I thought since I had the bond and with Infinium, even if it's dormant, I would help find the Cimmerian relic." He noted the Queen and Dalia glanced at one another. Gwyniera stared at Miller in exasperation, but Miller's face was stone. Killian couldn't understand why the man didn't want to search for the relics, or perhaps Miller didn't want *him* to search for the relics.

"Would you please excuse Killian and myself for a moment. There are some things I'd like to discuss with him." Dalia immediately obeyed as if she were grateful for the opportunity to leave Killian's presence. Maurelle nodded, but had a look of slight irritation. Still, she left with a floating grace through the door. Gwyniera left with her nose in the air and not a backward glance at Killian.

When the door closed, Killian looked at Miller awkwardly. The older man stood in front of the grand window that seemed to be his peaceful place. Whenever Miller tried to gather his thoughts he always stared at the unusual greenish-orange sun as it bobbed in the unique atmosphere surrounding the Praetorium.

"Sir, is there a reason why you don't want my help with the relics?" Killian was surprised at the bitter undertone in his voice. He couldn't help it. He felt his insides harden; he was angry that a man who hadn't shown faith in his abilities was still trying to hold him back. After Nathaniel's betrayal he wanted to stop the Trinity even more; he'd seen what they were capable of.

"Miller," he raised his voice at the old man, "answer me!"

Intense, heart-wrenching guilt and anxiety overwhelmed him. Killian toppled to his knees, it had been a long time since he'd been so overwhelmed with emotions, but he never remembered the sensation to be so debilitating. He gasped for breath and tried to gather his senses. Miller bent down and helped him off the ground. His dull blue eyes were misted with tears. Killian clutched his chest, he didn't know how to function with the searing pain of sorrow flowing through his body.

"Don't fight it, Killian. I'm sorry, I can't help how I feel. I know it's uncomfortable for you, especially now, but accept it in and it will get easier." Killian's eyes widened, Miller had never acknowledged he knew anything about the odd happenings of his dormant power, but he tried to listen.

"How did you know I was feeling something?" Killian gasped as the discomfort lifted. Miller gave him a small smile.

"I know a great deal about you, Killian. I know you think I'm trying to keep you back from your potential and I don't blame you for being frustrated, but... I also know how desirable Infinium is. It was enough to corrupt my oldest, dearest friend. I would selfishly ask you to...please reconsider fighting against the Trinity." The old man looked at him with pleading eyes, yet somehow Killian sensed that Miller knew he would have to find the relics.

"I'm not going to be the only one looking for them, but sir, for months now you and others have told me about the bond with the relic. I'm the logical choice to find at least one of them. Maybe we can find the other guardians and they can help find the remaining two." Killian spoke softly, still confused at Miller's strange request.

Miller nodded. "I just...can't lose you too...like...like I lost your mother."

Killian gaped at the man. He remembered Nathaniel saying Miller was close to his family, but he didn't know what kind of relationship Miller had with his mother. "What do you mean, sir?" His voice was shaky as he anxiously waited for the reply.

Miller stood and squared his shoulders confidently toward Killian. His deep blue suit shimmered in the bright sunlight. "Killian, I'm your grandfather. Your mother is...was my daughter."

Killian's heart skipped a beat as he gawked at the man. Miller's shoulders visibly relaxed as if it was the greatest relief to finally unload the secret. Killian was speechless, though questions bombarded his mind. Miller stroked his thick mustache and returned to his seat in front of Killian.

"Forgive me for not telling you. I thought it would keep you safer if others weren't aware of our connection. I know I'm being selfish for asking you to stay out of this fight, but...you are my only family." Miller gave a sad smile and chuckled. "And because of that, I know you will *not sit* out from the fight. You are so much like your mother and father. Strong. Brave. But, I want you to understand everything before you make your choice."

"Miller...I..." Killian didn't know what to say. He looked at the man and could feel his love and concern for him. It made sense why he had been so protective since he'd arrived, but there was one question he needed an answer to. "Why didn't you keep me here? Why did you send me away? I know you and Nathaniel were the ones that separated me from my grandmother."

"Yes, but I also helped Rhetta run with you." Killian stopped and stared at the man.

"You what?"

"After your parents' and Grandfather's deaths, Rhetta and I decided you had to be taken from the Praetorium until we could uncover the traitor. I introduced her to Dalia several months earlier when Dalia was brought in as an advisor for the Relic. Dalia agreed to help conceal you both since she believed the relic was infused with a stronger power and had heard rumors the Trinity was seeking the relic. If I had known Infinium was infused in it, I never would have left your side. But it was so concealed even Dalia, the foremost expert, didn't recognize the power immediately."

That was the one secret I kept from Nathaniel, that I was an accomplice to your disappearance. I played ignorance when we finally found you. Nathaniel was so adamant we find Rhetta and the relic and I thought it was because he was worried about the Trinity finding it. Now I see what a fool I was. He wanted the power for himself. I should have caught on when he wanted to execute Rhetta. I objected and she was banished. Then I asked him to send you to Terrene. I still believed the Praetorium was unsafe for you. Nathaniel agreed and promised to keep guardians for you. Every few years we gave you a new one, in the event the Trinity compromised a guardian. I wanted you so completely safe even I didn't know where you were." Miller hung his head and quickly wiped his eyes. "If I had known the life you were subjected to, I would never have allowed it to go on for as long as it did. Nathaniel assured me you were safe, so I never pressed the issue. It caused somewhat of a rift between us when you came home and I discovered how you were raised." Miller sniffed and returned to the grand window again, obviously trying to hide his emotion.

"Miller," he began quietly, "it wasn't your fault. And I wish I could sit this out, but after the lengths Nathaniel went for Infinium and the relics, I can't imagine what the Architect of the Trinity will do. I can't let them destroy Terrene. And neither can you."

Miller smiled at him and nodded. "You can't blame me for asking. So, with this information about our true relationship, I hope we can get to know one another better." Killian nodded in agreement. Miller cleared his throat and his demeanor shifted away from loving grandfather back to dedicated Ponderi leader. "Right then, if you wish to go against the Trinity you have to go through training with Infinium. It is the strongest power we know of, and it will place a target on your head. But when you learn to use it and control it, you will become their greatest threat as well."

"Dalia told me when it's dormant I only have side effects, it's pretty difficult to control."

Miller signaled him to come to an enormous, gold framed mirror on the wall. "Take a look Killian, do you think you bested Nathaniel with so much blood loss on luck?"

Killian looked at Miller skeptically as he peered at his reflection. He stepped back in surprise. His physique had always been athletic, with lean, toned muscles. But now his shoulders were more broad, his arms bulged beneath the thin fabric of his shirt. Even his face seemed more defined, and his blue eyes had a faint orange circle that surrounded the pupil. His hair had lightened to a bright auburn, and fell into his eyes as it had before prison. But it wasn't just his physique that shocked him. Along the sides of his neck he saw strange marks. They were pointed, almost like several arrows pointing upward. The marks were a light reddish color, like they had been carved into his skin. The skin rippled like a scar as he rubbed his fingers along them. Placing his hand on the back of his neck he felt the same raised arrow-shaped marks rising from the area between his shoulder blades to the base of his head. The marks spanned the width of his neck and with three coming to the front of his body from the center of his neck on each side.

"What are these," he asked anxiously, rubbing his hands along the red, raised marks.

"Infinium activated during the attack from Nathaniel. Dalia informed us that is the mark seared into your skin. The activation pulses through your body, so you actually physically change. It's like a brand from the formula. The active formula has altered different aspects of your body, but more importantly, has accessed more of your brain which allows you to be more powerful. You have more brain capacity than normal people. The phenomenon of the marks and the physical changes appear to be your body's reaction to the chemical change."

"It's active?" Killian asked fearfully. He didn't feel confident enough to control it. He had wanted more time to learn about Infinium so he could avoid the formula destroying his brain. His thoughts drifted to the tale of Axel, he'd lost his mind and he was the creator of the formula.

"Yes, Killian, that is how I knew you were feeling things with more intensity. When we saw you after we took you from Nathaniel, we knew something had happened. Dalia instantly recognized the marks and told us. Infinium fought back, it didn't want to die since it is a part of you. The power activated to energize you. Didn't you wonder how you destroyed the dagger?"

"My mind was so foggy, I didn't really think about it."

"The human mind is the most powerful thing in the Hemisphere, but we don't use all our potential. Different races, like Cimmerians use different areas of the brain, which is why they have magical abilities. Glaciens use a different area, making them masters of the environment and elements. Ignisians are strong and fierce, the best warriors in the Hemisphere. You, Killian, have Infinium which was designed to unlock *all of those* areas. You have the abilities of each realm, but magnified and stronger. You can control elements and the environment even better than the Empress, so Infinium destroyed the minerals that made up Nathaniel's dagger at your command." Miller's eyes were twinkling in excitement and awe at the significance of the power.

"This is unbelievable. Dalia didn't explain all of that in detail when we spoke."

"I didn't know you had spoken with her, but Dalia is quite leery to share much detail, with good reason. She doesn't know who to trust either and she has seen the negative aspects of the formula. She probably didn't want to overwhelm you with too much."

"Miller," Killian said in a hoarse whisper. "Nathaniel got to Dalia. That's how he knew how to take Infinium. But he told me he wasn't the only one. We need to talk to Nathaniel and find out who else he's working with. He insinuated they were here in the Praetorium."

"Killian," Miller said rubbing his forehead as if trying to push out a resilient ache. "Nathaniel isn't talking. He won't say a word to anyone. We have him locked in the holding cells beneath the building. I wouldn't recommend speaking with him. I...I've never seen him like this to be honest. He looks...*evil*. He's been totally corrupted. I wouldn't trust a word he would say anyway at this point."

Killian nodded and paused for a moment before speaking. "Miller, do you mind if I take some time to process all of this before I meet with all the other leaders?"

"Of course, Killian. I'm sure you're overwhelmed. Take all the time you need. I'll find you when the council meets again."

Miller walked over to him and put his hands on his shoulders. "I'm glad you know the truth. I know you've been through enough betrayal to last you a lifetime, but I need you to know you can trust me. You are my only grandchild and remind me so much of my sweet Marie. I'm very grateful you are safe, and I will do all I can to ensure you stay that way." Miller wrapped his arms around Killian's shoulders and embraced him tightly. Killian returned the embrace, overcome with the affection he could sense from both himself and Miller. He knew Miller could be trusted, the emotion was genuine and real. For the first time, he was grateful to have Infinium activated. Distinguishing genuine emotion among others, he was sure would be useful.

Pulling back from Miller, he smiled and left the room. "Oh," he turned sharply, "someone broke into my room before the Peridus." Miller's face was shocked, and frightened. "They left a warning about enemies at the games. Their face was hidden, but I thought I should let you know someone was able to get in."

Miller said nothing, but nodded slowly. His face was thoughtful as he pondered who it could have been. The old man gave Killian a kind smile as he stepped into the hallway.

Killian felt a pang of guilt. Miller as far as he knew was the only person who truly sought his safety, but inwardly he had decided to go against the old man's wishes. He had resolved to find a way to speak with Nathaniel. The holding cells were something he'd never heard of and he had no idea how to find them, but he would try. Nathaniel held the answers to who was behind it all...he held the answers to everything.

***

By the time his friends found him in the familiar, comforting entryway, the sun had turned its soft lavender color and a dim twilight seeped across the exotic lawn of the Praetorium. He'd spent several hours planning how he would find Nathaniel and what he would say.

"Killian," Mercedes' quiet voice called to him. He whipped his head around and smiled, seeing her along with the rest of his friends brought him peace. Mercedes' eyes widened as she took in his face.

"Wow, what happened to you?" Dax asked in his blunt manner. Killian had forgotten about the change in his appearance and suddenly felt self-conscious.

"What happened indeed?" Sophia said in a sultry voice, drifting her eyes over his muscular body. Mercedes scowled and Dax pouted behind her. Killian chuckled but felt his face flush in embarrassment.

"Infinium activated. I guess it changed a few things, like giving me these ugly marks all over me like some kind of demented scar," he answered lightly, trying to brush off the event as if it weren't important. He brushed his hair aside revealing the red, raised arrow-like scars.

"Sweet, I didn't notice those when you were covered in all that blood," Blake said running over to look at them. "Now I'm not the only tatted one." Killian laughed thinking of Blake's tattoo on his neck.

"I guess you can call it that," Killian said. Mercedes had slowly made her way over to him and took his hand in hers. Killian squeezed it harder remembering their passionate moment after the attack. "I never asked you and Sophia if you were okay after you were taken out of the Peridus."

"It was fine. The pressure sensors slowed me down. Then we just ended up in a dark room until someone ushered us to a hallway where we could join the crowd."

"Speak for yourself!" Sophia shouted. "I was dragged away by a horrifying spider-bat creature that smelled like dying fingernails! Then to make it worse, after I finally settled down, Killian comes bursting into the crowd covered in blood!"

Killian's face flushed vaguely remembering pushing through the crowd after the attack. "Speaking of all that blood, Blake how did you find me after Peridus?" he asked, curious.

"We knew something was wrong as soon as we stepped into the simulator," he explained, and Dax nodded. "All the finalists were together in one simulation, but not you. Somehow your door diverted you. Now we know Nathaniel programmed it to divert you into an enclosed portion of the room when you crossed the threshold. I wanted to turn around and find you right away," Blake admitted angrily, "but once you're in the simulation, you have to finish it before you can get out. As soon as we made it through I found the leaders. Gwyniera didn't show much interest, but Egan and the queen left with me immediately. I admit I never expected to see Nathaniel behind that door."

"We've been worried about you," Mercedes said. "I can't believe Nathaniel tried to..." She seemed to struggle with the words.

"Kill him?" Dax bellowed. "Traitor. We all were duped, no one saw it coming. He had the entire Peridus set up to get you alone. If you didn't make it to the simulation, he had it programmed to divert you to that same room. You didn't stand a chance." He folded his bulky arms across his large, bare chest.

"Honestly it was Lucan that found the right room," Blake admitted.

"What? Lucan, the recruit Lucan who hates me?" Killian said amazed.

"Yep, he has a keen sense of hearing, almost animal-like. He heard you arguing and shouting behind the walls. Maurelle used her power to start blowing into the steel trying to find the room. I'm just glad we found you when we did."

"Me too. Remind me to thank Lucan," Killian said softly.

"I don't know if I can take much more excitement," Mercedes said lightly, though there was a tone that seemed quite serious.

"Well," Killian began, "I actually just learned Miller is my grandfather." His friends stared at him with wide eyes. Blake laughed out loud after several moments.

"That makes so much sense now."

"What does?" Killian asked.

"For all the years I've been here, I never heard Miller say anyone's name more than Killian Thomas. He was always trying to discover how you were, but your case was so classified no one knew except a few select people. When I was assigned as guardian, the man gave me the third degree on how crucial your protection was. It makes a lot of sense now. I thought he was just a cantankerous old man most of the time...almost a control freak about how we offered protection."

Killian smiled. In a strange way it comforted him even more, to know during all those years he felt alone and abandoned someone was behind the curtain worrying, and trying to check on his wellbeing. Inside, he wished Miller had learned how he was treated, he knew the man would've removed him immediately.

"So what does it mean to have Infinium activated?" Mercedes finally asked.

"I don't really know. I feel stronger, I feel more connected with emotions and things like that. Miller said I need to be trained, he's pretty concerned about people trying to get Infinium after Nathaniel's attack."

"See Dez, now he's strong enough he can keep an eye on you from your strange admirer," Sophia chuckled. Mercedes glared at her trying to silence her. "What?" Sophia shrugged her shoulders, "it's true. I mean not that you weren't strong before Killian it's just that..." Dax nudged her shoulder to stop her from digging a deeper hole. She shot a fiery glance at him then folded her arms across her chest, pursing her lips.

"What is she talking about?"

Mercedes looked embarrassed, but her emerald eyes were genuinely perplexed when she met his. He sensed her anxiety about the subject, and it signaled a protective instinct inside of him. He wanted to know if someone was upsetting Mercedes, and he wanted to put an end to it. "Mercedes, is someone bothering you?"

"No," she said shaking her head. "It's just a little...strange. Everywhere I go, somehow I see him. The building isn't *that* big, so it's no surprise when you run into people, but it's just...*all the time*."

"Who is it?" Killian said fiercely, his blood burning again, all the way up the strange marks on the back of his neck.

"Egan," she said in a soft voice. Killian's body calmed quickly.

"Egan? Ignisia's chief?"

"I told her it's nothing to worry about," Dax said quickly. "Egan is monitoring everyone with the other leaders. It's just a coincidence." Sophia blew out her lips making a strange noise and rolled her eyes. "It's true. Egan would never do anything dishonorable." Dax huffed.

"I'm sure he wouldn't," Mercedes said, trying to get the subject changed.

"Even so, keep an eye on it," Killian commanded. He leaned in closer to her and lowered his voice so the others wouldn't hear. "Seriously, tell me if it makes you uncomfortable. We can't be too careful anymore." She nodded and gave him a grateful smile.

"Well, it's been a wild two days hasn't it?" Blake said wistfully.

"Seems like we've got quite a wild ride coming up," Dax agreed.

"After what's happened," Killian began, a determination in his voice "After what the Trinity proved they're capable of, I'm ready to do anything necessary to get the relics. They won't ever stop until they win. To them it doesn't matter who is killed, children, women, elderly, they're capable of it all."

"We need to stick together," Blake added. "If we can't trust each other, who can we trust?" The group of friends nodded.

"Tomorrow training begins," Killian said turning his attention back to the fading, peaceful lavender sun. "Remember who we're training for. An entire realm depends on us for their lives. A storm is coming, but we'll be ready. I know we will." Mercedes gripped his fingers and held them tight in her hand. The others nodded in agreement as a solemn silence filled the entryway. Each finding their own motivations, their own reasons to defend a realm full of innocents from the bloodthirsty, cunning society.

Killian's mind drifted to the darkness below the building. The pull to venture to the mysterious underground prison was relentless. Almost as if it was beckoning him.

I'll be waiting.

The hushed voice was so vivid and clear Killian whipped his head over his shoulder looking for the source. No one was there.

"What is it?" Mercedes asked when she noticed his change of attention.

"Nothing, I just thought I heard..." he looked at her curious eyes and forced himself to smile. "Never mind, it was nothing." Killian kissed her forehead and pulled her close to him, ignoring the murmurs from the others. He knew the voice. Nathaniel. It only solidified what he had to do. The battle was about to begin, he could feel it. Nathaniel held secrets crucial to understanding the Trinity.

Killian stared at the dim sky with the colorful twinkling stars. His body burned in anticipation and excitement for his secret mission. Soon he would find his way to the underground prison, which was surely heavily guarded. It was time to put the unbeatable power to good use. He would find Nathaniel and force him to reveal the truth; the old man deserved a visit from him. He would consider it payback for the multiple scars covering his body. Killian smiled. This time he would be ready for the Trinity, but they wouldn't be ready for him.

Acknowledgments

There have been endless amounts of people who have supported me and helped me along this long journey of completing my first full length novel. I must first thank with all my heart my husband, Derek, for his endless input and wonderful suggestions—he really could make a career out of developmental editing. He has been the one to roll his eyes and put my hands back on the keyboard when I want to quit and never write again. I want to thank my patient children for giving mom the chance to spend quiet time writing, but also giving me the needed breaks of Lego building or snuggles. You all have inspired this novel in some way and I hope you enjoy finding bits of each of you strewn along the pages.

I want to thank my parents for inspiring me to keep writing and always raving about my little poems and short stories you had to read when I was a child. You taught me how to work and reach for the stars. I'm thankful for Katie, my sister, who has read every word multiple times and offered insight as a book lover. Even though we live apart, I feel like you're right here when you've helped me with this project. I'm thankful for Aubrey, my other sister for taking the time to read my blurbs, the book, and inspiring my mantra of the arrow, even though you are so very busy with your endeavors. Your help is irreplaceable. Thank you to my brother Dane for helping me stay logical and figure out the direction I wanted to go to reach my goals the fastest. For Shalee and Landon, the youngest siblings, for reading this book right after your wedding when most people wouldn't have offered. Thanks to Sara, Tom, Larry and Crystal. You, as Beta-readers, helped me work through so many kinks along the way, but also helped me feel like I had a story full of potential and awesomeness that I kept writing even when I wanted to throw it all away. I hope I can get your input for other projects down the road. I know you're excited for my relentless emails!

Thanks to the editors at www.wonderouswords.com for helping me smooth out the edges and catching all those funny grammar mistakes.

Thank you to Debbie Cassidy for your amazing cover design. I appreciate it so much.

And finally, I would like to thank all the readers and future readers. The success of *The Lost Relics* is all because of you. Thank you for helping my dreams become a reality.

All the best,

LJ Andrews

About the Author

LJ Andrews has been reading since she was five, and writing since she was six. She loves reading and writing anything fantasy to escape the day to day we call reality. However, historical fiction allows her dream of owning a Scottish castle satisfied, and her bank account in the black.

After earning a formal degree in Occupational Therapy she worked lovingly with the geriatric community for five years. Often during the treatment sessions she was fascinated with the marvelous journeys and adventures her elderly friends had experienced, and something great happened. The writing bug entered her brain and stories began to flow out. Since then she has earned a copy editing certificate from the American Copy Editor Society, and Poynter News University. Running a freelance editing business has given L. J. the opportunity to spend time reading other masterpieces before anyone else, while writing her own exciting stories.

L.J. lives with her husband, three children, two dogs and two rats...yes rats, in a small town nestled in the mountains of Utah. She enjoys playing with Legos, Batman, and toy cheetahs, making chocolate chip cookies, and of course writing stories when all her little people are sleeping.

You can follow LJ here: www.ljandrews.com

Other Books:

The Lost Relics: Trinity Rises

The Gateway

Made in the USA
Middletown, DE
18 July 2017